He w **as**

It was not a word that she would men, but it suited him. *Don't keep staring at the gorgeous mouth*, she told herself firmly. It was his eyes that drew her most strongly. They were every bit as mesmerizing as she remembered. In the shade they were the color of a faded eucalyptus leaf. As he looked away into the sunlight, they shone like silver coins.

Forcing herself to focus, she asked the first of the many questions that jostled for a place on her lips.

"Why have you appeared to me now?"

That broke the spell. A slight frown creased his brow and he pulled his eyes away from hers. "Because you are in grave danger."

OTHERWORLD
PROTECTOR

JANE GODMAN

MILLS &
BOON

Published in Great Britain 2015
by Mills & Boon, an imprint of Harlequin (UK) Limited,
Eton House, 18-24 Paradise Road, Richmond, Surrey, TW9 1SR

© 2015 Amanda Anders

ISBN: 978-0-263-91827-4

89-1215

Harlequin (UK) Limited's policy is to use papers that are natural, renewable and recyclable products and made from wood grown in sustainable forests. The logging and manufacturing processes conform to the legal environmental regulations of the country of origin.

Printed and bound in Spain
by CPI, Barcelona

Jane Godman writes in a variety of genres including paranormal, gothic and historical romance, and erotic romantic suspense. She also enjoys the occasional foray into horror and thriller writing. Jane lives in England and loves to travel to European cities, which are steeped in history and romance—Venice, Dubrovnik and Vienna are among her favorites.

A teacher, Jane is married to a lovely man and is mum to two grown-up children.

While writing this book I was diagnosed with a brain tumor. I'm one of the lucky ones. My tumor is low-grade and slow-growing. I'd like to dedicate this book to my fellow brain tumor fighters and those who care for and support us.

Chapter 1

Stella Fallon was in the process of discovering that there is nothing so hysteria inducing as the realization that you have given up your job and traveled to a new country, spending every penny of your savings in the process, in pursuit of a dream that doesn't exist. Okay, so it had been a crap job. And the savings had just about covered her plane ticket. As she stared up at the vast crumbling mansion, these extenuating circumstances did not provide Stella with one single morsel of comfort. If the house was empty—and it certainly looked that way—she was officially homeless, jobless and, once she had paid the taxi fare, had exactly one hundred euros to her name.

"This is the right house, senorita. For sure." The driver repeated the statement he had made a few minutes earlier. While his tone was patient, his eyes were wary as they met hers in the rearview mirror. Possibly he could sense her rising panic. He might even have been cursing the fact that, from the long line of eager tourists and experienced businessmen waiting for taxis at the airport that night, he was the one who ended up with this quirky-looking girl. Whatever his emotions might be, he was clearly fearful of not getting his cash and impatient at being kept waiting now that he had delivered her to her destination.

"It can't be." Although the driver had spoken in Spanish, she responded in English and he made a helpless, uncomprehending gesture. Stella corrected her mistake. *"No es posible."*

"Sí. This is the address you gave me. La Casa Oscura—" he gestured into the pitch-blackness beyond the car windows "—it is well-known in this city."

La Casa Oscura. The Dark House. Except it shouldn't be dark. According to the emails Stella had received, it should be lit up in welcome for her. Or, if "lit up" might be construed as an overenthusiastic approach to greeting a new junior employee, there should at least have been some sign of life. There was none.

"You want me to take you to a hotel in the city center for tonight? That way you can come back in the morning. Check the place out in daylight."

The suggestion made sense, and Stella was about to dent her precious hundred euros further and agree. That was when she felt it. Felt *him.* There was the familiar flicker of movement on the outer edge of her vision. She knew from experience there was no point in trying to capture it. He existed only on the periphery. Looking directly at him would cause him to disappear. But it was enough. Wellbeing, warm, mellow and welcome flooded her veins. Her protector was here.

"No." Taking out her wallet, she counted out the right number of notes for the fare and added a tip.

"I can wait here until you are inside," the driver offered

as he pocketed the money. Stella could almost see him assessing the possibility of being featured as the bad guy in the following day's tabloid headlines.

Cabbie abandoned lone Brit-girl tourist at death house, saying "I wanted my supper!"

"I'll be fine," Stella assured him and he shrugged a doubtful shoulder. She could hardly explain her newfound bravado to him. As she clambered out of the car, juggling her backpack and laptop case, the driver hauled her wheeled suitcase out of the trunk. With a final glance over his shoulder and shrug, he returned to the car. Stella waited for him to drive off before she turned to look up at the house. The darkness here on the hillside above the city was so all-encompassing that what she saw was the outline of the hulking building and none of its detail. First impressions were everything, and this one definitely didn't *feel* comforting.

Although the house itself, like its name, was cloaked in obscurity, there was enough light from the street lamps for Stella to make her way unhindered through the vast wrought-iron gates. Thoughts of medieval prisons and torture chambers sprang into her mind. All useful ideas for future game projects, she assured herself, making a mental note. Her feet crunched onto a gravel drive. This, in turn, opened out onto a large, paved square and Stella noticed, with a feeling of profound relief, that there were several cars and motorbikes parked to one side of this area. In the darkness, she could not distinguish makes or models. One of the cars was definitely low-slung, sleek and probably expensive. Moncoya expensive? At the very least, the cars were evidence that the house might not be an abandoned ruin, after all.

Stella commenced a crab-like gait—dragging the huge suitcase, backpack and laptop bag—across the square to the house. As she did, her movements triggered a series of blindingly bright, fluorescent floodlights. It was surreal. If she looked up, would she see a hovering UFO? Or would she be surrounded by armed guards, dressed in black uniforms emblazoned with the gold Moncoya Enterprises *M*, and made to lie facedown on the ground while they searched her luggage for signs that she was a spy for a rival company?

Reminding herself that a fertile imagination was a necessity, not a liability, in her line of work, Stella continued up to the now clearly visible front door. This was a huge, green-painted structure, set within a vast facade of faded terra-cotta stone. The floodlights cast an eerie gloom that made the house appear to be suspended in space.

Stella didn't quite know what she had expected. *Relocation to Senor Moncoya's Barcelona residencia will be a requirement of the post.* That was what the email had said. Since she'd have agreed to anything—*Relocation to the moon? Where do I sign?*—for a job with Moncoya, she hadn't really thought this bit through. *Story of your life,* she told herself as she pressed the bell next to the front door. *No wonder that peripheral protector of yours has to work overtime.*

The door was opened, not—as a tiny part of her had hoped—by Ezra Moncoya himself, but by a grungy-looking youth with dreadlocks and a beard that was plaited.

"You must be Stella," he said, throwing the door wide as he grabbed her suitcase and laptop bag. "We've been expecting you."

As she stepped across the doorstep into the vast white-and-chrome foyer, Stella knew her first impression had been wrong. She was in the most right place she had ever been.

Cal watched as Stella stepped over the doorstep of La Casa Oscura and the door closed behind her. As if the house itself was swallowing her up. He chided himself for the overimaginative foolishness of such thoughts. He had always known that this time would come—had known it since a time long before Stella's birth. This precise moment was the reason he had taken the assignment, even though watching over mortals was beneath him in so many ways. Nevertheless, he had to take a moment to wonder at the staggering recklessness of his charge. Unlike Cal, Stella had no idea of who she was, of either her lineage or her destiny. So surely a little bit of caution would not have gone amiss in the circumstances.

He smiled reminiscently. She had always been the same. Even from the earliest age, the little girl with the spiky blue-black hair and wide green eyes had been a trouble magnet, hurling herself from one dangerous situation to the next with a bring-it-on fist pump and a grin. Her behavior had been so far outside Cal's expectations that, on Stella's sixth birthday, he had sought an audience to request advice on the matter.

"Never doubt the gravity of what lies ahead. For her or for you." The Dominion, one of the leading angels of the fourth choir, had worn the traditional long gown, hitched with a golden belt. As a symbol of the seriousness in which he held his task of regulating the duties of lower angels, he had carried a golden staff in his right hand and the seal of his office in his left. Although Cal was easily equal in rank and power to the Dominion, by that time he had been fighting on the side of the angels for so long he always felt slightly overawed by such overt symbols of celestial authority. "When you joined us, you were handed the most demanding of tasks. Now, through this girl, yours is the responsibility for ensuring that peace is restored so that the border between the living realm and Otherworld remains intact."

"I understand and have gladly accepted the burden you placed upon me. It is just—" Cal had thought back to the escapade that had prompted him to request this meeting. It hadn't been *that* bad, he had reasoned. No one had been injured. The truck driver should have known better than to leave his vehicle unlocked with the keys in the ignition. And who'd have thought the skinny little girl Stella had been back then would have been able to get the hand brake off anyway? "I had not anticipated that a major part of my role would be to keep her alive until the prophecy can be fulfilled."

"You must do whatever it takes," the Dominion had assured him with a dignity that befitted his position.

So he had. What he hadn't known then was how much he would enjoy it. Even now, nineteen years after the "do whatever it takes" conversation with the Dominion, Cal still found Stella's cheeky grin irresistible. He'd broken a few rules along the way. They both had. There had been occasions when he'd had no choice but to materialize to help her out. It wasn't exactly forbidden, it was just not recommended. Distance was the key to a successful relationship between protector and charge. The difference for them was that, unlike other mortals, Stella was conscious of Cal's presence even when he didn't appear before her in human form. That caused him some anxiety. She should not have been aware of him, of course. That wasn't normal. But Stella was not an ordinary charge. And he had just watched his far-from-average charge walk into the situation he had dreaded since the day she was born.

The time had come. The prophecy was about to be realized at last. While the coming change in their relationship saddened him, Cal's fighting spirit was roused by the prospect of action. This moment signaled the transformation they had all been waiting for. Casting a glance heavenward at the unusual formation streaking the sky with its three golden tails, he moved through the thick terra-cotta wall and followed his charge into La Casa Oscura. Or—as it was known throughout Otherworld—Moncoya's lair.

"This place is amazing." Stella placed her backpack down and turned in a circle to get the full effect. The faded beauty of the neoclassical facade she had glimpsed outside was in complete contrast to the stark modernity of the interior. The entire lower floor of La Casa Oscura was one vast, open-plan room and the whole of the rear wall was glass, affording a soaring, dramatic view across the nighttime city. At opposite right angles to this, another full wall was taken up with rows of computers and games consoles, each of which was linked to its own enormous plasma screen. Circular seating islands had been created at random intervals, breaking up the white-tiled floor space. In one corner, there was a sensory area with bubble tubes, soft lighting and—Stella noted as she completed her twirl—two men asleep on large beanbags. A shelf lined with hundreds of glass jars, filled with every kind of sweet, cookie and candy imaginable, sat alongside a soft drinks machine. It was a grown-up playroom.

The man who had opened the door to Stella nodded his agreement and gestured to the drinks machine.

"Get you something? I'm Diego, by the way."

Stella accepted a bottle of chilled water gratefully. "Do you live here?"

Diego snorted. "Only the privileged few get to actually stay here in *la casa*. The rest of us drop by when there is a big project to work on or a deadline to be met." He nodded in the direction of the sleeping men. "Thirty-six hours straight. We've been trying to iron out a kink in a new games title. Just about cracked it. Some people can't take the pace. So you're the crowd fund girl Moncoya's been raving about."

Stella felt a blush tinge her cheeks. *Moncoya* and *raving* were not words she ever thought to hear put together and then applied to her. It was the stuff of every gamer's fantasy. "Is he here?" She tried not to sound too eager.

"Moncoya? He doesn't greet new employees in person, you know."

Her enthusiasm popped like bubble gum on a pin. Of course he didn't. How stupid of her to ask. Just as she was about to stammer out an apology for her foolishness, the front door opened and, with perfect timing, Ezra Moncoya walked in. Even if Stella had not spent an obsessive amount of time doing internet searches for her new employer over the past week, she would have known him anywhere. *Let's face it,* she thought, looking into the most unusual eyes she had ever seen, *unless you had lived as a hermit in a remote cave for the past twenty years, you could not fail to recognize Ezra Moncoya.* And to an aspiring games designer, Moncoya was a god. He had been Stella's idol for as long as she could remember. While the other girls in the children's home had pictures of boy bands on their bedroom walls, Stella had Moncoya advertising posters, snippets cut from magazines and game covers.

He was of less than average height with a slight build, but Moncoya's presence instantly filled the vast room. He wore evening dress, but managed to bring a touch of his unique flair to the conventional outfit. Tuxedo and trousers in midnight blue were perfectly contoured to his slender physique, and he wore a cravat in place of a bow tie. It was his face, however, that drew—no, commanded—Stella's attention. It was a face that graced the cover of thousands of electronics periodicals as well as the gossip pages of every international newspaper and magazine. Moncoya's chiseled beauty was legendary, almost as well-known as his sexual prowess, but nothing had prepared Stella for the reality of the man. How had she reached the age of twenty-five without knowing you really could have your breath taken away by the presence of another human being? Moncoya ran a hand through his signature mane of tousled, morning-after hair, its highlights ranging from honey gold to caramel. The diamond studs in his ears caught the light. Until that instant Stella would have laughed if someone had told her she could find a man who wore black nail polish and blue eyeliner attractive.

It was those eyes that drew her in and captured her, she decided. Bluer than a summer evening, the irises were edged with gold as if encircled by fire. The effect was devastating. Once you looked into Moncoya's eyes, you couldn't look away. *Not even if your life depended on it.* She shook the foolish, intrusive thought away.

It didn't seem to concern Moncoya in the slightest that Diego, after an initial blink of shock at his employer's entrance, had faded away, leaving them alone. Or that, without the benefit of an introduction, a girl he had never met was gazing at him in spellbound silence across a distance of several feet. A slight smile touched his lips and he moved forward, holding out both hands.

"Stella Fallon. You are everything I hoped you would be." It seemed a strange comment since, in those few seconds, she had no way of demonstrating the abilities for which he had hired her. Such was the force of his personality that she took the outstretched hands. The oddest feeling, like a slight electric shock, shimmered from her fingertips then tingled throughout her whole body at his touch.

Get a grip, Stella. He probably has this effect on women

all the time. Stella collected herself with some difficulty. "Senor Moncoya, I want to thank you…"

He had gone. Releasing her hands, he strode away to the glass wall at the rear of the room. Stella hesitated. Away from the power of those eyes, doubt washed over her. *Was that it? Was she dismissed? Or was she meant to follow?* When Moncoya glanced, with a touch of impatience, over his shoulder, she got her answer and hurried to join him. For a few minutes they stood side by side, their reflections staring back at them from the window's mirrorlike gloss.

Stella tried to see herself through Moncoya's eyes. Short. Well, he wasn't tall so that was good, wasn't it? *Stop it, Stella. Nothing is going to happen here.* Slim. A bit too slim. *Okay, I'm on the skinny side.* Short, spiky hair. Hair that was a lot shorter than his. Wide eyes and pixie features—like a gremlin, a former boyfriend had once said…during a fight. Vintage dress and combat boots. It was her favorite look. 1950s movie icon meets steampunk rebel. Not the kind of woman for a man like Mon—Moncoya pressed a button and one of the glass panels slid back. With old-fashioned courtesy, he bowed slightly, indicating that Stella should precede him. She stepped out onto a wide terrace and inhaled the midnight scent of orange blossom. The entire city of Barcelona, lit up like a child's fairyland, was spread out below them.

"Welcome to your new home."

Stella turned to Moncoya with shining eyes, wanting to voice the thanks she had attempted earlier. As she did, her peripheral vision kicked in again, the movement urgent enough to make her pause. The feeling of contentment she got from knowing her protector was there was as powerful as ever, but this time there was something more.

Something equally strong. She had never before experienced this particular sensation from her shadowy guardian. She took a second to examine the new perception. It felt a lot like a warning.

Chapter 2

As a child Stella would have long, imaginary conversations with her protector while playing with her toys. In these, his answering voice was quiet and masculine. He was the one person who always had time for her. He said what she wanted to hear. With him she felt safe and loved. If she was upset or fearful, she only had to think of him and he would come to her. It didn't matter that he didn't exist beyond the outer reaches of her vision, or that when she blinked he was gone. He was as real to her as any of her foster carers or teachers.

Stella had been three when her parents were killed in a car crash. When she pictured that day it was as a sharp turn in the road, a change in the path of her life. Behind her was a meandering, sweet-smelling country lane, lined with flowers. Ahead there was a gray concrete highway with nothing on either side to alleviate the monotonous view.

Every attempt had been made to find adoptive parents

for her. "She has no other family and—I don't know what it is, maybe it's because she's such a fey child or always lurching into mischief—but she doesn't seem to *take*, if you know what I mean. And she should have grown out of the imaginary-friend phase long ago."

Stella had overheard that fractious comment one day as she sat outside the matron's office in the children's home waiting to take her punishment for her latest transgression. It had set the tone for a childhood spent alternating between kindly foster homes and a series of trying-too-hard-to-be-homely institutions. It didn't matter. She always had *him*.

No one else listened when Stella talked about the monster that lived under her bed. It didn't matter where she slept, the monster would be there awaiting her arrival. Although its eyes were dark, sometimes they burned ember bright. In the dark reaches of the night, it whispered Stella's name in a low, scratchy voice. The monster wanted Stella. Not just any little girl. *Her.* She would squeeze her eyes shut and her lips would form a silent plea for the monster to leave her alone. Her protector always came in answer to those appeals.

If she didn't look directly at him, she could see the protector's tall shadow on the edge of her vision. Somehow it was easier in the dark. Once, in the children's home, the curtains had not been fully closed and a sliver of moonlight from the streetlight outside had sneaked through. Briefly, it had illuminated his face, allowing her eager gaze to drink in his square, determined jaw, fine mouth and silver-gray eyes. She had been startled into turning her head to stare directly at him, and he had instantly disappeared. From then on, he had taken care not to allow her any further close-up glimpses.

He spoke to the monster in a guttural language Stella

didn't recognize. Not aloud, of course. Instead the whispered words seeped into her subconscious. The monster would whine and attempt to cling to the floorboards in response. As her heart pounded out a rhythm of relief, Stella would sense the monster's defeat and hear its slithering departure. Over the years, Stella came to understand how it worked. Even to accept it. The monster would always be there. It would always want her. But she would be safe... so long as her protector was near.

Now, for the first time in her life, the monster was gone. She had been so tired the first night after her arrival that she'd tumbled into bed in the strange room on the casa's upper floor and not given it a thought. After five nights in Moncoya's Barcelona mansion, she felt she could officially say her bedroom was a monster-free zone. And all it had taken to bring about this purge was a two-and-a-half-hour international flight. Maybe monsters didn't have passports.

Stella sometimes wondered if her monochrome childhood was responsible for her neon-color imagination. Whatever the cause, her mind was a constant whirl of ideas. When she was young, color, shape, music and poetry all vied for her attention. As she grew up and became more discerning, she had become more focused. Honing her natural artistic skills in college, she had pursued her ultimate dream by completing a master's degree in computer games design. She had left school twelve months ago to seek a job in London. In the most competitive field imaginable, slap in the middle of a recession.

The question was always the same. "What have you done?"

The answer never varied. "Nothing yet."

Her awesome, hard-won qualifications counted for nothing. It was a vicious circle. *Give me a job so I can prove myself. Prove yourself and we might give you a job.* She took a routine office job to pay the bills on her tiny studio and spent her evenings dreaming up new ideas for games. She met up with a few university friends for drinks one weekend, and they had discussed their various ideas. The subject of crowd funding came up. It was how "Supernova Deliverance," an online survival game with a supernatural theme, had been born. In its turn, it had led Stella to this job.

The email from Moncoya's personal assistant had come on a cold, miserable day. One on which her job had seemed more boring than ever. It was fate, she decided, her heart skipping several beats as she read and reread it. Senor Moncoya had followed the progress of the crowd funding project with interest. He was particularly impressed with the way she had laid out the conceptual framework and her graphics development skills. There was a temporary internship at Moncoya Enterprises in Barcelona. Would she be interested?

"I have to reply today!" Realizing she had spoken aloud, she had retreated back behind her computer screen, her mind whirling with possibilities.

There was a brief job description. *Ability to visualize compelling social games. Knowledge and insight of game balance. Strong design and drafting skills.* Key phrases danced around her mind as she typed her resignation letter. *Fluency in Spanish an advantage. Must sign a confidentiality contract.* Good thing she'd chosen to take Spanish at school.

"Muchas gracias, Senor Moncoya. Te amo mucho."

Since she had joined his company, Moncoya had given her no reason to withdraw that declaration of undying love. Okay, so he had some very odd friends and they liked to party hard. But if Moncoya wanted to hang out with a group of people who looked like stylish punk rockers that was his business. She caught occasional glimpses of his friends and was struck by two things that they had in common. They were all stunningly beautiful, and she wondered if that was a deliberate choice of Moncoya's. Being so striking himself, did he choose to surround himself with others who were similarly good-looking?

The other thing they shared was a style idiosyncrasy. Each of them wore the same contact lenses. They all had the same curious ring of fire around their iris as Moncoya. Was it a statement? A tribute to Moncoya? Or was Moncoya's own yellow burst of fire also the result of contact lenses? Out of interest, Stella had searched the internet for it. She had found something called "central heterochromia" that apparently would have got you an automatic burning as a witch in the Middle Ages, but even that didn't come close to the blaze of color exhibited by Moncoya and his party people. She had shrugged it off. As a fashion statement it was extreme, but Moncoya *was* extreme. It was part of his charm.

There had been a horrible misunderstanding a few nights ago when some of Moncoya's friends had taken a shine to Stella and seemed to feel she was an important guest rather than realizing she was just a very junior employee. They had wanted her to join the party, and she'd been forced to make a hurried exit. Somehow she didn't think the amused tolerance Moncoya had so far demonstrated toward her would survive any attempts to gate-crash into his social sphere.

Stella was aware of the occasional exchange of looks between the other game design employees. She had overheard one or two barbed comments. She suspected she was meant to hear them.

"Why is *el jefe* still around? Never known him to hang around *la casa* for more than a day. Two at most."

"Could it have anything to do with his new pet? The little crowd funder protégé? He calls her his star."

"She's a bit young for Moncoya, surely? Although, come to think of it, she does have that elven look he likes so much."

Diego had chimed into the conversation then. "Ease up on her, guys. She knows her stuff, that's for sure. And her artwork is spectacular."

A job she loved. A boss she liked. And no monsters. This new turn in the road offered her a whole new direction. The drab highway was forever behind her. Ahead lay a winding, challenging mountain pass. She was ready to forge upward along this new scenic route.

"He doesn't need to send his foot soldiers to lurk under your bed anymore, Stella. Not when he's sitting right next to you." *And hoping that very soon he'll be joining you in that bed.*

Cal could feel the frustration pouring off him like sweat off a cage fighter. He wanted to storm over there, drag her away from Moncoya and all the way back to the only place he knew for sure he could keep her safe. When there were other people around it was so difficult to watch out for her. University had been problematic and so boring. Cal had yawned through the lectures and seminars that fascinated Stella. All those kids, all rushing somewhere. London especially had been the worst place to guard her.

Because it wasn't just Moncoya he had to look out for. In a way Moncoya was the least of his problems. He snorted with laughter at that thought and mentally rephrased it. Moncoya was a dangerous bastard, but at least he would be predictably terrifying. It was the others, the unknowns, who posed the greater problem. Because word of the prophecy had trickled out. It had been inevitable.

So many centuries had passed since the prediction was first spoken, and then written. So many great scholars had frowned and debated over its meaning. One of Cal's worst fears throughout that time had been how the vague wording might be interpreted. Evil can twist any meaning to suit its purpose. And fragile Stella would be on the receiving end of those twists.

Confrontation with Moncoya was inevitable. But, as the apocalyptic time drew closer, who else was hunting Cal's precious charge? Was the man on the bus really just a sad loner who got a hard-on from rubbing himself up against young women? Turned out he was. Could the woman who had run toward Stella with a closed umbrella extended in front of her like a weapon during rush hour really have been late for an appointment? Cal couldn't take that chance. A strategically extended foot and the woman had gone sprawling into the gutter while Stella continued on her way oblivious to any danger, real or imagined. As it should be. All in a day's work. No thanks necessary.

He *didn't* want thanks. Or even acknowledgment. What he had never envisioned when he took this assignment and laid his plans for this day was that he would be forced to watch as his charge gazed worshipfully into the fiery eyes of the very being from whom she should be shrinking. On reflection, he supposed it was only to be expected. Moncoya's touch, like that of all his kind, was known to be heady and intense. Moncoya, the most powerful of them all, could, it was said, induce euphoria to the point of spiritual, even physical, ecstasy with the lightest touch of his fingertips. Cal curled his lip at that. He'd believe that particular piece of Moncoya propaganda if he felt it for himself. Not that the little manikin would ever have the nerve to touch him, let alone come close to him. Not after the last time. Nevertheless, the new, dreamy look on Stella's face seemed to confirm the rumor that Moncoya's touch, once felt, had such a profound effect on the psyche that it evoked a desperate yearning to experience it again.

"More wine?" Cal looked up as the cause of his bad mood held the bottle of Rioja over Stella's glass.

"No." She shook her head, placing her hand over her glass a fraction of a second too late so that the ruby liquid ran over her fingers. She laughed, lifting her fingers to her lips to lick the droplets away. "I want to get back to that platform tonight. There are still some issues with fine-tuning the graphics."

They were seated on the terrace at the back of the house enjoying its spectacular views over the city. The evening sky was a tapestry of coral and lavender threaded through with streaks of gold, and the air was heavy with the scent of summer flowers. Stella wore a sundress that looked as if it was made from six stitched-together handkerchiefs. From his position leaning against an olive tree to one side of the terrace, Cal studied her face thoughtfully. For the first time ever, she was wearing lip gloss. His heart sank further and he found himself torn between conflicting emotions. Moncoya's presence made him want to behave like the overprotective father in a sitcom and tell her to get inside and cover up. Another part, possibly the stronger part, insisted in forcing his eyes to linger on the slender expanse of her thighs. It was an oddly possessive emotion, new and strangely exhilarating.

The sky darkened swiftly to night and bats flew in relay from the eaves of the casa to the street lamps and back, greedily grabbing any insects in their path. Moncoya leaned closer to Stella, and Cal clenched a fist against his thigh, willing the tousle-haired mongrel to give him an excuse to intervene, at the same time knowing he was powerless to do anything. Because this was as it had been ordained and he, of all people, could not deflect the course of the prophecy.

Just as Moncoya's hand moved to within an inch of the pale flesh of Stella's upper arm, a monumental crash reverberated around the garden. The ground trembled as though in the grip of a brief but violent earthquake, and a cloud of red dust flew up several feet from the terrace.

"Go inside." Cal watched approvingly as Moncoya thrust Stella toward the open door. This was a first. Who'd have thought he'd ever find himself in agreement with Moncoya? He was aware that, although she followed the instruction, Stella hovered half in and half out of the casa, gazing at the point of impact in fascination.

Moncoya lowered his head and stretched out his arms, and the grotesque beast that had just fallen to earth drew itself up to its full height as it faced him. Moncoya appeared tiny in comparison. Grudgingly, Cal admired his courage. Moncoya spoke softly in a lilting language. The whole night stilled. The dust cloud settled. The creature bared its teeth in a snarl. Moncoya spoke again and it unfurled wings that spanned at least eight feet. Nevertheless, it appeared pinned to the spot.

Cal, growing tired of Moncoya's dawdling methods, stepped forward and smashed his fist directly into the gargoyle's hideous face. The creature sank into a crouch, its glowing eyes searching the darkness for the invisible assailant. Moncoya's head snapped up and Cal took a second to mutter a curse. He had been determined not to reveal his presence to Moncoya. Not yet. Now Moncoya was aware of his existence, although he still didn't know who Cal was.

"Time to catch up on your beauty sleep. God knows, you need it." Cal delivered a swift, painfully accurate dropkick to the side of the gargoyle's head. With a curious grace, the huge creature collapsed back into the red earth. Its natural defense mechanism kicked in and its flesh turned instantly to stone.

"Who is there?" Moncoya's voice rang out.

Cal moved close, allowing his breath to touch the smaller man's cheek. "Your worst nightmare," he whispered. Moncoya's eyes narrowed to slits of pure fury as he turned in the direction of Cal's voice.

"What just happened?" Stella stepped back onto the terrace, her own eyes huge and very green as she stared at the recumbent gargoyle.

"A meteorite of some sort." You had to admire Moncoya, Cal decided. The man could smoothly tell a bald-faced lie.

"That isn't a meteorite!" Stella had begun to stomp across the garden in the direction of where the stone creature had fallen. Even though Moncoya reached out to halt her, his intervention wasn't necessary. Before she reached the pile of rubble, Stella turned slowly back to the house, her expression changing. Cal knew that look well. It was a combination of suspicion and stubbornness.

Moncoya shrugged. "Does it matter?" He gestured for her to be seated but she ignored him.

Cal waited for her to say it did matter. Willed her to see Moncoya for what he really was. To finally understand why she had been brought here...

The wariness vanished from her face as she looked at Moncoya. Frustration chased away Cal's brief feeling of optimism when Stella began to laugh. "I suppose another glass of wine won't hurt before I get back to work."

Chapter 3

Stella would have known her protector anywhere. She had stored up the memory of those curiously light eyes, that strong jaw, the perfection of his mouth. It was as if, in that brief instant of seeing him all those years ago, her mind had taken a mental photograph. That was how she knew the man at the beachside cafe was watching her. Not just ogling a random girl in a swimsuit. Not smirking with amusement as she struggled with the tie on her bikini top and almost flashed the whole Barcelonan beachfront as she emerged from the water. No, he was watching her because it was *him*, and that was what he did.

Although in his own form Stella's protector stayed on the edge of her vision, she knew he sometimes came to her in human form. She would get that feeling—as if warm honey had been injected into her veins—and she would know. He was the lifeguard at the swimming pool when she slipped and hit her head. Or the electrician who fixed the faulty wiring in her apartment.

Once she had been jogging in the park when a dog ran toward her. She hadn't been alarmed at first but, out of nowhere, a figure had streaked past her and wrestled the animal to the ground. The beast had clamped its jaws onto the man's forearm, but luckily he wore padding so that its teeth did not sink into his flesh. Some sort of dog training exercise, Stella had thought as she ran past. Then the familiar soothing feeling had come over her and she had paused to look back. Although they had been there only seconds earlier, there was no longer any sign of either the man or the dog.

Another time, after a night out with friends, she had been about to get into a taxi when a line-jumper had shoved her out of the way and stolen her cab. Her initial fury had died away as the sweet warmth flowed through her. A collective gasp of horror had risen from the watching partygoers as the taxi pulled away straight into the path of an out-of-control truck. The cab had spun wildly, like a toy in the hand of a giant, before banging to a stop. Its rear end was crushed like a concertina. Stella had shivered in her thin party dress as she gave a witness statement to the police.

"There was no one else in the car," the police officer assured her. "Luckily. Anyone in the backseat would have been smashed into a million pieces against that wall."

The closest she'd got to actually seeing the real him was when she actually was involved in a car accident. She'd been sixteen. A rebellious, studiously unorthodox sixteen-year-old who jumped on the back of the motorcycle of her latest crush. When her protector pulled her from the wreck that time, the only precaution he'd been able to take was to pull his cap down low over his face. She supposed it was because he didn't have enough time to do anything else before the gas tank exploded.

"Don't keep hiding from me. I like who you are," she had told him just before she lost consciousness.

That was what she said again now as she tugged a wrap over her bikini and marched up to the table where he sat.

"Huh?" He looked up in surprise as she took the seat opposite.

"I said I like who you are."

"Thanks." His grin was surprisingly boyish and shy. "I think."

Stella's heart did a funny little flip as if it had suddenly developed an extra beat. He looked so much younger than she'd expected. He hadn't aged at all. They stared at each other.

Finally, she spoke again. "All this time."

"I know."

He was beautiful. It was not a word Stella usually associated with men, but it suited him. Despite the coiled muscular strength of his body, his face was artistic. If she didn't know otherwise, she'd have guessed he was a painter, musician or poet. It was something about those high cheekbones, the narrow nose and strong jaw. *Don't keep staring at the gorgeous mouth,* she told herself firmly. It was his eyes that drew her most strongly. They were every bit as mesmerizing as she remembered. In the shade they were the color of a faded eucalyptus leaf. As he looked away into the sunlight, they shone like silver coins.

Forcing herself to focus, she asked the first of the many questions that jostled for a place on her lips. "Why have you appeared to me now?"

That broke the spell. A slight frown creased his brow and he pulled his eyes away from hers. "Because you are in grave danger."

She leaned forward excitedly. "Is this about that meteorite?"

"There was no meteorite, Stella."

"I knew it! Never mind what Ezra said—" She broke off. "What's your name?"

"My name is Cal."

She studied him with her head on one side. "I thought it would be more dramatic. Gabriel, Raphael or something like that. But I like it. It suits you. So tell me about this meteorite that wasn't a meteorite, Cal."

"It was a gargoyle."

Stella wrinkled her nose. "Like the statues you get on churches and cathedrals?"

"Some of them do spend their daytime hibernation crouching on buildings, yes."

Stella watched him in fascination. *Hibernation? Crouching?* Those words ascribed a life force to something that could not be alive. How could he speak of something like that so calmly? Her mouth felt uncomfortably dry, and she decided to focus on the mundane rather than the bizarre. "I've left my bag down on the beach. Can you get me a bottle of water? I mean, do angels carry cash?"

He grinned and signaled to the waiter. "When I'm here, Stella, I do normal, mortal things. Plus some other stuff."

"It's the other stuff that's starting to bother me." Stella took a long swig of water. "Okay. How did a stone statue drop out of the sky into the garden of the casa the other night?"

"It glided."

"Of course it did. Stone is well-known for its aerodynamic qualities."

He started to laugh. "You're so...*you*. Even though they have wings, gargoyles can't fly. They glide. So it glided into Moncoya's garden. I think they use the updrafts, the same way a bird does." He mimed a gliding motion with his arms outstretched.

"Cal, are you seriously trying to tell me gargoyles are living creatures?"

"Not in the sense that humans are. Gargoyles are supernatural beings. During the day they are stone. At night they are flesh, blood, bone and muscle." He tapped a fingertip against his temple. "Not much in the brain department, sadly."

Stella exhaled slowly. "Okay, because you are you—and I've lived with the reality of you all my life—I'm going to suspend every rational instinct and try to believe you when you say that gargoyles can glide. So we've done the 'how.' Now the 'why.' *Why* did that particular gargoyle drop in on us the other night? Was it just a social call?"

"It had been sent to get you, Stella."

"Sent to get *me*?" The word came out as an undignified squeak, and she fought to get her voice back under control. "Who by?"

He shrugged. "I haven't been able to discover that. Yet. There are a number of possibilities."

Stella glanced over her shoulder. "This is a joke, right? It's a reality TV show or something. Any minute now someone will jump out with a microphone and we'll all laugh about how I fell for this."

"You know that isn't going to happen."

She sighed. "If I hadn't known you all my life, I might have been able to convince myself this was some sort of prank. Unfortunately for me, you exude your own mystical gravitas. So this mystery person who sent a gargoyle after me is the grave danger you've come to warn me about?"

He shook his head slowly. "I can deal with gargoyles. They're a nuisance, but easy to put back in their box. I can also take out whoever sent it." The declaration should have sounded macho and boastful, but it didn't. On Cal's lips, it was a simple statement of fact. "But there is a very powerful being who wants you, Stella. This is one thing I am totally sure of. He wants you very badly and he is known for his determination. You must be on your guard."

"And this being is…?"

"The king of the faeries."

"I'm guessing we're not talking pretty little winged creatures who live at the bottom of the garden."

Cal shook his head. "This isn't a child's fairy tale. Faeries are ancient beings of wonder and enchantment. They have great physical beauty while they bring dire peril in their wake. Their power for destruction is enormous."

"So how will I recognize the king of the faeries when he comes for me?"

"You already know him." Stella had a sudden and overpowering premonition that she did not want to hear Cal's next words. He said them anyway. "His name is Moncoya."

Steam swirled around Stella and she exulted in the sensation, allowing the water to play over her aching shoulders. Too much time hunched close to a computer screen left her with a crick in her neck that felt as if it was here to stay. After several minutes of soothing warmth, she turned the shower to cool. The Spanish evening was still and sultry. It felt as if there should be sangria and flamenco guitar awaiting her, not a laptop and a pizza. Stepping from the shower, she wrapped herself in one towel and dried her hair with another. When she emerged from the bathroom, she was startled to find Cal sitting on her bed. He was wearing only a pair of ancient cutoff jeans, and the sight of his golden torso did something unmentionable to her insides.

"I suppose I should be glad you stayed out here," she said, disguising her inappropriate reaction with sarcasm.

"I promise never to join you in the shower." His gaze swept over her body, registering the fact that she was wearing nothing but a thigh-skimming towel. The corner of his mouth lifted in appreciative acknowledgment. "Not without an invitation anyway."

The smile was almost irresistible. Almost. The memory of their last encounter was still fresh in Stella's mind, however. Gargoyles and faeries and supernatural threats to her safety. It was all very well having a personal bodyguard—and, it really, really helped that hers was so gorgeous—but she wasn't going to be drawn into all the weird stuff. She had told him as much down at the beach. It seemed he had not got the message.

"I'd like to get dressed." She maintained a dignified tone.

"Pretend I'm not here." Cal turned his back.

It was on the tip of Stella's tongue to order him out of her room, when it occurred to her that she wouldn't know if he'd actually gone. It was probably better to have him here, where she could see that glorious expanse of tanned, muscled back while she threw on her shorts and top, than send him away.

"Are you my guardian angel?"

Stella threw herself down on the bed, lying on her back, with her hands laced behind her head. The room was furnished in a traditional Spanish style with walls that were painted in warm, soothing terra-cotta tones. The floor tiles were a mosaic of blue and gold, and carved, dark wood furniture lined the room. A ceiling fan made lazy circles above her head. Cal seemed to debate joining her and then sat on the floor at the foot of the bed, stretching his long legs in front of him. From the angle she had chosen, all Stella could actually see of him now was the lower half of his legs and his bare feet. Just as she decided he wasn't going to answer the question, he spoke.

"It's hard for me to answer that because the concept of a

guardian angel has been created by humans. Mortals have built a set of rules around something they do not understand because they want to be able to explain it."

Stella threw a cushion in his general direction. "Answer the bloody question."

The cushion flew back at her. "In my experience, mortals don't like it when the response is not what they want to hear."

Tired of not being able to see him, she moved to the other end of the bed and lay on her stomach so that her face was only inches from his. "Are you being enigmatic to annoy me or are you trying to tell me I've got the terminology wrong?"

"Both."

He grinned and Stella watched in fascination as a dimple danced at the corner of his mouth. It wasn't something she'd ever thought about, never having been able to get close to him before, but Cal did not conform to the blueprint of physical perfection that should surely be a prerequisite for an angel. It was those minor imperfections—the gap between his front teeth that was a fraction too wide, the tiny star-shaped scar at the corner of his right eye, the unruly lock of hair flopping onto his forehead, the golden-brown stubble—that made him such a stunning-looking man. And that in itself was surely wrong. Weren't angels meant to be asexual? But, if what he was saying was correct, she needed to unlearn everything she thought she knew about angels.

She linked her hands together and propped her chin on them, enjoying being close to him. It was a strange sensation, like getting to know someone she had been acquainted with all her life. Or coming face-to-face with a pen pal in whom she had confided her most intimate secrets. Getting to know him? Who was she trying to fool?

She'd stored up the memory of his face ever since that long-ago moonlit night. Wasn't falling for your guardian angel forbidden? She frowned, trying to remember the results from the time she'd searched the internet for it. She was fairly sure horrible things would happen to heaven and earth if an angel and a mortal ever made love. Unless that bit wasn't true? Her heart gave a hopeful little skip. *Getting a bit ahead of yourself, Stella,* she told herself firmly.

"Are you all right?" Cal's voice brought her back to reality. "You've gone very red."

"It's what we humans do in the heat. I did a lot of research about guardian angels. I did it so I would know all about *you*. Are you telling me it was all wrong?"

She thought the look in the depths of his shimmering eyes became guarded. The laughter and teasing were gone. "Some of it almost certainly was." His voice was colorless. "Guardian angel or not, can we do what I came here for? Can we talk about how I intend to keep you safe from Moncoya?"

Stella sat up abruptly. "Not this again."

"Yes, this again." Cal reached out a hand, but she evaded him.

"I need a cold drink." Slipping from the bed without another word, Stella left the room and made her way down the stairs.

Chapter 4

Cal swore under his breath. He could hear voices from the lower floor, which meant he could go down there only if he was invisible. Invisibility meant he would not be unable to interact with Stella, which in turn meant he could not try to convince her of the danger she was in. Every minute she spent with Moncoya was enabling the faerie king to draw her deeper under his spell. Such was the power the so-called "little people" could wield when they chose. Not that Stella appeared to be in need of much persuasion. Helplessness was a new sensation for Cal. It was not one he relished.

It bothered him that she thought of him as her guardian angel, although, in many ways that was exactly what he had become. Not by choice, and there was certainly nothing angelic about him. His thoughts recoiled from the memories that had led him here. It didn't matter how he had come to be in this role. Whatever label Stella gave him, his job was to protect her and he couldn't do that if he stayed up here and couldn't see what she was doing. Sighing, he followed her.

Cloaked by invisibility, he reached the foot of the stairs and cast a swift glance about the vast room. Stella was standing by the drinks machine, sipping water from a glass. There was no one else around and Cal frowned. He had definitely heard voices. A glance at the glass wall showed him that the panels were closed. Shadowy movement in the dusk beyond the terrace caught Cal's gaze and he walked over to get a closer look. His attention was diverted as Moncoya entered behind him through the front door. Stella didn't notice and the faerie king paused, eyeing her rear view appreciatively. Cal couldn't really blame him. It was a particularly tempting sight.

Moncoya's embroidered waistcoat hung open over a white dress shirt and he wore skintight black leggings tucked into glossy riding boots. His hair was tied back in a ponytail. Momentarily, Cal caught a glimpse of the yellow ring that lit his eyes. How could Stella not see that there was something fundamentally wrong about this guy?

"Buenas noches." Moncoya strolled forward and Stella swung around to face him. Although she smiled, there was a touch of nervousness in her expression. *Good. I've managed to plant at least a seed of doubt,* Cal thought. "Something troubles you?" Moncoya's eyes raked her face.

Stella shook her head. "It's this heat." She took another sip from her half-full glass and Moncoya observed the action through narrowed eyes. It was clear to Cal that Stella was uncomfortable. Moncoya, his faerie senses so closely attuned to the feelings of others, would certainly pick up on it.

"*Sí*, it is very warm. May I?" Moncoya stretched out a hand for the glass. Cal recalled, just in time, that a faerie could claim a mortal for its own by luring the person into sharing food or water. Before Stella could hand over the glass, Cal reached out an invisible hand and snatched it from her. It shattered on the tiled floor.

Stella's exclamation of shock echoed in the vast space. "I'm so sorry! I don't know how I came to be so clumsy."

"Be careful." Moncoya spoke mechanically. "Your feet are bare. You must move away from this area while I clear away the glass."

Biting her lip in chagrin, Stella followed his instruction. Moncoya knelt to collect the shards of glass. He looked up and straight at Cal. Cal froze, even though there was no way Moncoya could possibly see him.

"So the little star has a protector. How sweet." The ring around Moncoya's azure eyes gleamed with red fire, the way his sidhe underlings' eyes did when they skulked under Stella's bed. His voice was low and feral. "I don't know who you are, but I can guess who sent you. No matter. A little rivalry adds spice to the conquest."

With that, he walked over to Stella and slipped a possessive arm about her waist. Cal was left watching in helpless rage as his charge turned an apologetic smile on the faerie king. He weighed his options. Go over and intervene? It would give him great pleasure to sink his fist into Moncoya's smug face, but there was unforeseen danger in that sort of action. Naively, Cal had assumed he would be able to warn Stella of the danger and she would believe him. He had not envisioned a scenario where she refused to listen. If she went willingly to Moncoya—or any of the other warring factions—all would be lost. And he knew his stubborn charge all too well. If he went after Moncoya with his fists swinging, he could not predict Stella's reaction. She might view Moncoya as the underdog. What if she decided to punish him by siding with Moncoya? It was a chance he couldn't take. He had to get her to listen to him…or force Moncoya into revealing his true nature.

The movement in the garden drew Cal's attention again. It had become more obvious now. It was as if the darkness itself was swirling up against the window, shifting and changing shape as it pressed against the glass. The voices he had heard earlier were clearer now. Soft and persuasive, they murmured an incantation. Another sound, like giant beating wings and distant hoofbeats, caught Cal's straining ears. Stella appeared not to notice these out-of-place sounds. Moncoya, his hearing as finely tuned as Cal's, looked up with a frown just as the first crack appeared in the giant wall of glass.

Cal faced a difficult choice. He couldn't remain invisible and shield Stella with his body. Materializing was dangerous because Moncoya would see his face. He would know whom he was dealing with. But Cal's first duty was to his charge. Those thoughts took a fraction of a second. Then he reacted like lightning. Materializing, he grabbed Stella by the hand and threw her—protesting loudly— down onto one of the oversize cushions as far from the window as possible. Before she could bounce back up again, he covered her body with his own.

He was just in time. The entire glass wall at the rear of the casa imploded, showering the room with shards of glass. Moncoya's howl of fury rose above the sounds of mayhem as the shapes of the night poured into the room.

"Who dares approach Moncoya in his lair?"

"Lair?" Despite Cal's efforts to keep her completely covered, Stella wriggled partially out from under him and turned her head to see what had happened. But Cal kept her pinned in place with one of his legs spread across her body. He knew her too well. If there was danger, his feisty charge was likely to throw herself right into the thick of it.

The amorphous mass of the darkness began to shift and three winged figures could now be seen within the quivering cloud. Although their features were indistinct, their figures were female and they were on horseback. Moncoya lifted his hands and the formless horses reared up as though in fright.

"What are they?" Stella's breath was warm as it tickled Cal's ear.

"Valkyries." He answered her absentmindedly. His thoughts were occupied with escape, his eyes measuring the distance to the door. "Be ready to run when I give you the word."

"You know why we come." One of the Valkyries moved slightly ahead of the others. Her voice was compelling and echo-like. As the Valkyrie spoke, the shapes around her shifted as though straining to get closer into the room.

"Your audacity is beyond astounding. I have staked the first claim. She belongs to me." The words were spoken in a booming voice that was totally unlike Moncoya's usual subtle tones.

"You wrong us. We do not come for the star. Ours is the task of escorting the fallen." Cal wasn't sure if he was imagining it, but he thought the Valkyrie's voice seemed to be fading.

"I will give you fallen aplenty. With her at my side, the conclusion to the battle will be swift and bloody, the outcome final. Otherworld will be mine."

The Valkyrie's horse lunged nervously as, laughing, Moncoya took a step forward. He raised his hands again and the dark cloud changed, becoming a swirling smoke cloud before gradually dispersing. In its place, as if by magic, Moncoya's party friends began to pour in through the gaping wall. Laughter and music filled the room as they danced across a floor somehow miraculously clear now of glass and debris. The change in atmosphere brought even more theater to the scene.

"Now," Cal urged and, to his relief, Stella leaped to her feet and kept pace with him as he ran for the door. As they burst through and into the night air beyond, he grabbed her hand, hauling her to the parked vehicles. Selecting the largest and most powerful of the motorbikes, he swung himself onto it, gesturing for Stella to get up behind him. She obeyed, clasping her arms tightly around his waist and pressing her cheek into his back.

"Can you start it?"

He fished the keys out of his pocket. "It's mine."

The engine roared to life and they screeched out of the drive just as the door of the casa flew open.

"I'm so glad I've got you for my guardian angel," Stella yelled as, both barefoot and clad in shorts, they streaked down the hill into the busy city streets.

"Who told you I was an angel?" Cal shouted back over his shoulder, cutting across a stream of traffic.

"Can we talk about this on the way? Because I for one would like to put as much distance between us and Moncoya as I can." Cal was throwing clothing into a suitcase while Stella sat curled up in a chair in his hotel room, watching him. Despite the heat, she was clad in one of his hoodies. The sleeves were rolled back and, when she stood up, it hung almost to her knees. Her feet were still bare.

"Talk while you pack. You can start by telling me about Otherworld."

He ran a frustrated hand through his hair. "Otherworld is a realm inhabited by supernatural beings. It exists alongside the world of the living, but is invisible to most humans. The intrusion of the Otherworld into this one does take place, but, when that happens, it is mainly unobtrusive and harmless."

"Are you talking about ghosts?"

"Ghosts are the most common manifestation of an overlap between Otherworld and the world of the living, yes. But ghosts are not the only beings to inhabit Otherworld. If they were, my job would be much easier. Ghosts are generally not aggressive, although there are breakaway groups within their numbers, notably banshees and poltergeists. The Ghost Lord is not one of those leaders who seeks to take control of the whole realm of Otherworld." Cal snapped the suitcase shut and looked around, checking the room to make sure he had collected all of his belongings. "Let's go." He glanced down at her feet. "We'll get you some shoes on the way."

Stella followed him out of the room. "It sounds complicated."

"Tell me about it. Just as this world has its different countries and races and religions, so Otherworld has its own dynasties. It is not a physical realm, but it is as fiercely fought. Debates rage as furiously there as they do here. Battles are as bloody, if not more so. The difference is that the weapons used are deadlier and the methods employed are more ruthless. It is my task to ensure that the war for Otherworld does not spill over into the world of the living."

"Sounds like a hell of a big job for one man." *Where in all of this do you find the time to babysit me? And why?* Stella massaged her temples, trying to get rid of the ache that was forming there.

Cal chucked the suitcase into the trunk of a particularly nondescript car, and then held the passenger door open for Stella. She slid inside. It had not once occurred to her not to go with him. Her every instinct cried out that he was her only hope. Against what, she had no idea.

"Car. Bike. You must have known we would have to make a quick getaway," she said as Cal started the car.

"I know Moncoya."

Stella shivered. She wasn't ready for that conversation. "Who are the aggressors in Otherworld?"

The city traffic was heavy and Cal joined a line of cars heading for the suburbs. "It changes over time, with different dynasties fading in and out of prominence. The vampires are always at the forefront of any conflict. Their prince has caused us problems on and off for the past few millennia. Rage is the most powerful underlying motivator for the vampires." He grinned down at her stunned expression. "Makes them bloody difficult to negotiate with, I can tell you."

Stella swallowed the obstruction in her throat. "You mean proper vampires? The full-on, bloodsucking kind?"

"Is there another kind?"

"But you just said that the overlap between Otherworld and this world is harmless. If vampires are real and they drop in and out to feast on human blood, I wouldn't exactly say they do us no harm," she argued.

Cal appeared to give it some thought. "I see what you mean. They do harm those individuals they feed on and ultimately transform into new vampires, that much is true. In the grand scheme of things, their proclivities don't fundamentally change the earthly realm. It's something vampires have always done. It's a bit of a nuisance, especially when we get a high-profile case that has to be covered up. It doesn't change the status quo, however, so there's no real damage done."

Stella covered her mouth with one shaking hand, regarding his profile with eyes that were wide with shock. As he drew up at a red light, Cal turned and returned her gaze with a question in his eyes. When she lowered her hand, her lips trembled on something that was an attempt at a smile. "A bit of a nuisance? Cal, what the hell is happening here? And why am I part of this Otherworld madness?"

Cal's eyes ached. Neon advertising signs, overhead lights and the relentless stream of headlights coming in the opposite direction had taken their toll. It was only just over an hour since they had left Barcelona, but his intense concentration on the road and who or what might be following made it feel as if he had been driving forever. Squinting slightly as he read the road signs, he was relieved to see that they were approaching the city of Girona.

"Tell me again why we couldn't get a flight from Barcelona Airport?" Stella spoke for the first time since they had left the shopping center on the outskirts of the city, where they had stopped to get fuel and the cheap plastic sandals that now encased her feet. Cal had managed to avoid the question about how she came to be involved in the Otherworld uprising by claiming it was a complicated story and he needed to concentrate on getting them to safety. Stella had huffed at him, but accepted his admittedly pathetic excuse. He wondered now if she really wanted to hear the answer. Sooner or later, it was a conversation they would have to have. He wasn't looking forward to it. Bloody Valkyries. What had possessed *them* to get involved before there had even been any fighting? Their job was to gather up the fallen, not come storming in causing havoc before the first blow had been struck. But these were strange times. Ever since the three-tailed comet had first appeared two months ago, tensions in Otherworld—always heightened—had fizzed to the surface like champagne bubbles pressing at a cork.

"They will expect us to go to the main airport. It's the

first place they'll look. Hopefully, by the time they think of the smaller airport at Girona, we'll be out of here."

Stella mouthed the word *they* to herself but said no more. He was worried about her. It was a feeling that went beyond the obvious concerns for her safety. She looked very small and lost in his well-worn hoodie. Cal experienced an overpowering, urgent desire to reach out a hand and touch her. To smooth the spikes of her hair into place or stroke her cheek. Determinedly he kept both hands on the wheel and fixed his gaze back on the road. Forced himself to remember that he was a protector, not a nursemaid or something more intimate.

The gargoyle had been an interesting, although not entirely unexpected, diversion. Gargoyles were generally solitary creatures. Nevertheless, Cal very much doubted that the one that had descended in such a cumbersome manner into Moncoya's garden had arrived there on its own behalf. Gargoyles were not noted for their mental agility so it was highly unlikely the creature itself had been responsible for planning the offensive. A mind more cunning than that of a grotesque figure that spent its days crouching on the side of a church had thought up that little scheme. Because, even without Cal's intervention, the lone gargoyle had never stood a chance against the might of Moncoya. Which meant it had probably been sent simply to discover if Stella actually was at La Casa Oscura. If it had found her alone and succeeded in snatching her while it was there…well, that would have been a nice bonus for whoever sent it. So who had commissioned a gargoyle to enter Moncoya's lair on a reconnaissance mission? There were, as Cal had already said to Stella, a number of possibilities. None of them was pretty.

The arrival of the Valkyries had overset his plans in a way that the gargoyle had not. The Valkyries were not warriors, they didn't take sides. Their disorientation signaled that the powers at work were more sinister and disruptive than anything even Cal had encountered before. He couldn't have left Stella in the middle of the mayhem that had been taking place back at La Casa Oscura. And yet, wasn't that exactly what was meant to happen? Wasn't it her destiny to be launched into the midst of the uprising at this point in time? No. He shook his head. He knew now that the forces gathering were greater and more volatile than he had anticipated. Something had changed. Therefore he had to alter his plans accordingly. The confrontation would come, that part of the prophecy was inevitable. And Stella would be part of it. That too had been foretold. *My job is to equip her for what lies ahead. It was bad enough when I knew what she was facing. I cannot allow her to go into this new unknown without preparing her. And this change of plan would have nothing to do with how you felt when Moncoya put his hands on her?* He ignored the insidious little voice in his head as he followed the road signs for the airport.

"Where are we now?" Stella shifted in her seat and blinked at the unprepossessing view of industrial units in the darkness beyond the window.

"Approaching Girona. I need you to get on the internet and book us on the next plane to England."

She bit her lip. "This is a bit embarrassing, but I haven't got any money."

He threw a quick grin in her direction. "I know. You never do. Reach over and get my jacket off the backseat. There's a credit card in my wallet."

"Angels with credit cards, what next?" Stella wriggled around until she'd retrieved his jacket. "Oh, I forgot. You get all antsy when I call you an angel."

Cal was conscious of her scanning his profile in the

close confines of the car but he deliberately didn't respond to either her words or her scrutiny. After a shrug, Stella busied herself with her phone. "We're in luck. There's a flight to Manchester in three hours and they have seats available. Oh, and when we get on that plane, Cal—" her voice was restored to something approaching its normal tone "—I have one or two questions to ask you."

"It might be best to save the conversation for somewhere more private." *There you go putting it off. She has to know. You can't protect her forever from what she is.*

"You might be right. But the question you can start with right now is why the bloody hell I've just paid for our fares using a credit card belonging to someone called Emrys Jones?"

Chapter 5

Watching Cal while he slept might actually be addictive, Stella decided. The sculpted perfection of his chest rose and fell in time with his rhythmic breathing. The skin of his neck, exposed to her gaze as his head rested against the plane window, was incredibly smooth, with a bronzed sheen that was just begging to be touched. Long eyelashes fanned his cheeks and his lips were slightly parted. Temptingly so. *You are annoyed with him, remember? That doesn't go away just because he happens to be gut-wrenchingly gorgeous.*

Cal was her most enduring memory, the one true constant in her life. No one else had stuck around. She had convinced herself he was her guardian angel, had even— she blushed now at the memory—daydreamed about him falling in love with her. Yet he was undeniably prickly about the label. If he wasn't an angel, who was he? Or perhaps the question should be *what* was he? One thing was for sure, he was definitely flesh and blood right now. And his human form was doing something utterly primeval to her nerve endings. Nevertheless, the puzzle of his identity had never been far from her mind since she had first seen him at the beach. Considering what had been going on in her life just lately, it was quite remarkable that Cal managed to occupy so much of her thoughts.

She wondered if she should be more distressed at the events of the past few days. But, if she accepted the reality of Cal—and, throughout her life she had not just accepted him, she had welcomed him—then she had to also acknowledge that there was a whole paranormal world out there that she didn't understand. It was true that the manifestation of it all at once in the form of gargoyles and Valkyries and Cal taking on this delectable human form was unbelievable. But perhaps there was a reason for that. La Casa Oscura might be within some sort of magnetic field or something. She still couldn't get her head around how Moncoya, one of the most famous men in the world, could also find time to be the king of the faeries. More important, from a basic survival point of view...

"What the hell has any of this got to do with me?" She addressed the question to the sleeping beauty next to her. Cal didn't stir.

Grudgingly, she had accepted his explanation about the credit card. "I have no idea what's going to happen with Moncoya so we need to be prepared for any eventuality. I have a number of cards all in different names. It's not exactly legal in the mortal realm, but it's a necessity in the face of what our faerie friend might throw at us."

She hadn't asked the most obvious question about what Moncoya might throw at them. She had a feeling she might find that out the hard way. Instead, she'd gone for another, equally important, question. "Is Cal your real name?"

A heartbeat, nothing more, before he had answered her. "Yes."

She had shown no further qualms about using the credit card again when, having left the car in the airport parking lot, they had checked in at a desk thronged with weary-looking tourists. "Our flight leaves at two a.m. Come on." Cal had grabbed her wrist. "We've got time to get you some new clothes." The nonexistent Emrys Jones had paid hefty airport terminal prices for skinny black jeans, sneakers and a light blue sweater. Hoodie, tacky plastic shoes, shorts and tank top had all been dumped in a restroom bin. It was a reminder that everything she owned was back at La Casa Oscura.

Now Stella was crammed into the narrow seats of the economy flight, with Cal's broad shoulders overlapping her personal space and his long legs bent at an awkward angle so that his knees pressed against hers. They were about half an hour from landing in England and he'd been asleep since takeoff. She prodded him sharply in the ribs and he opened one eye.

"Nice to see you remain alert and watchful at all times, Mr. Protector."

He yawned and stretched. "It's an act." Stella raised a skeptical eyebrow and he grinned. "Well, I fooled you, didn't I?"

Stella cast a sidelong glance at the youth who sat on her other side. He had on headphones and was engrossed in his handheld game throughout the flight. "Tell me about Moncoya."

"Moncoya has ruled the faeries for several centuries. He was not in the direct line of succession, nor was there ever any expectation that he would inherit the title. His claim was tenuous at best. In fact his only qualification, at that time, was his ruthlessness. Moncoya and his sidhes infiltrated the residence of the former king during a celebration. In the middle of the night, when everyone was sleeping, they rose up and slaughtered any who did not support them, including the king. Until that time, violence was not the faerie way. The faeries were thrown into total disarray, and Moncoya took advantage of the ensuing chaos to impose his will on them. He has ruled by fear ever since."

Stella made a winding motion with one finger. "Go back a bit. What is a sidhe?"

"If you picture the faeries as a nation, a bit like Britain, then there are many nationalities within it. The sidhes make up the majority of the population. They are the 'little people' of Celtic legend." Stella thought of Moncoya, who was just above her own height. "They are endowed with incredible physical beauty and are able to coexist with humans. Traditionally faeries have had the ability to shapeshift, but Moncoya frowns on it as it doesn't fit with his modernizing ideals. Although Moncoya was elevated to the faerie gentry when he took the throne, he is a sidhe and he surrounds himself with loyal fellow sidhes."

"So the party people at La Casa Oscura...?" Stella supposed she already knew the answer.

"Sidhes. They are Moncoya's bodyguards."

"I don't understand how he can be the Ezra Moncoya he is in this world and also be the faerie king. You don't get to build up one of the greatest games empires in the world without putting the hours in. If he has to keep dashing off to rule his faerie empire in Otherworld, I just can't see how he manages it."

Cal grinned. "It's called magic. And Moncoya has such an iron grip on the faeries, he has no real opposition to his rule. He also has a very powerful weapon at his disposal... his two consorts."

"Isn't a consort like a queen? Does that mean he has two wives?"

"No. In Moncoya's case his consorts are his daughters. He has trained his twin daughters, Tanzi and Vashti, to be his most powerful weapons."

"What I don't understand is why, if he has all this power over the faeries, he would want a presence *here*. Why bother with the pretense of being mortal at all, let alone this sexy, high-profile celebrity persona Moncoya has deliberately cultivated?"

Cal turned his head and gazed out the window for a moment. The plane was beginning its descent and, looking past his profile, Stella could see the lights of the towns and villages below them. When he spoke, his voice was quiet and curiously regretful. "That's where you come in, Stella."

"Finally."

Cal turned back to look at her. "When I spoke of the beings who exist just beyond mortal sight, and who reside in the realm of Otherworld, there is one I did not mention. This one does not always choose to dwell in Otherworld. He, or she, will be born mortal and may, therefore, walk this mortal realm unnoticed. This, the most powerful of them all, is a rare and usually solitary being, with the ability to weave the most intricate of spells. Creating light within darkness, animating the bodies of the dead and exerting absolute control over the spirit realm. This being has no need of legions or battles, not when, with a single incantation, every undead entity within Otherworld and beyond will bow before this being in abject submission."

Something about the solemnity of his expression made Stella's heart flutter alarmingly. She tried to hide her nervousness by keeping her tone light. "Who is this being?"

"I'm speaking of the sorcerer known as a necromancer."

When she evinced no surprise, a slight frown creased his brow. "You've heard of it?"

"Sure have. Level Eight skills set. Very difficult to achieve. A couple of the guys in my halls at university managed it, but they were real stay-up-all-night-gaming geeks." She laughed at his expression. "And you have no idea what I'm talking about."

The frown vanished and he smiled in a slightly bemused, and utterly adorable, manner. "I really don't."

"'Crypt Wars,'" Stella explained. When Cal still looked uncomprehending, she elaborated further. "It's a computer game. Pretty basic stuff. You progress through the levels in turn and take on different forms as you do. The higher the level, the more powerful the being. Necromancer was Level Eight, just above fire-breathing dragons and just below carnivorous skeletons."

"I'm not going to go into just how flawed that hierarchy is right now, but let me assure you that necromancers do exist outside the world of computer games. And necromancy is a spectrum, ranging from low-level skills such as conversing with the deceased to complete control over the undead, as I have described."

"They do? How cool is that?" Stella fastened her seat belt. All around them the businesslike bustle of the plane preparing to land continued regardless of their strange conversation.

"Quite cool, until you realize the lengths to which each of these leaders would go in order to get a necromancer on their side."

Stella thought carefully about it. "Oh, I see. If the vampire prince you mentioned, for instance, had a necromancer on his side, he could have a spell cast that would render Moncoya powerless to harm him. Powerless to do anything much at all, in fact."

Cal shook his head. "Not quite. Moncoya is not undead, having never actually been alive in the mortal sense of the word. So, although a necromancer could have some control over him, it would not be absolute. The spell would work the other way around, however. If Moncoya got his hands on a necromancer, he could exert total control over the vampires, phantoms and therianthropes—or were-creatures as they have become known—within Otherworld as well as some of the lesser undead. It would also be possible, if necessary, to summon the earthly dead from their graves and raise an army of corpses. If Moncoya could do all of this, his dream of ruling all Otherworld would be realized."

"A corpse army? How horrid!" Stella wrinkled her nose. "You said necromancers are rare, so I'm guessing none of the warring factions currently have one working with them."

"Correct. You already have a very astute grasp of Otherworld politics, Stella. My sources tell me that Moncoya has uncovered the identity of possibly the most powerful necromancer of all time. The arrival of this unparalleled sorcerer was predicted centuries ago by another great necromancer, one whose very name has become enshrined in legend."

"Who was that?"

"You would know him by the name he took during his time on earth. At that time, he called himself Merlin."

"Well, yes. As sorcerers go, they don't come much more well-known than Merlin," Stella conceded. "You said necromancers are mortal, yet you just said he took the name Merlin here on earth. That implies he wasn't human."

"That's because he wasn't. Merlin was a hybrid. He was born of a mortal mother and a nonmortal father."

"And there is really someone around today who Merlin predicted would come along and be this all-powerful necromancer? That's mind-blowing stuff. I'm surprised he's managed to keep it quiet. You'd think the press would be all over him like a rash. Talk about celebrity status." Stella leaned across him as she spoke to look out the plane window. They were close enough to the ground now to see the lights of the individual cars, although, given that it was now the early hours of the morning, they were few and far between.

Cal's breath was warm on her cheek when he spoke. "The necromancer of the prophecy is not yet aware of his or her own powers."

"If that's the case, how does Moncoya know who it is?"

"Merlin's prophecies are well-known, but often cryptic. This one is no different." Cal quoted the words, like a child remembering lines from a play. "*When the three-tailed comet returns to Iberia's skies and the brightest star has seen five and twenty harvests, then he who claims the heart of the necromancer star will unite the delightful plain.* During Merlin's time, Otherworld was referred to by many names, one of which was 'the delightful plain.'" He was watching her face closely.

"You're right. That is a pretty vague prophecy." She leaned back in her seat. Cal's eyes seemed to bore into her and she frowned, trying to get a sense of what he was attempting to convey to her. Her mind was stubbornly refusing to process what was behind his words. Part of her—a really big part, the biggest imaginable part—didn't want to do this next bit. The plane wheels touched down in the same instant that it hit her like a punch in the gut.

"Oh, no. No. *No.*" She shook her head to punctuate the increasingly emphatic words. "Stella means star... And I'm twenty-five? And the comet appeared when I arrived in Spain… Iberia? Come *on*, Cal, this is all too far-fetched for words."

In the end, it wasn't the fact that he didn't try to persuade her or even the trace of pity in the silver depths of his eyes that struck the most fear into her heart. Those things no longer mattered. Not when, just as the plane taxied to a halt and the passengers began to unbuckle their seat belts, she looked again at the youth next to her.

He smiled directly at her and she was momentarily dazzled by the faun-like perfection of his features. His eyes were his most striking feature. Even greener than her own, the irises had an outer ring of pure gold. As the implication of his beauty dawned on her, she turned to Cal. He was staring over her head at the young man. In the merest blink of an eye later, she looked back again. Despite the fact that the plane doors were still closed and the aisle was filled with passengers waiting to disembark, the youth had gone.

Chapter 6

"I don't understand how he could be there one second and gone the next." Stella was almost running to keep up with Cal's long strides, but he didn't indulge her by slowing down.

"A sidhe can move faster than you can blink."

"Can they also make themselves invisible?"

"No. It's much more likely he shifted. He will have simply changed his form and become one of the other passengers. Someone you wouldn't look at twice. The harassed-looking woman over there whose roots are showing or the grumpy old guy with the cane."

They were walking briskly, weaving through the throng of people, following the signs to passport control. "What does it mean? Him being there...sitting next to me?" Even to her own ears, Stella's voice sounded very small.

"It's a message from Moncoya. He's letting us know we can't hide from him. Keep hold of my hand." As he spoke, Cal's eyes were scanning the crowd constantly.

"Believe me, I have absolutely no intention of letting go." To prove it, Stella twined her fingers more tightly between his.

"Shit." This comment was dragged from him as he assimilated the fact that all of the automated passport control machines were out of order. Three manned desks were open and long, slow-moving lines had formed at each. They joined the end of one of these.

"This must be a coincidence. Surely?" Where had that nervous flutter in her voice come from?

"Perhaps."

As words went, that one was less than reassuring. Stella cast an anxious look around her. The room was a huge, high-ceilinged, impersonal square. Other people were pouring in behind them so going back the way they had come was not an option. The only exits were beyond the barriers at which passengers had to display their passports. Two uniformed police officers stood to one side of the desks, surveying the crowd of people. In the line for the desk to the right of theirs, four young men clad in colorful ponchos and hand-knit alpaca sweaters caught Stella's eye. They all carried panpipes and looked like walking advertisements for the Peruvian tourist industry. On closer inspection, it seemed they had not fully embraced the Andean lifestyle, since each one of them wore a headset beneath his wide-brimmed leather hat.

The line shuffled slowly forward. Stella was aware of the tension in Cal's whole body that was somehow managing to communicate itself to her through the clasp of his hand. Turning to look at the line to their left, she was briefly distracted by the antics of what appeared to be a bachelorette party. Clad in tiaras, tutus and—bizarrely— galoshes, the six women looked as though they had been partying hard for days. "Have I missed some hot new trend? What is it with the headsets?" Stella wondered, noting that the women in the bridal group were all wearing them under their tiaras. Cal, tightly wound with inner tension, didn't respond.

As more passengers surged in from newly arrived planes and the room became even more crowded, they were increasingly jostled. Still holding Stella's hand in one of his, Cal also drew her close, sliding his other arm about her shoulders so that she was pressed up against the hard muscle of his chest. In spite of the circumstances, Stella took a moment to enjoy the sensation. "No matter how chaotic it gets, don't move away from me."

Stella glanced up at him, at the taut muscles of his jaw and the rigidity around his eyes. Was he tired, or was there something more to it?

Just then the poncho-wearing group shimmied closer and one of the men caught Stella's eye. As he did so, he spoke into his mouthpiece. Immediately, the other three men turned in her direction. They were all remarkable for one thing. Their good looks. She glanced across at the women in the bachelorette party. The disheveled, hungover look of minutes earlier was gone. Each one of them could have been a glamour model, except for one fact. They were all tiny.

"Er, Cal…"

"I know. It doesn't matter what they do, stay in contact with me."

"There are police officers over there." Obediently, Stella pressed herself tighter against him. "Can't we go to them and explain what's going on?"

"Stella, have you ever met a police officer shorter than you?" He was right. She glanced across at the two police officers, and one of them gave her a friendly wave. He was so handsome he might have just stepped out of a trailer as the romantic lead in a film. Sadly, his lack of inches meant he was never going to get that sort of starring role. Panic settled somewhere between her chest and her abdomen, making breathing difficult.

"What can we do?" They were completely surrounded now.

"If you are indeed the star Moncoya seeks—and you are the only one who doubts it, by the way—you can help me get us out of this."

"How?" Stella shuddered as one of the tutu-clad women came within inches of them. Her lips drew back, showing very small, perfectly even white teeth. The expression was somewhere between a smile and a snarl. The ring of fire around her irises blazed bright.

"We will be stronger together." Cal's voice, usually the softly spoken, masculine tones of her childhood imagination, sounded completely different. Now, it had become a rich baritone, full of fire and majesty, echoing around the soulless room and bringing an abrupt end to the impromptu party. Stella looked up at him and watched in fascination as the silver light in his eyes shone more brilliantly than ever. The glow in their depths would shame the purest moon beams on the darkest night. It must be her imagination—of course it was—but it was almost as if the concentrated beam from Cal's gaze was brightening the room, shimmering and glistening on each object it touched.

From nowhere, her invisible friend, Cal, had been transformed into a commanding presence of mountain-shattering proportions. Without moving, or speaking, he was dominating everything around him, and the sidhes promptly abandoned any further attempt to disguise their identity. Hissing and showing their teeth, they drew back slightly. *Beauty really is only skin-deep,* Stella thought. She was surprised she could string a coherent thought together at all, let alone make it a flippant one. Other passengers, sensing the sudden change in mood, also began to distance themselves.

The air around the two of them seemed to thicken and quiver. Stella had the oddest feeling that, if she reached out a finger, she would encounter a springy resistance. It was like being encased in invisible Bubble Wrap. Stella and Cal were alone, surrounded by a circle of irate sidhes and a more distant ring of wary onlookers.

"We're out of here. Nobody is going to stop us." Cal spoke again, still in that incredible, Shakespearean voice. Keeping his arm around Stella so that she walked in step with him, he began to move toward the passport desk. Nobody did stop them.

"Majesty will come for his star," one of the poncho-wearing sidhes, braver than his fellows, whined at them as they passed.

"Majesty can fuck off."

A collective seething rasp rose up around them. *"Galdre. Deófolwítga."* Memories came flooding back to Stella. It was the language of the monster under the bed.

They had reached the desk now. Stella looked nervously at the immigration officer, seated in his booth. She had a horrible fear he might be handsome enough to take her breath away. He wasn't. He was middle-aged, balding and looked as if he wanted to be elsewhere. Probably tucked in his bed. He also seemed oblivious to the jittery atmosphere, merely gesturing through the thick glass panel for them to step forward.

"My girlfriend is feeling unwell. These people were good enough to let us come through before them," Cal said, and Stella was relieved to hear his voice lower several tones and approach something like normality. He held his passport out to the official on the desk and gestured for Stella to do the same. "Thanks, guys." He raised his hand in a friendly wave to the line of people behind them as they passed through the barrier. Gripping Stella's hand hard, he marched toward the two sidhes dressed as police officers. They moved to block the exit.

Looking down at Stella's worried expression, he grinned. "That was fun. Ready for the hard part?"

Confronting a couple of angry sidhes in a public place, with a crowd of Moncoya's foot soldiers snapping at his heels, would not have been Cal's first choice of ways to give Stella an introductory lesson in how to deal with the threat posed by the faeries. A quick glance around showed he had no choice. Despite the early hour, this was an international airport going about its business. There were so many people milling around that the chances of bystanders getting caught in the cross fire were high. Doubtless the sidhes were counting on that. Cal's reputation for protecting the innocent was well-known. Moncoya had derided him for it often enough. All of Cal's ingenuity as well as his powers were going to be needed if he was to get Stella out of this and away to safety while ensuring no one else got hurt.

Those thoughts took seconds to flash through his mind as he and Stella walked toward the exit. The two sidhe police officers remained in place, blocking their path. A family with young children was just behind them.

Cal was unconvinced about the concept of fate. He had met the three goddesses who sat at their spindles spinning the threads of human destiny. His opinion of their motives and effectiveness wasn't high. Perhaps it was because they were condemned to a dull, lonely spinster's life for all eternity, but, in his many centuries of experience, he had discovered that they enjoyed making mortals suffer. Cal was of the school of thought that believed people made their own destiny. It helped if, like him, one wasn't mortal, in which case the influence of the goddesses was hugely reduced. At that precise moment, however, he could have kissed one, or even all three, of the ancient crones. Because, for once, they chose to intervene at exactly the right moment.

As Cal and Stella got within a few feet of the exit, the mechanized doors swung inward. This startled the two sidhes, who had been standing with their backs against the panels. One of them began to protest, but the words died on his lips as three real police officers strode into the hall and paused just inside, looking around. Cal could tell they were genuine law enforcement officers. For one thing they were as tall as him. And none of them could, by any stretch of the imagination, be described as pretty.

"...reports of a commotion down here," one of the officers was saying to his companion. He barely glanced at the sidhes. "Probably nothing, but the sergeant wants it checked out."

"Come on." Not waiting to hear any more, Cal dragged Stella with him, past the police officers, through the doors and into the arrivals hall.

He should have known it wouldn't be that easy. Freedom, and the opportunity to lose themselves on a bus or train or in a taxi, was just yards away. As they made their way past the crowds waiting at the luggage carousels, Cal could feel dozens of eyes following them. He was willing to bet that most of those eyes bore a fiery ring around the outer edge of their irises. Sure enough, as soon as he moved toward the set of doors that would lead them to the outside world, a crowd of passengers—each of them predictably short in stature—moved into place, barring their way.

Cal slowed in his stride, casting around himself for something—anything—that would help them escape. To one side of the arrivals hall there was an official motor cart. It had been hooked up to an electric charging station.

"What are you doing?" Stella cast a look over her shoulder. "They are coming through. We need to make a run for it or we'll be surrounded."

He threw a quick glance behind him and caught a glimpse of colorful ponchos and pink tutus. Hauling Stella with him, he made for the vehicle.

"Jump in." Even though the look she gave him was one of pure horror, he was profoundly glad when she did as he asked. He unplugged the vehicle from its charging dock and squeezed into the seat next to her. His knees came up almost to his chin in the cramped space.

"You're going to have to supercharge this thing to get it past that lot." Her eyes were huge and very dark green as she nodded in the direction of the doors, where the sidhes were now converging, waiting for them. There were a few anticipatory grins cast their way.

"I knew you were a girl after my own heart." Cal grinned down at her. "Hold tight."

"Hold tight?" Her expression was incredulous. "You don't seriously think this thing is going faster than we can walk, do you?"

Cal didn't reply. Instead, he focused his attention on the connection his foot made with the cart's pedal. Summoning all his supernatural energy—now was not the time to screw things up—he intoned slowly and forcefully, *"Onettan. Swiftnes."* The machine lurched, its electrical engine whirring loudly. He exhaled a sigh of pure relief as it raced across the tiled floor, gathering speed as it went.

"Cal, did you just tell this thing to go fast?" The cart was practically flying now, its tires burning rubber as it hurtled toward the sidhes. Stella lurched against him in the confined space. "And—my God, I can't believe I'm actually going to ask this—did it *understand* you?"

"No. It's only working through me. If I take my foot off the pedal, it will go back to the way it was." All around them, sidhes were diving out of the way of the speeding machine. "Once we're through the doors, get ready to jump."

The automatic doors opened as the luggage cart approached, and Cal had time to assimilate the surprised faces of several taxi drivers on the pavement as they charged through the gap and out into the open air.

"Now!" He dived off one side and saw Stella go the other way. The cart made a startled whirring noise and ground to a halt in the middle of the road, causing a minibus to swerve around it. Leaping to his feet, Cal grabbed Stella's hand. "You okay?"

She nodded and they broke into a run. Cal decided that making for the train or bus station within the airport complex would be too dangerous. Better to get away from the area completely and find another way into the transport system.

The pavement sloped away from the airport building and they were close to a multistory parking ramp when the two sidhes disguised as police officers emerged from its entrance. Cal looked over his shoulder. If they turned back, the dozens of sidhes in the arrivals hall would be waiting for them.

He stopped. The sidhes were mere feet away. Twin smiles lit their fiery eyes. They took several steps closer.

Cal raised his hand. *"Fýrwylm."*

Flames shot from his fingertips toward the sidhes, showering them with sparks. Their smiles disappeared and were replaced by wary looks.

"That the best you've got, *galdre*?" Although the sidhe licked his lips nervously, he took a step closer.

"No. He's got me." Stella placed her hand over Cal's. "What do I need to do?"

"That's my girl," he murmured, grinning down at Stella. "Think with me. Match your thoughts to mine."

He could see the concentration on her face. Her brow furrowed with the effort. Then he felt it. A surge of power, like a jolt of electricity, pulsed through Cal's body. This time when he raised his hand, together with Stella's, the bolt from his fingertips resembled a flamethrower. He had known she would be strong, but this was beyond even his expectations.

"Fýrwylm." Stella repeated the word he had used, and the flames burned even brighter. Muttering, the sidhes shrank back. "What language am I speaking?"

"Anglo-Saxon, the oldest form of the English language." Cal led her forward, clearing their way by spreading a circle of fire ahead of them.

"How do you say *bastard*?"

Cal started to laugh. "It was the same word then that it is now. Or you can say *dóc*, which means illegitimate mongrel." He didn't add that he'd been called that himself a time or two over the centuries. Usually by Moncoya.

"Okay. *Fýrwylm*, you sidhe bastards."

There were shouts now from the airport building and the sound of sirens. The two sidhe police officers had disappeared.

"Time to go." Cal urged Stella into a run again. There was no way he wanted to have to explain what was going on to a genuine police officer.

"Did I really just do that?" Stella held her hand in front of her face, studying it as she ran.

"You did." He looked back to see police cars and fire engines converging on the multistory parking ramp.

"What else can I do?"

"Let's get away from here to somewhere safe. Then I can show you." He smiled down at her, catching her hand and pulling her through a hedge into a field. "Or maybe *you* can show *me*."

Chapter 7

Stella slumped into a seat in the café. Despite the fact that she had not eaten for—she frowned in an effort to concentrate—over twenty-four hours, the sight of the tea and muffin Cal placed in front of her caused her stomach to pitch and roll uncomfortably. And it wasn't just the lack of food, of course. A night with no sleep and the need for a long, hot shower were also taking their toll. Oh, and the vicious, bloodthirsty faeries who were on her trail. Yep, that lot would destroy your appetite anytime.

"Eat it." Cal's voice was stern as she pushed the plate aside.

"Where are we again?" She hadn't really taken much notice of the signs as, wearily, she'd followed him from the train after a five-and-a-half-hour journey.

"Carmarthen." Stella regarded him blankly and he elaborated. "It's in South Wales."

"I know where it is. I just don't understand why we're here." There was a rising note of unaccustomed fretfulness in her voice. Stella didn't like it and decided to drown it with tea. The brew was strong and slightly too hot. Its effect was revivifying and she sat up straighter.

"It's on our way." The café was set in a side street adjacent to the station. It was the first place they had come across after leaving the train. It was quiet now and Stella couldn't imagine that it would get much busier once lunchtime arrived in the next hour. Two elderly women lingered over tea and cake at a table near the window and a man in overalls was reading a newspaper and eating bacon and eggs. The proprietor, a sour-faced woman, who appeared to derive very little joy from her chosen business, was watching the news on a television set with the sound turned down.

"On our way. That's really helpful, Cal. On our way to where exactly?" The tea had gone some way toward restoring her appetite and Stella bit into the muffin. Its sweetness jarred her teeth but she could almost feel it sending a boost of energy directly into her bloodstream.

"The only place where I know for sure I can keep you safe."

"Cal, I really cannot get my head around this. If I am a necromancer—let alone *the* necromancer of Merlin's prophecy—wouldn't I have known about it before now?"

He took her hand and Stella was conscious of the muffin crumbs and stickiness adhering to her fingers. His eyes, those beautiful, strange eyes, were probing her face. Wanting something from her, but she wasn't sure what. "Don't you know it?"

She started to shake her head, then stopped. His expression caught her attention and snagged on something deep inside her subconscious. It was as if a domino knockdown had been set in motion inside her head. One tiny memory triggered another, until the whole series fell into place. "Oh, my God, Cal."

His voice was infinitely gentle. "When you were four years old, not long after your parents died, you were placed with a family in Suffolk. Do you remember?"

"I'm starting to." *Don't make me do this.* The images, so long buried, were scrambling to the surface now with a vengeance.

"It wasn't your fault, Stella. You just told them what you saw." Cal ran his thumb back and forth over her hand.

Unshed tears burned her eyes. "Imagine how they felt, those people who took me into their home. Their own little girl had died six years earlier. She was run over, and they couldn't have any more children. They were supposed to be my forever family. Instead, on my very first night in their home, I told them I'd seen their daughter standing at the foot of my bed. I knew her name, described every horrific detail of her injuries—" she gulped in a mouthful of air "—I told them she blamed them for her death. No wonder they couldn't launch me back to the children's home fast enough." She blinked the tears away. "How did I manage to shut *that* out of my mind for all these years?"

"Because it was bad. Because you didn't want to remember something that hurt you so much."

She hung her head. "It wasn't the only time."

"No. It's the reason you never found a permanent home."

Stella gave a wobbly laugh. "And I thought it was because I couldn't stay out of trouble."

"I think that was a big part of it, too. No one knew how to handle the little whirlwind who flooded their house or painted their dog blue and then had long conversations with their dead grandma."

"Except you. You never abandoned me."

He reached out a hand and ran his knuckles down her

cheek. His touch heated her face as though there was some residual fire remaining from all the flame-throwing antics back at the airport. "I never will." He laughed, lightening the mood. "I happen to think the world needs more blue dogs."

Stella studied one of her hands as if she had never seen it before. It was the hand she knew so well. Small, with artistically narrow fingers and neat, unvarnished nails. It was hard to believe it was the same hand that had wreaked havoc on the sidhes just hours earlier. "So I really am a necromancer? I've been so successful at hiding those instincts that allow me to see dead people that I'd almost forgotten I had them. But there must be a world of difference between that and being able to summon the spirits of the dead, surely?"

"It's simply a matter of honing the skills you already have. Even the finest necromancers have to practice their art."

"I still don't understand how Moncoya made the link between Merlin's prophecy and me."

"He has been looking for you for a very long time. He knew, of course, when the three-tailed comet would come. And he thinks you sent him a sign."

"Me? No way...wait. Oh, hell. It must be the game, 'Supernova Deliverance.'" Stella pulled in another deep, steadying breath. Cal took hold of her hand again, and the warmth of his palm on hers was comforting. She focused on that. "When I wanted to crowd fund the game, Moncoya saw an outline of my idea. That was what prompted him to offer me the job. The main character has powers like those you described and...well, let me show you." She took out her phone. Before she could get the game up on the screen, the woman behind the counter turned the television volume up louder, distracting her.

"Manchester airport remains closed after a possible terrorist attack early this morning." The news anchor's brisk tones accompanied images of a line of fire engines outside the multistory parking garage's smoke-damaged exterior. "Details remain unclear and police have said it is too soon to speculate about who is responsible. They wish to speak to this man and woman in connection with the incident." Images of Cal and Stella checking in at Girona airport filled the screen. The images were grainy, but unmistakable. "The public are urged not to approach this couple, who may be armed, but to contact the police immediately with any information."

Stella glanced from the television screen to the woman behind the counter. She was staring back at them with panic in her eyes as she spoke into her phone.

"This is the last leg of the journey. We're almost there."

Cal could see that Stella was flagging. Her face was pale with weariness, her mouth set in a grimly determined line. She hadn't said much when they left the café, simply following in Cal's wake as he had thrown the money for their food and drink down on the table and made a swift exit. She hadn't even asked where they were going as they made their way past the ice-cream-colored buildings and along the narrow streets of the oldest town in Wales.

"What'll it be?" he had asked, running a hand through his distinctive mop of chestnut hair. "Shave it off or get a hat?"

"Hat," she'd replied, with a look of horror. And that was why, despite the bright sunlight, he was wearing a knitted skullcap pulled low over his ears. Stella, who at least was dressed in different clothing from that in the police photographs, had purchased it for him from a craft stall on the town's outdoor market. They passed through this bustling thoroughfare on their way out of Carmarthen and into the countryside beyond.

"Shouldn't we go to the police and at least try to explain what happened?" Stella asked now as they trudged up a steep hillside.

"How do you propose we start that conversation?"

She chuckled and the sound chased away some of his own weariness. "How about we just take a couple of corpses with us and let them do the talking?"

"Spoken like a true necromancer. Seriously, going to the police is exactly what Moncoya wants us to do. Think about it, Stella. He would like nothing more than to get you away from me. What more effective way to do that than to get us both placed in police custody?"

"You think he's behind this terrorist nonsense?"

"I know he is. You have no idea what he's capable of. I, on the other hand, know him only too well. If we were arrested, the first thing that would happen is that the police would place us in separate cells. That would suit his evil majesty right down to the tips of his highly polished fingernails." His mouth was a hard, thin line. It was what tended to happen whenever Moncoya was the subject of conversation.

"Couldn't you get us out of a police cell?" She reached out a hand for his, and although he felt the gesture was automatic, it tugged at something deep inside him. Something that had not been touched in a very long time.

They had arrived at the summit of the hill now. Cal paused and smiled down at her. He would never get tired of looking at her heart-shaped face with its huge green eyes and that incredibly expressive mouth. It was a mouth that could do sulky and sultry like no other he'd ever seen. Right now, it was breaking into a grin that was half shy, half teasing. "Of course I could get us out, but do you want to be on the run for the rest of your life?"

The grin vanished. "Isn't that what we are doing now? This feels a lot like running to me."

"We were coming here anyway. This was part of *my* plan, not Moncoya's."

"To come to the top of a hill in Wales?" Stella eyed him with obvious suspicion. "Don't tell me, I'm going to become a wild woman of the woods."

"Close. Come on." Keeping hold of her hand, he pulled her with him as he began to descend the other side of the hill. This place had that effect on him. It refreshed him. That was the reason he always came back. Coming here with Stella was something he had never envisioned. Would she be able to sense how special it was? Why did it matter so much that she should? The questions became superfluous as, apparently infected by his pleasure, Stella broke into a run. Pulling him with her, she laughed as they picked up speed and the summer breeze cleansed their faces of the long, weary hours of traveling.

"Stop, you madwoman." He pulled her to a halt. "We're not going all the way to the bottom."

They were about halfway down the slope and Cal led Stella into a small, dense copse. In the darkest part of this wooded tangle, he pulled aside thick fronds of overhanging ivy, uncovering the concealed entrance to a cave. The white limestone rock was barely visible beneath its covering of lichen. Even if a rambler chanced to wander off the hill path and into the trees, in this gloomy light the person would walk right past the cave. You had to know what you were looking for. More important, you had to be looking with the right eyes.

He felt suddenly nervous as he waited for Stella's reaction. The arched entrance to the cave was high enough to walk through upright, and she studied this in silence for long moments. Then she turned to him with eyes that sparkled with excitement. "Can we go in?"

The entrance led them into a small cavern. It was large enough for Cal to stand upright inside it, but he could have stretched out his arms and touched both walls. Reaching up into a natural shelf in the rock, he took down a flashlight. Beyond it, the cave narrowed and Cal led Stella into the gloom, shining the light ahead of him.

"Just keep one hand on the wall and watch your step. The floor is uneven in places."

They walked for a minute before the corridor opened out into a large circular space. The beam of the flashlight illuminated the scene. There was an old sofa and two chairs, a bookshelf and a table. Stella took in these details, blinking at Cal in surprise. "Someone lives here?"

"We do. For the time being." Cal handed her the light and went over to the bookshelf. Taking down two old-fashioned oil lamps, he set about lighting them. Soon there was a warm, strangely homely glow about the place.

"No, seriously." He glanced up from his task, holding her gaze. "You are being serious."

"I told you I was bringing you to the only place I knew I could keep you safe. This is it."

Stella flopped down onto one of the chairs. "After the hours of traveling, revelations and confrontation, in spite of the fact we're in a cave, this actually feels incredibly comfortable. Where will we sleep?"

Cal pointed to an arch in the cave wall. "The bedroom is through there. I'll take the sofa."

"And this may be a bit of a girlie thing but..."

"There is no bathroom." He started to laugh at her expression. "There is a stream just outside. It flows down into a deep pool. As long as you don't mind the cold, it's perfect for bathing. This cave has been inhabited on and off for centuries, so there is even a well for drinking water."

"I was actually thinking of something more basic than bathing." Even in the flickering golden lamplight, he could see that she was blushing.

"It is a bit primitive, I'm afraid. Think Victorians and chamber pots."

Stella lowered her head into her hands and, as he observed her shaking shoulders, Cal had a horrible feeling that she might have started to cry. When she looked up, her face was a picture of laughter.

"In the space of twenty-four hours we've become desperate fugitives from justice."

He studied her in concern. "Can you get used to it? This is the one place I guarantee Moncoya won't come." *Just don't ask me how I know that.*

"I can get used to anything if I can get my head down right now and go to sleep."

"Come with me." He held out his hand and pulled her up from the chair. Carrying one of the lamps, he led her through to where a bed fitted neatly into what turned out to be a small alcove in the cave wall. Cal dragged a large trunk out from under it and took clean pillows and bedding out of that.

Stella watched him with round eyes. "You've thought of everything. Or did you know this was going to happen?" He busied himself making the bed and didn't reply. She tried another, this time an unexpected, question. "How old are you?"

It was a question he always treated with caution. He tried his standard answer. "The exact number of my years is something even I cannot tell for the passing of time means little to me."

"Is that a roundabout way of saying you don't know?"

Cal started to laugh. "You could say that."

"So there's no point worrying about how many candles we'll need on your next birthday cake." Stella tugged off her sneakers. "I think I'm going to sleep for about a week." She lay down, her eyes closing as soon as her head touched the pillow. "Cal?"

He had turned away, but he moved back to the side of the bed. "Yes?"

"Stay with me." Her voice was soft with drowsiness. "Please."

He hesitated for a moment. Then, kicking off his own battered shoes, he lay down next to her, fitting his body along the length of hers. Stella took his arm and draped it around her waist, murmuring something incomprehensible. Despite his own tiredness, Cal lay awake for a long time listening to her breathing as she slept.

Chapter 8

Stella had fallen into the deep, dreamless sleep of exhaustion, waking only once in the night. At first she had struggled to identify where she was in the all-enveloping darkness. Then, as her memory returned, she sought to pinpoint what had woken her. She had been lying on her side with her back to Cal, who still had one arm draped across her body. The rise and fall of his breathing brought his chest into contact with her shoulder blades, warming and comforting her.

"Darnantes." He was still in the grip of a deep sleep and the single, anguished word seemed to have been torn from his lips. Stella knew then that it had been his voice that had disturbed her slumber. The word meant nothing to her, but it clearly meant something—and it would seem that it was something hateful and poisonous—to Cal.

He spoke again, this time muttering a sentence or two. The words were disjointed and unintelligible to Stella, but there was something about his voice that touched her. It resonated with pain and a sorrow that was both powerful and heart wrenching. Intuitively, she had turned and wrapped her arms around him, drawing him closer to her. The action seemed to comfort him and, pressing his face into the curve of her neck, he had fallen silent once more.

The next time Stella woke, Cal was gone. He had left one of the oil lanterns beside the bed so that Stella could at least see, even though she had no idea how long she had slept. She rose, grimacing at the ache in her limbs and the fact that she was still wearing the clothes she had traveled and then slept in. Holding the lamp out in front of her and following the sound of tuneless whistling, she emerged from the cave to find Cal stirring a pot that sat in the middle of a roaring fire. He looked up, grinning at Stella as she approached.

"Good afternoon."

She blinked at him. It was impossible to judge time, either in the darkness of the cave or here in the shadowy gloom of the bower. It was a strange sensation. Debilitating and yet curiously liberating at the same time. "Really?"

"Not quite." His hair was wet and, as she drew nearer, she could smell the clean scent of his freshly soaped skin. Jealousy and attraction immediately went to war inside her. Jealousy won…but only just.

"You've bathed," she said, unable to keep the slightly accusatory note out of her voice.

"You can, too. Breakfast will be ready when you're finished." He pointed to where he'd draped a towel and a wash bag over a tree branch. He jerked his thumb behind him. "Just follow the edge of the cave wall for a few yards and you'll come to the pool I told you about. The water's cold, but crystal clear."

Stella plucked at the cloth of her jeans. "I haven't got any clean clothes."

"That's where you're wrong." He stepped aside and there, just behind him, next to the cave entrance was a suitcase. Not just any suitcase. It was Stella's suitcase. The one she had left behind at La Casa Oscura. She eyed it as if it was a coiled snake.

"How the hell...?"

The questions crowded to her lips. *Who had packed her belongings? How had her suitcase been delivered here? Was there an international Cave Courier Service? Did Moncoya know her stuff was gone?* In the end, she asked none of them. She was here with a man whose eyes shone with a magical silver light. He had been her invisible protector throughout her life. At the same time he had been guarding her from harm, it seemed he had also been leading a double life as some sort of interworldly peacekeeper. She had seen flames shoot from his fingertips and heard him speak a dead language in a voice that was not his own. He had brought her to a cave that she strongly suspected was hidden from mortal sight. In spite of all this, she trusted him. He had driven monsters out from under her bed and drop-kicked a gargoyle for her. And now he had taken the trouble to fetch her clothes. Given everything else that was going on, did it really matter how he had done it? She decided it didn't.

Which was how, twenty minutes later, she came to be eating her breakfast dressed in a pair of frayed and faded denim shorts. It was impossible to see this garment since the oversize sweater she wore over it reached almost to her knees. Her favorite battered combat boots completed the ensemble. She was clean—having bathed in the crystal waters of a pool that, while they were cool, should actually have been arctic. She suspected that might be another

Cal-related phenomenon—and now she was eating near-perfect porridge and fresh fruit. Okay, she was technically a suspected terrorist on the run from the police. And, she was getting used to the idea that she was a very desirable property in the eyes of the ruthless warring vampires, faeries, were-creatures, phantoms and various other nasties of a mythical place called Otherworld. Nevertheless, Stella was beginning to feel more like herself again.

"Who'd have thought living in a cave could be so luxurious?" She smiled up at Cal.

"We aim to please." Cal brought his own breakfast over and came to sit next to her on the flat rock where she was perched. They ate in companionable silence.

"You said this cave has been occupied on and off for centuries. Has it been handed down through generations of the same family?" Stella kept her voice studiously casual. That was the problem with Cal. He knew her too well for guile.

"Not quite." His own voice was distant.

"Just the one occupant for a long time, then?" Stella probed a bit further. "One careful owner? A hermit, maybe? It's certainly private enough."

He laughed, but it was a hollow sound, one she wasn't used to from him. She thought how quickly she'd become attuned to his moods. "It is only private within the confines of this bower. Venture outside of these trees and you may well stumble upon those who seek this very place."

"Cal, you may have recovered from the traveling and the faerie fisticuffs of yesterday, but I haven't. My brain is like mush. Stop talking in riddles."

He was definitely edgy, his eyes wandering restlessly around their leafy encampment. "Merlin was born in Carmarthen, Stella. This is his cave."

"You probably know more about this than I do—" Stella

dredged deep into her memory for anything she had heard about the legendary sorcerer "—but does anyone really know for certain where he was born? I thought there were as many legends about Merlin as there were about his protégé, King Arthur. I'm certain I read somewhere that his cave was below the castle at Tintagel in Cornwall."

"I didn't say this was his *only* cave." The unease of a few minutes ago seemed to have gone and his smile, the one that did something strange to her midsection, had returned.

"Ah, I see. He was a wizard of property." It was curiously silent inside the canopy of trees, as if they were the only living creatures for miles. "What happens now, Cal? We can't stay here forever."

"No, we can't." His voice struck her as endlessly sad. "The prophecy must be fulfilled."

"If that means what I think it does…" Stella made a movement as if to bounce up from her sitting position, but Cal caught her hands.

"Hear me out." She tried to pull away, but he persisted. "Please?"

"It doesn't matter what you've got to say, Cal. Necromancer or not, star or not. There is no way I'm going to fight Moncoya or any other beasties just because some ancient cave-loving wizard who died hundreds of years ago said I should." He kept his eyes fixed on her face, and eventually she subsided back into a sitting position. "Okay. I'll listen, but you won't change my mind."

It was a moment or two before he spoke, as though he had mentally rehearsed what he wanted to say. "The modern view of Merlin is the one you have just described. The white-bearded, dark-robed, elderly wizard who masterminded King Arthur's rise to power. But you're right. Legend has muddled what we believe we know of him.

For centuries, scholars have even debated long and hard about whether he existed at all."

"Do *you* believe in his existence?" Stella was mesmerized by Cal's expression. It was trancelike in its intensity. He gave a short nod. "Then he must have been real."

A slight laugh shook his shoulders. "Thank you. Believe me, I appreciate your faith in me. The powers bestowed upon Merlin encompassed much more than sorcery. He was given the ability to interpret dreams, to cast spells—in fact there has never been another, before or since, so talented in that respect—and to shape-shift, although his skills in that respect have, I believe, been exaggerated. Like you, he was also given the gift of necromancy. I know you do not view it as a gift yet. But it is just that. A great gift and one that must be handled with care. He was also endowed with an aptitude for invisibility."

"You said Merlin was a hybrid. Is that how he came to have these powers?"

"Yes, he inherited his mortality from his human mother and his…" the pause seemed to hang in the air for a very long time "…other talents were bestowed through his father."

"Who was his father?" Stella told herself firmly that she hadn't lowered her guard, hadn't forgotten to be annoyed that he was going to try to persuade her to enter into this frenzied Otherworld insurgence. It was just that the story was so fascinating and Cal told it with such passion that she couldn't help being drawn into it.

He shook his head and, with the action, seemed to shake off his reflective mood. "It isn't important to what I'm trying to explain. You see, Merlin's greatest gift is the one that is the least acknowledged. His prophecies are unerringly accurate, Stella."

"First time for everything." She shrugged. "He's had a

good track record. What is it? At least a millennia and a half since King Arthur was born. No one is going to blame Merlin for getting this one wrong."

"You don't understand why the coming of the necromancer star is so important. How could you? It is only part of a wider prophecy. One that has already unfolded faultlessly, just as Merlin foretold." He tightened his grip on her hands and shifted position so that he was facing her, his knees just touching hers. As always, the points where his body came into contact with hers had a soothing effect on her senses. Cal's eyes had darkened to the color of a storm-laden sky. "The barrier between Otherworld and this mortal realm is a fragile one at the best of times, Stella. Sometimes it is worn thin. Since Moncoya came to power, it has been tested in a way that has never been known before. The intrusions into this earthly world by dark forces are increasing by the day. If the battle for Otherworld is not swiftly concluded—and the prophecy tells that unity can only be achieved by he who claims the heart of the necromancer star—so that order can be restored, then this world will perish."

Stella closed her eyes, shutting out the beautiful gloom of the silent bower and the earnest face of the equally beautiful man before her. "Are you seriously telling me I'm the only hope you have of saving the world?" she asked, opening her eyes.

"I'm saying you are the best hope we have." And she knew, from the expression in the now chalice-bright depths of his eyes, that it was true. Beyond doubt.

"Who is *we*?" The words came out on a long exhale of breath. "Who are the good guys, Cal? You said you're not an angel."

"No, *I'm* not. But the good guys, as you call them, *are* angels. Otherworld does not obey the same laws as the earthly realm but, if it helps, I suppose you could think of angels as an international peacekeeping force. If you apply the same logic to their opposite number, in other words to demons, they are a series of anarchists, each group hell-bent on overthrowing the established order and causing as much mayhem as they can in the process. They, of course, are delighting in and exploiting the current chaos."

"That does help with the imagery. Where do you—just you, Cal—come into this?"

His grin was slightly lopsided and always heartbreaking. "I'm on the side of the angels. It's my job."

She withdrew her hands, bending her head so that she could fiddle with a thread on her sweater. What had she wanted him to say? *"To hell with the rest of the world, I'm only here because I care about you, Stella"*? Even though she knew she was being unfair, his words hit her like a slap across the face.

"I understand it now. You never were my guardian angel. I've been wrong about you my whole life. You were just doing a job. Protecting me so that you could get me to Otherworld to fight for the angels."

"Stella, believe me, it was never like that to me…"

She looked up, smiling brightly, determined to hide the fierce pain that seemed to be trying to tear her heart in two. "So this is Necromancer Boot Camp, right? I'll wash these dishes and then you can tell me all about our training program. I warn you now, you'll have your work cut out getting me into shape."

She snatched up the breakfast bowls and, keeping her shoulders squared, walked quickly away before he could speak again.

Cal swore under his breath. It wasn't meant to be like this. He was supposed to be above getting too close. That was why he had taken on the role of protecting Stella. That and his knowledge of the prophecy, of course. That was why the Dominion had chosen him. Why one of their number, the one who was his personal contact within their angelic choir, had come to him with the proposition in the first place. The task they had asked of him had been exactly as Stella had supposed. *"Guard the necromancer star against harm for five and twenty harvests. Then escort her to Otherworld so that the prophecy may be fulfilled."* So why was he sitting here worrying that she might be crying her eyes out as she washed the dishes? Why did he feel he had betrayed her trust? And why the hell did he want to go to her, wrap his arms around her and reassure her that of course he cared more about her than anything else?

Because, against his will and his judgment, he did care about Stella. He cared more than he wanted to admit. It was the one thing he had sworn never to do. Not after the one time he had opened his heart to another had ended with such disastrous results. Somehow, somewhere along the way, the liking and admiration he had felt for the spiky, funny little girl he thought he knew had changed. Since he had allowed Stella to see his mortal self, their relationship had shifted focus. Without him noticing, she had burrowed her way into his heart in a new and exciting way. He had to constantly remind himself to stop watching her. Too often he discovered his eyes were feasting on the delicate perfection of her face, the perfect line of her neck or those adorably pert breasts. Looking away didn't help much. His mind still managed to spend too long dwelling on the sparkling expression in her green eyes, the luscious curve of her lips and the musical sound of her laughter. *Admit it, Cal, you've got it bad.*

He was like a schoolboy in the throes of his first crush, getting a hard-on just thinking about her. *Here we go again.* In spite of the gravity of his thoughts, he adjusted his jeans now to accommodate the erection that was straining against the stiff cloth. If the circumstances were different, this would be the most exhilarating emotion he had ever known. In a life that had encompassed centuries of magic and mayhem, that was saying something. Instead, these feelings he had for Stella were doomed. They must be buried, never to be revealed. Along with so many other things.

There was one thing he could do for her. Stella had been gone for five minutes already, but time was ephemeral to Cal. A conversation with the Dominion should remove him from the warded safety of the bower for hours. He could ensure, however, that it took him away from his role as Stella's bodyguard for only the blink of an eye.

"No." When he outlined his proposition, the angel's serenity was unruffled, his certainty that he would be obeyed absolute. "You are too valuable to us. I cannot permit you to do this."

"Then this is where we part company." Cal began to walk away.

"My friend, think about what you are doing. Would you place the well-being of this mere girl above that of all mortality?" The angel's voice rang out, halting Cal in his tracks.

Mere girl? Had anyone ever punched an angel? Cal swung back to face the Dominion. "You can't have this both ways. For the past twenty-five years you've been telling me to watch over her because she is the only hope mankind has. Now, all of a sudden, *I'm* the one who's become too precious to sacrifice. Make your mind up."

"It was never part of our arrangement that you would fight alongside her. Your task was simply to get her there."

"I'm changing the arrangement. As of now." Cal felt

his jaw muscles stiffen. "Or I'm walking. And if I walk, I take her with me."

"You would not do that. Not after Darnantes…"

Cal threw up a silencing hand and, for the first time—probably in all eternity—the angel took a step back. "You know better than to speak to me of that!"

"Where would you go?" The angel's tone was softly persuasive. "It would shame me to offer you threats, but there can be no hiding place in the earthly realm or in Otherworld. For you or for her."

Cal laughed and the sound, echoing in nothingness, was not a pleasant one. "I think we both know better. You know with whom you are dealing. You know what I can do. We have been on the same side…until now."

"There is no need for this. We cannot afford to lose you. Yet, believe me, I do understand your concern for the girl. Let another accompany her. Lorcan Malone, maybe? It is about time he ceased his restless wandering and came into the fold." Cal remained stubbornly silent. The angel repeated his earlier words. "You are too valuable."

"You assume we will lose. The prophecy asserts otherwise."

The Dominion shook his head. "I know better than to attempt to debate the words of the prophecy with you. Go then. Do what you must." He shook his head. "You disappoint me."

Cal grinned, his heart suddenly lighter. It might be reluctant permission, but at least it wasn't condemnation. "It would not be the first time, would it?"

Back in the bower, he looked up as the crackling of twigs underfoot signaled Stella's return. Her eyes looked suspiciously red, but she met his gaze with a smile. If it was forced it was a good attempt. Sketching a salute, she stood to attention. "Private Fallon reporting for duty, sir!"

Although he wanted nothing more than to take her into his arms and kiss away the trace of tears that lingered on her cheek, Cal fought down the impulse with a Herculean effort. He had to do all he could to ensure her safety. He had taken a huge step toward that already today. Their relationship was destined to be one-sided. Sharing who he was could never be part of it.

Rising to his feet, he walked to her. "Shoulders back, Private," he said sternly, playing along. "There's not much of you, but not to worry. We'll make a necromancer of you yet."

Chapter 9

Being a necromancer had its compensations. For one thing, Stella was never again going to have to worry about being stuck in a power outage without candles. Not when Cal announced that her first lesson was going to be how to create light within darkness.

"So do we do this with wands and crystal balls?" Determined not to allow him any glimpse of her true feelings, she adopted a flippant attitude.

"You've been watching too much television."

"You're not going to put on robes and a pointy hat? I was hoping for the full magician's outfit." She studied Cal in the shaft of bright sunlight that managed to find a slanting path through the trees.

"Then you'll have to control your strange fetishes. What you see is what you get." He indicated his standard uniform of naked torso and cutoff jeans.

What she saw usually made her mouth go dry with

longing. *Not today,* she told herself sternly. If she was to remain aloof from him she must also strive for immunity from the honed perfection of his body. Stella continued to rely on glib comments in an attempt to cover her nerves. "I'm sure Merlin would have worn robes to do *his* stuff."

"I can tell you categorically that, contrary to anything you may have read, seen or heard, Merlin did not wear robes."

"How do you know?" She challenged. Then, as if a sudden thought had occurred to her, she clasped her hands together in mock delight under her chin. "Cal! Were you there? Did you *know* Merlin?" she teased.

"Can we get on with this, please?" His voice held a hint of impatience.

"I'm just a bit nervous," she explained as he led the way into the cave.

"You have always had this power. You just need to learn how to harness it."

"I don't understand what that means." She wrinkled her nose in confusion at Cal as they made their way into the labyrinth and even deeper underground than their living quarters. "Telling me to 'just learn how to harness it' is not particularly helpful."

In reply, he extinguished the lamp he was carrying, and the darkness around them instantly became so thick and black it hurt her eyes. No matter how hard she blinked, her vision wouldn't clear. She couldn't find even a sliver of light on which to focus. Because there was none.

Cal placed his hands on her shoulders, and that slight familiar tremor, like a very faint electric shock, zapped through her at his touch. "This is not a spell." His voice was different. Not the big, commanding tones of the airport. It was softer and lower, mesmerizing as he almost chanted the words. "No incantation is needed to achieve this. All you must do is reach inside yourself and find the will to make it happen."

His chin was touching her shoulder, his breath stroking her cheek with a warm caress. She wanted to turn her head and explain that she couldn't think of anything else with him so close. Or kiss him. Forget being hurt and confused. Just turn her head and kiss him. Instead, she forced herself to focus on his words.

"All magic brings great responsibility. We must remain aware, at all times, of the consequences of what we do. Never act in haste, never allow negative energy to control you. That must be the difference between us and our enemies. The bringing forth of light will not be the same for you as it is for me. It will be a personal thing. All you have to do is reach deep inside yourself and find it. Feel it. It is already there, Stella. You are the necromancer star. Light is a powerful force within you."

So she stood completely still in a darkness so coal black it felt as if it was pressing in on her chest and suffocating her. She tried to discover within herself that which she did not understand. Gradually her mind shut out the awareness of Cal standing close by, of the clean, masculine scent of his flesh, of the soft, rhythmic sound of his breathing. Her injured heart tucked away the bitterness of his abandonment and betrayal. That wasn't going anywhere. *Deal with it another day.* Slowly, at a point low in her abdomen, a tingling sensation began and spiraled slowly outward.

With it, on a level just above conscious thought, came a new awareness. *This is my destiny. This is who I am.* The knowledge had lain dormant within her for so long. Even the main character in her "Supernova Deliverance" game had been part of that knowledge. A girl who held the power of the stars within her own body. *Sound familiar, Stella?* No wonder Moncoya leaped at the chance of getting her to Barcelona. It was as if she had waved a flag at him announcing her readiness to be his weapon.

It seemed right to lower her head and raise her arms upward and outward to shoulder height. Adopting the same stance Moncoya had taken when he faced the gargoyle, she allowed the thrilling sensation to radiate out from her middle and through her whole body. A flicker of light, so faint and fleeting it might have been her imagination, appeared at the same height as her outstretched arms.

"I did it!" She turned to where she thought Cal was standing.

"You can do better." His voice was farther away than she expected.

"Challenge accepted," she replied through gritted teeth. The second time was so easy it startled her. Within seconds, she had the cave lit up like a carnival. Laughing, she turned again to Cal, chattering in her excitement. "I really can do it! I thought I might have to keep my head bent and my arms out, but I don't. Then I was scared it would do something to my insides. You know, drain all my energy. But it's weird. It's sort of invigorating. I could go even brighter. Do you want to see?"

He shook his head, smiling. Even through her euphoria it struck her that there was something sad about that smile. "You are better even than I was the first time I tried. That's lesson one over. You have established a belief in your own ability, which will make the lessons to come easier."

Over the course of the following week, Stella's belief in herself had grown daily. With it the emotional gulf between her and Cal seemed to widen to a point where it was insurmountable. Gone was the intimacy of that first night. The closeness of holding him and being held by him might have been a dream. Now, after they said a stilted goodnight, she went to her lonely bed while Cal curled his long limbs onto the sofa. Stella had offered to swap, but he had curtly refused. Yet, despite the growing distance, the attraction she felt toward him was stronger than ever. It was so fierce it actually burned. She couldn't explain it. He had hurt her beyond anything she had known before. Oh, she accepted that he had not intended to cause her pain. That much was true. How could he know what he had done to her heart when he told her she was just a job to him? Cal couldn't be expected to understand that he was all she had ever had. Everyone else in her life had abandoned her. Never Cal. He had been the one she had come to depend on. Her constant. *Admit it, Stella, just once, just to yourself.* He had been the one she thought would always love her. Only now she knew he didn't care about her at all. Probably, on some level, he quite liked her. She thought he did. They laughed at the same things. There was a warm light in his eyes when they rested on her. But he would happily hand her over when the time came and move on to the next assignment. Well, it was up to Stella to hide her feelings and cultivate the same businesslike approach. She thought she was doing a good job. On the whole.

Except when he smiled at her as he was doing now and her stomach did a funny little backward somersault. She still had a bit of work to do on that. They were sitting high on the hilltop above the cave. The day was clear and bright, and fluffy clouds scudded the sky as though a great artist had wiped indigo paint onto white cloth. It was the first time they had left the security of the bower since the day they had arrived, and Stella was feeling anxious.

"Stop looking over your shoulder. You are the necromancer star. The greatest of them all." His grin widened. "And I'm not bad either. Together we can fight off anything."

"I'm scared on two levels. I'm wondering if those ramblers down there—" she pointed way below them to the fields, where four or five people, their coats a bright splash of color, were walking "—might turn out to be sidhes, and I'm also scared about what you're going to ask me to do. Creating light in darkness is all very well. Raising the dead? I'm not sure I'm cut out for that."

Instead of responding, Cal swept a hand wide, indicating the valley below them. "There is a story about the land that surrounds this hill. It is said that many centuries ago there was a farmer who was famed for breeding the finest white horses. He was approached by an old man of noble bearing. The man had long white hair and a flowing beard and he carried a staff. He wore the robes of a monk from an earlier period in time. Sound familiar?"

Stella nodded. "Merlin...but you said the stereotype wizard of legend was not necessarily the truth about him."

"I did, but let us not forget his ability to shape-shift. It probably suited him, on that occasion, to look the way legend portrayed him. Perhaps it made him appear more commanding. Merlin asked the farmer to sell him five white horses and told the man to name his price. When the man refused, Merlin allowed him a glimpse below the soil of the valley where a vast army of warriors slumbered in deathly sleep. Each soldier had a white horse tethered at his bedside and a sword across his chest in readiness for battle. All except five, who still awaited their steeds. The man bowed before Merlin and gave him the horses without taking a penny in exchange."

"I should think so. You wouldn't mess with Merlin, would you?"

Cal's shoulders shook with silent laughter. "Probably not. My point is that the warriors Merlin showed the farmer slumber here still. They await your command, Stella."

"Me?" The word sounded a lot like a squeak. "Oh, bloody hell. No, you do it."

He draped an arm around her shoulders, drawing her close against his side for a few seconds. *Just for encouragement. Nothing more,* she told herself firmly. "Summon them, Stella."

"Those people down there will see them. We'll draw attention to ourselves," she protested. "The police will be on us before you can say 'flame-throwing airport terrorists.'"

"They will see nothing that we do not permit them to see."

"I don't know what to say in order to call them." It was a final, desperate attempt to put off the inevitable.

"The words are unimportant. You are the necromancer star. They will come when you command them."

Rising to her feet, Stella looked around her at the slumbering scene. It seemed impossible to believe she was about to do as Cal asked. And yet that newfound part of her—her necromancer soul—thrilled to the test he had given her. When she spoke, she barely knew her own voice. She certainly did not recognize the first word that left her lips. Nevertheless she knew what it meant.

"Hidercyme. Come here. Come to me."

And they came. So slowly at first that she began to think nothing was happening. Then she realized that the trembling sensation she felt did not originate in her own limbs. It was coming from the very ground on which she stood. The trees themselves began to shake. Smaller stones broke loose from the restraining soil around them and skittered wildly down the hillside. The sky darkened and a breeze rose up from nowhere. Stella had time to notice the ramblers lifting their faces skyward as though looking for signs of rain and turning their collars up.

A huge gash appeared in the valley floor as if the verdant pastures had been torn apart by the hands of an angry giant, and then the warriors, each mounted on his white steed and clad in chain mail, rode out. Mere minutes later, the whole valley floor was filled with the massed ranks of a great ghostly army. Each man held his sword across his chest and bowed his head in homage. And yet, as Cal had predicted, the group of ramblers continued on their way, unaware of the spectral legions surrounding them.

One man rode forward and up the slope, pausing a few feet away from them. He addressed himself to Stella. "My men are yours to command, *breguróf steorra*. We have been in readiness for your word throughout these many centuries and more."

Obeying her instincts, Stella stepped forward, reaching up to briefly clasp his gloved hand where it lay on the pommel. "Thank you, Grindan, your words mean much to me." How did she know what to say, let alone know his name? Yet she responded to the inner voice that prompted her.

With a nod to Cal, Grindan the Faithful dismounted. Taking Stella's hand on one side and Cal's on the other, he faced the serried ranks of warriors and raised their arms aloft. In response, each soldier silently raised his sword. A thousand blades pierced the morning sky, yet no whisper of sound penetrated the solemnity of the moment. Without speaking, Grindan released their hands and returned to his horse. With another nod, he mounted his steed and returned to his men. Within seconds the vast army had vanished into the cleft within the valley floor. Hardly a minute had passed before normality was restored and the countryside returned once more to its undisturbed state.

Stella stood absolutely still, hardly daring to breathe. Then, abruptly, she sat down on the grass, hugging her knees up under her chin for comfort. "What did he call me?" She squinted up at Cal, who was standing with the sun behind him, and he moved so that he could sit next to her.

"*Breguróf steorra.* It means 'majestic star' or 'mighty star.'"

She was quiet again for a long time. Then she turned her head. The look on Cal's face made her draw in a sudden, urgent gulp of air. "Merlin did that? Because he knew that one day I would need them?" He nodded. "My God."

She raised a shaky hand as if to brush her hair back from her face and then lost track of the action, so that her fingers faltered in midair. Cal caught hold of her wrist, stilling the movement and restoring her to calm. The urgency in his eyes deepened as he raised her hand to his lips, tracing her palm with his tongue. With a sound somewhere between a sob and a laugh, Stella fell into his arms and her lips parted in response to the prompting of his. She had wondered for so long what it would be like to kiss Cal, but the reality was so much more than she had imagined. She had dreamed of tenderness. The truth was harder and more demanding. His beautiful mouth, with its full lower lip, plundered hers. As he drew her closer and deepened the kiss, the stubble along his strong jawline rasped against her tender flesh and she shuddered with pleasure. As his tongue explored the depths of her mouth, she gave a moan of surrender, pressing harder against him. Something about the sound and the action seemed to break the spell and, slowly, he drew back. The silver of his eyes was dulled to pewter.

"I'm sorry. That should not have happened."

Rising to his feet, he reached down a hand to help her up. Stunned, Stella allowed him to assist her. Part of her wanted to refuse, to stay where she was, to make sense—if there was any—of what had just happened. Both the appearance of the army and the thunderbolt intensity of the kiss. But the ever present shadow of Moncoya loomed in her mind. Reluctantly, she followed Cal back to the bower.

Something had been bothering Stella. Something other than the devastating kiss that must—it seemed—never again be thought of, let alone repeated. She decided to speak to Cal about what was on her mind, even though she suspected she might not like his response. Since he seemed to be doing his best to avoid her, she had to go looking for him. She finally found him sitting at the edge of the pool. He appeared lost in thought.

"The prophecy says that he who claims the heart of the necromancer star will be the one to rule Otherworld, right?"

He looked up at her, shielding his eyes from the dappled sunlight that was sneaking through the trees. She could tell by the wary look in his eyes that he had probably been dreading her next question.

She lowered herself to sit next to him on the rock and threw a pebble into the pool, watching the ripples it made. "What does that mean exactly? For me?"

"No one knows for sure," he said, after a long pause.

"Could it mean there are some factions—dynasties, I think you called them—in Otherworld who would like to rip my heart out of my body and lay claim to it that way?" There, she had said it aloud. *Laugh at me, Cal. Call me an idiot. Please.*

He clenched his fist on his thigh as though warding off a sudden pain. "There are those who have interpreted it that way."

"Who are they?" Stella was pleased with the way her voice stayed so calm.

"The most bloodthirsty dynasties, apart from the faeries, are the vampires and the therianthropes, notably the werewolves. They are the ones who like the image of claiming the heart of the necromancer in a literal sense. I suspect one of them might have been responsible for sending the gargoyle to check out Moncoya's casa. My money would be on the wolves. The vampire prince tends to have more subtlety."

"But Moncoya wants…what, exactly? Is his idea of claiming my heart to win my love?" She strived to get the flippant note back. It didn't quite work.

"Yes. Moncoya has been boasting that he will make you his queen. I was surprised at that, to be honest. He's not known for doing the decent thing, so I'm still unsure of his motive."

"That must be why his party pals were so delighted with me." Stella thought back, with a slight shiver, to the over-enthusiastic welcome she had received at La Casa Oscura. "I thought they held orgies or something, and were on the lookout for new recruits. If only it had been that innocent."

"The problem from your perspective is that he's not really interested in whether you agree to the wedding or not."

Stella frowned. "I don't understand. If he has to claim my heart, surely he needs me to love him and therefore it follows that I would have to go to him willingly. If he forces me to marry him, he won't have my heart. He doesn't fulfill the prophecy."

He shook his head. "Don't try to apply mortal values to Moncoya, Stella. He believes you will belong to him once he has had sex with you. Whether you consent or not is immaterial to him. If he can claim your body, he has your heart anyway. Faerie values."

"Nice." Stella grimaced. "And they said romance was dead."

"He's an evil bastard, Stella. Flowers and chocolates are not his style. All he wants is to stake his claim to you."

"Um, Cal?" Stella spoke quietly and he bent his head close so that he could hear her. "It feels weird discussing this with you, but if Moncoya is relying on me being a virgin we have nothing to worry about."

"I know." His voice was equally quiet.

Stella looked up quickly. "Oh, shit! Cal, please tell me you weren't there!"

"Of course I wasn't." He looked horrified. "What do you take me for? I just know everything there is to know about you, that's all."

"Phew. Anyway, surely we have nothing to worry about if I'm not all pure and innocent. He can't claim me if I've already been—for want of a better word—*claimed*."

"Mortals don't count."

Stella put her head on one side. "That's a bit unfair. I mean, sure, one or two of them could have done with a few tips in the technique department." Despite the gravity of the situation, she couldn't help laughing at his shocked expression. "But there were a couple who weren't bad."

"Not bad? Oh, Stella. You deserve so much better than not bad." He shook his head in mock sadness.

"And you would know all about that, would you?" she teased, her head on one side. It was such a relief to be able to joke with him again. As soon as she said those words, the mood between them changed. Out of nowhere, Stella found it very difficult to breathe. Found herself, not for the first time—even before the kiss—imagining what sex would be like with Cal. Wondering if it would indeed be better than not bad. Wanting to find out. And she knew, by the look in the liquid silver depths of his eyes, that he was thinking exactly the same things. Heat flooded every part of her body.

"Stella, we can't…" She never did discover what they couldn't do. For the first time, the peace of the bower was shattered by another living creature as a huge falcon swooped low and then landed in the lower branches of a tree that overhung the pool. It eyed them with its head cocked curiously on one side while flapping its wings to make a sound like a hand clap muffled within silken gloves. Then, with a single, rattling cry, it rose again into the sky. Raising his face heavenward, Cal watched until the bird was a tiny, dark speck in the blue overhead. Stella, on the other hand, was watching Cal.

"What was that about?" she asked. Because she could tell by his expression that the bird's appearance meant something to him.

"It was a message from a friend. A warning that danger is on its way."

"Moncoya?"

"I don't speak falcon, Stella, so I don't know the details." His smile was reassuring. "Remember...you're on the winning side."

She wasn't convinced. "I think I'd rather be on the winning side back in the cave." She bit her lip. "Will you come with me? I know you don't want to be around me much right now..."

He draped an arm about her shoulders. "Stella, I always want to be around you. That's part of the problem."

Chapter 10

You can't love someone you don't trust. Stella decided she should get that as a tattoo. Because saying it—over and over like her own personal mantra—sure as hell wasn't working. Even setting aside the lack of trust for a minute. She still had no idea who, or what, Cal was. So she couldn't possibly have allowed herself to fall in love with him. No one would be *that* stupid. Would they?

That was what rational Stella told herself. And for long periods of time, she almost managed to convince herself. Today, reason wasn't working. Rational Stella was nowhere to be found. Irrational Stella had taken herself for a dip in the refreshing waters of the pool and was now stretched out full length on a rock at the water's edge. She lay on her back, allowing the cool stone to soothe her skin as the heat of the day faded into late evening. Gazing up at the overhanging trees, she permitted her mind to play a tantalizing game of "what if?" Or even to dwell on possibilities. Possibilities such as what might happen when this was all over. When Moncoya was defeated and Otherworld was safe, might there still be a place for her in Cal's life? Every good guy needed a sidekick. And now that she had overcome her initial disbelief, Stella had to admit she was getting pretty good at this necromancing lark.

"Cal and Stella," she murmured, trying it out to see how their names sounded together. As a new superhero pairing, of course. Nothing more. "Stella and Cal." That sounded better. Oh, dear God, whom was she kidding? Next thing she knew she'd be carving their initials into the nearest tree trunk.

No, she told herself. She was not being giddy. On the contrary, she was being practical and professional. Future-proofing her assets, which were her supernatural talents. She could, of course, think about returning to the semisafe world of games design once this was all over. Use *those* talents. Be safe and secure. Oh, for the days when the scariest thing she could imagine was not having Wi-Fi. She smiled at the thought of her phone—usually grafted into her hand—lying at the bottom of her suitcase, uncharged and unloved, since her arrival here. Could she go back to that time before she had known she was a necromancer? As crazy as it seemed, she didn't think she could. So, if she got out of this madness alive, even if Cal didn't want a partner, business or otherwise—despite all her lectures, her heart gave a funny little skip at *that* thought—it seemed her future must include the dead.

Stella wrinkled her nose. Not in disgust at the thought of a life spent engaging with the deceased. That no longer troubled her. Cal had done his job well. He had tried hard to convey to her that being a necromancer was a privilege. She understood completely what he meant when he said that she must harness her skills, that they were an art form to be revered and practiced. The ability to listen to and care for those who had passed beyond the veil of mortality was a responsibility conferred upon very few. Stella didn't know where her strange gift had come from, but she was determined to take it seriously. No, it wasn't that thought that was bothering her all of a sudden. It was something far more immediate and physical. She sat up abruptly.

What was *that awful smell?*

It reminded her of a trip to the zoo as a child in the company of one set of foster parents. It had been a swelteringly hot summer day and, even though Stella had desperately wanted to see the giraffes, the stench from their enclosure had been so overwhelming she had been forced to turn away. For some reason, the clean scent of the freshwater pool and surrounding pines had been replaced by a new perfume. This one was reminiscent of rotten food, dung and urine, and damp earth. Not a great combination. It was definitely animal in origin. But a glance around her revealed no clue to its source. Darkness was falling, but, even so, nothing about the familiar scene had changed.

Dismissing it as the results of an overactive imagination—maybe all her thoughts of death had summoned an illusory aroma of the grave?—Stella returned to her musings, sitting with her knees bent so that she could rest her chin on them. During the week that had followed the encounter with Grindan's army—returned now to their waiting repose—she had honed her skills even further. She had even raised no objection when Cal suggested a nighttime visit to the cemetery just outside Carmarthen as her next opportunity to commune with the dead.

It had been a film-set-perfect midnight with a full moon riding high above rain-laden clouds. The graveyard housed centuries of the town's dead, and many of the stones leaned drunkenly against each other as if for nocturnal support.

Several had been rent apart by deep fissures in their stone surfaces.

"We should have brought a flashlight," Stella had whispered, her teeth chattering in spite of the humidity caused by a looming storm.

Cal had arched a brow at her in the moonlight. "You can necromance us up more light than any torch," he had reminded her. "But it's best to do this without. They prefer the darkness."

"Okay." She had set her shoulders determinedly. "Let's get this over and done as fast as we can. Don't we need to kill a chicken, make the sign of a five-pointed star or light a black candle?"

"You watch way too many horror films and play some very dodgy computer games."

"Explain to me why, once I have raised them, they are not zombies."

"Because you are not enslaving them. You will offer them free will. They can choose whether to come to you and when to return to their resting place. When a necromancer raises a zombie, he or she creates a mindless, undead slave. It's not a practice I recommend. I've seen it go horribly wrong."

"As in the flesh-eating monsters of my iffy games?" Stella scanned his face in the moonlight.

Cal nodded. "And worse. This will be nothing like that."

And he was right. It hadn't been the way she had envisioned. She hadn't needed to give any commands. Almost as soon as she set foot inside the cemetery gates, she became aware of the shifting shadows. Darker shapes within the moonlit gloom. Willingly, they had come to her, rising up from their resting places, seeking her out, wanting to tell her their stories, and offering her their allegiance. Almost, it seemed, giving her their love. In the end, she had stayed in that lonely place all night, even when the heavens opened while lightning tore the clouds to shreds and thunder made the soft whispers of those long dead even fainter. Dawn had been raising a dim curtain on the rain-soaked landscape when she had walked back to the bower in silence. Cal, in tune with her mood, had offered no comment, either then or when she had gone straight to bed and slept until noon.

It had been that encounter, more than the spectacular sight of Grindan's eerie army, that had brought about this introspective mood. That and the fact that, no matter how hard she tried to push them aside, the feelings she had for Cal persisted. They were feelings that had nothing to do with the past. The image she used to have of her life following a road that changed course had been abruptly altered by the intrusion into her world of a faerie called Moncoya. There was no longer a road for her to follow. She had been thrust off the track and into wild, uncharted territory. It was up to her now to tear a path through the undergrowth with her bare hands. The Stella who had existed before that point had changed and, with that change, Cal's role in her life had become different. He would always protect her, she knew that. That night in the cemetery she finally understood why he chose the path he had. She had forgiven his comment about protecting her being a job. She knew she would do the same in his shoes. The obligation upon them—the weight they both bore—was infinite.

They were equals now. Not only in the power they wielded over the dead. They were evenly matched in the hunger they felt for each other. Cal wanted her as much as she wanted him. Stella had felt his yearning in the kiss he broke so abruptly. She caught it in his eyes as he glanced at her when he thought she wasn't aware of his gaze. Yet, when she looked deeper into those inscrutable silver depths, it seemed the barricades between them remained impregnable. For him, she sensed that the obstruction came from something in the past rather than the confrontation to come. For her it was simpler. It centered on the question that played on a continuous loop in her mind. *Who are you, Cal?* But, if she discovered the answer, would the barricades be lowered or raised? If she was going to like what she found out, why was Cal taking such trouble to keep it hidden?

Sighing, she decided to go back to the cave. Being in Cal's company wouldn't stop her thinking about him. Quite the opposite. But at least it didn't smell so bad underground. The stink was getting worse. She rose to her feet. As she did, her breath caught in her throat in shock. A man was hunkered down a few feet away. Although he was in shadow, his eyes gleamed like burnished gold as he watched her. Of all the thoughts racing through her mind—How had he breached the magical boundary Cal had placed around the bower? Where *was* Cal? Why did this intruder smell so awful?—the fact that he was naked barely registered.

Stella took an instinctive step back. The man bared his teeth in what might have been a grin. Or it might have been a snarl. At the same time, he rose out of his crouch and lunged, halting just a foot or two from her. Since his intention seemed to be to seize hold of her, she was unsure, at first, what it was that had halted him. It soon became all too horribly obvious. It was fully dark now, with only a faint trace of moonlight illuminating the scene through the branches that loomed overhead. It was enough for Stella to see the transformation that had his body in a powerful grip. She observed in horrified fascination the phenomenon of coarse strands sprouting all at once from every pore on his body so that he was immediately covered all over by thick, dark hair. There was a creaking sound, as if his bones were changing shape. Under her horrified gaze, the fingers reaching for her lengthened, tapering into vicious claws. Throwing back his head to reveal yellowing fangs, he howled once in the direction of the huge full moon before turning his attention back to Stella.

He moved forward until he was mere inches away, and the fetid odor of his body was almost pleasant in comparison with the old-blood scent of his breath. A movement in the trees above his head diverted his attention briefly. Stella did not look up, but the soft velvet flapping sound of a falcon's wings signaled the bird's presence.

"Oflinnan." Her voice was quiet but compelling as she addressed the wolf-man. "Cease."

He did, stopping in his tracks as if an invisible barrier had been raised between them. His lips drew back. This time it definitely was an attempt at an ingratiating smile. It failed. "Come here to me, little necromancer." His voice was a hoarse rasp, like fingernails grating slowly down a chalkboard. "Come give your heart to a man who knows what to do with it."

"Eat it, you mean?" Stella asked. Bravado and dark humor might have been misplaced in the circumstances, but she had a feeling that if she showed him any fear, her power over him would be diminished.

He laughed. Or perhaps growled. The bird rustled in the tree again. Distracted, the wolf-man looked up. "Tell your feathered friend to fly away out of here."

"He's no friend of mine. I thought he came with you." And yet, now that she thought about it, there *was* something about the falcon. The last time one had landed here it had brought a message for Cal. This was not the same bird. Stella had no idea how she knew that. She just did. For some reason she sensed that, for her at least, the falcon was a benign presence. It was a fleeting sensation, one she could not afford to dwell on.

Her mind had been off the wolf-man for a second or two, but it was long enough for him to spring forward on his haunches, teeth bared. She threw up a hand before he could grip her upper arms with those lethal talons, and her palm came to rest against the harsh pelt of his chest.

"Fŷrwylm." She hoped she had remembered the correct pronunciation.

It seemed she had. The wolf's howl of pain split the night in two as a ball of fire passed from Stella's open palm and into his body. The creature dropped to the ground, shuddering and groaning. A smell of mingled burning fur and flesh replaced the rotten animal scent that had invaded Stella's nostrils for the past quarter of an hour. It wasn't an improvement.

"Don't kill him. Not yet."

She looked up in surprise as the tree branches shook and the huge falcon flew down. As the bird landed beside her, it stretched out its vast, dark wings and drew itself slowly upright. Before Stella's startled eyes, the silken feathers disappeared and human flesh emerged. Within seconds, no trace of the bird remained and Cal was standing at her side in its place.

"You bastard," she said through clenched teeth.

"Sadly, that's always been one of the rumors about me," he replied with a cheerful grin. "But my parents aren't around so I can't ask them."

"You know that's not what I meant. You allowed this to happen. You let him get to me. It was a test. You were seeing if I could go it alone."

"And you did. But I was always right here if you needed me..." They were interrupted by a pitiful groan from the figure on the rocks at their feet. "A bit of light would be useful here, Stella. I'm surprised you didn't think of it earlier."

Casting a less-than-friendly look in Cal's direction, Stella focused her attention on lighting up the area immediately around them and then crouched to observe the injured wolf-man. She was shocked at what she saw. All trace of fur, fangs and claws was gone. He was just a skinny, scared youth and, although he glared at them with venom in his eyes, his fear was palpable. Angry red burns had melted away the pale flesh of his chest.

"Kill me, necromancer." The words were an anguished plea. "Bring my nightmare to an end."

"Who sent you?" Cal was close enough for Stella to smell the warm, fresh scent of his flesh. She focused on that for a second. He was the first good thing her nostrils had encountered since the sun had gone down.

"I don't know. Something drives me when the moon is full, but I don't usually know what I'm doing." The youth writhed as though hit by a fresh wave of pain. "This time, I heard a voice telling me to come here. Urging me to take the heart of the necromancer. Over and over." He clenched his fists against his temples. "I couldn't get that sound out of my head, no matter how hard I tried. So I came."

"Man or woman? Was there anything distinctive about this voice?" Cal asked.

"Man. And do you mean the lisp?" He began to shake. "I know what this is. I've read the books and seen the films. There's no cure for what I've become. I'll keep killing until someone stops me by piercing my heart with silver. Do what you have to do."

Stella rose to her feet, gesturing for Cal to move away slightly so that they could talk without being overheard. "Is that true? Isn't there anything else we can do for him?"

"He has been infected by the bite of a true lycanthrope—what has become known as the werewolf—and he is right when he says there is no cure. It is a curse that can only be purged by the death of the host." He glanced down at the boy, his face unreadable in the shimmering moonlight. Stella thought there was a trace of sadness in his expression. "We dare not let him go."

"Are you seriously telling me we have to kill him?"

"We have no choice, Stella. He said it himself."

She tried another approach. "We don't have a gun, let alone any silver bullets."

Cal held up his hand to reveal a slender but serviceable dagger. "Solid silver."

"You've done this before." It was a reminder, if Stella needed one, of the chasm of secrets that existed between them.

"Too often to count." This time his sadness was unmistakable.

"What does the silver do?" A glimmer of an idea, probably an outrageous one, was forming in Stella's mind.

"Silver is the element of the moon. Through its supernatural properties, it drives the wolf from the mortal body." He turned back to the shuddering figure. "Let me get it over with, Stella. It's unfair to leave him this way."

"Cal, wait." She grabbed his arm, stopping him as he began to turn away. "Just so I'm clear, as the silver pierces the human heart, it drives out all trace of the wolf?"

"Yes. Unfortunately, it also drives out the life force."

"The same life force that can be given back again by a necromancer?"

Chapter 11

"He's gone." Cal found Stella sitting in the corner of her bed with her knees tucked under her chin and her hands clasped around her calves. It was her favorite defensive position. He sat next to her and, as if by instinct, she rested her head on his shoulder. His mind tried to give him a warning but he ignored it. "I dressed the burns, gave him some clothes and money. He wouldn't stay until morning."

"Who was he?" Her voice had a slightly distant quality that troubled him.

"His name is Nathan and he's a student from Cardiff. He's twenty-two."

"Older than he looks. Does he remember any of it?"

Still dismissing those inner promptings, Cal shifted position so that he could slide an arm around her and draw her closer. She snuggled gratefully into his side. "Vaguely. He knows he owes you his life."

Cal wanted to say more. He wanted to let her know how

hard it had been to leave her to face the werewolf alone. When the falcon had brought him a warning that danger was approaching, Cal had faced an agonizing decision. He needed to discover whether Stella was strong enough to use her powers without the security of his protective presence. Lowering the barrier spell he had placed around the bower in order to permit the marauding wolf to approach her had been one of the hardest things he had ever done. Watching in his own falcon disguise as she faced the snarling fangs of her would-be killer had been even worse. It had gone against his every instinct to leave her to it and not intervene. In spite of that, his heart had been full of pride as he watched Stella face and then defeat the wolf.

He wanted to tell her as well how proud he had been of her for acting so quickly and bravely after he had lifted Nathan, holding him in a half-sitting position before plunging the knife into his heart. Nathan had barely enough time to nod briefly in a combination of acceptance and thanks, before the life died from his eyes. With it, something dark had risen from his body and hovered briefly above him before dissipating in the darkness like dust blowing on the breeze. Swiftly, Cal had withdrawn the knife and stepped aside. Stella had been shaking pitifully as, heedless of the blood gushing from the wound in Nathan's chest, she had knelt beside him, laying a trembling hand on his forehead.

"Awacnian." Cal had marveled anew at the way she intuitively knew which Old English words to use. If ever he had doubted that she was the necromancer star of the prophecy, this ability alone would have been enough to convince him. In Cal's own first language, she had told Nathan to awaken and, with a murmur, almost of protest, the young man had opened his eyes, gazing around him in wonder. At that point, Cal had sent Stella away.

"Does he remember how he became a werewolf?"

"Yes. He clearly remembers the wolf bite that brought about his transformation. It was after a night out with friends. He didn't have the money for a taxi so he walked home. Something, he thought at the time it was a mugger—he knows differently now, of course—jumped out on him from an alleyway. In a classic wolf attack, it went for his throat. Nathan thought he was dead for sure, but a group of passersby disturbed the wolf and it ran away before it could finish him off. He was taken to the hospital, stitched up and sent home. The police believed they were looking for the same attacker who had brutally murdered a number of young men in the same area. It was only when the next full moon came around that Nathan knew there was something very wrong."

"I only know of werewolves through the stories I've read in books. Tell me the facts."

"A true werewolf is a human being who turns into a wolf during the full moon. He or she has no control over this transformation. The condition came about many centuries ago, when a curse was placed upon a shape-shifter wolf by a sorceress. She took away his ability to shift by making him half human, but she also took away all that was human about him while he was in wolf form. True werewolves, when in the grip of their wolf self, are governed by uncontrollable rage and hunger for blood. They are driven to kill everyone they encounter, regardless of their human self. The curse causes these wolves to lose all control of their rational minds, and when they return to their human form, they remember nothing or very little of what they have done. They transfer their condition through a bite, assuming that the bitten human survives the attack."

"But, if werewolves are half human and live among us undetected most of the time, what place do they have in Otherworld?"

"Over time, the werewolf has mutated. Some—those of the true bloodline—continue to be human by day and wolf by night and have, on the whole, achieved a quite remarkable feat. They are able to maintain control over their bloodlust, although their other wolf instincts remain strong. A few are still under the control of the original curse and remain unaware of their inner wolf. Often, they end up in prison cells and mental institutions, unaware of the terrible deeds they have committed when the moon is full. They are becoming rarer. Others are full mutants. They remain in their human-wolf form at all times. They are the undead wolf pack who dwell in Otherworld. With strong leadership, they could be an imposing force. As it is, they resemble a pack of rabid dogs. The werewolves are a sorry story of nobility lost."

"Because of the curse? The first wolf must have done something pretty bad to cause a sorceress to take such a drastic step."

"No, if we are to seek badness within this tale, it lies in that sorceress. If ever there was a story of pure evil, Stella, she embodies it."

"Really? What was her name?"

"Her name is Niniane." Stella seemed not to notice the shift in tense. All her concentration seemed focused on his eyes. He knew they held within them a world—perhaps also an Otherworld—of memories and pain whenever he spoke that name.

He told himself he was glad when she shifted the conversation back to Nathan. "If Nathan was a true werewolf, how could he be sent to get my heart? And who sent him?"

"When he said a voice in his head commanded him, and that voice had a lisp, I knew immediately who it was. The wolves of Otherworld have been torn apart by infighting. Their loyalties are tested between one leader, named

Anwyl, who offers them stability, and another, named Nevan, who promises them power."

"Let me guess. Nevan has a lisp."

Her voice was a sleepy murmur against the flesh of his neck, and Cal tried not to dwell on how much he liked the sensation. "Got it in one."

"It's not all moonlight and lollipops, this necromancing business, is it?"

He laughed. "There's often moonlight involved, but lollipops? Not so much."

"I necromanced the hell out of that poor boy." She lifted her head and he felt her eyes on his face. "The first time with the fire. If he had been in human form then, I'd have killed him."

"If you hadn't done that, he'd have killed you. He was sent to get your heart, Stella." Just saying the words made his blood run cold. Nevan the Wolf had better lie low for several centuries after this stunt. "There was nothing human about him in that instant. It was him or you."

"Does it get easier to tell yourself that?"

He thought about it for a minute or two. "No. Try to get some sleep now, Stella."

"Will you stay here with me?"

This was very dangerous territory. Ever since he had brought Stella to this cave, he had been fighting the feelings she provoked within his mortal self. He had succumbed to those feelings once before. Had allowed himself to believe he could love as humans did. Doing so had almost destroyed him…and the rest of the world. It had led him to Darnantes and the deal he had been forced to strike with the Dominion. But this was different. Centuries had passed. He had changed. And Stella was not Niniane.

"Of course I will." Reminding himself that he was only part mortal, and that he had strength and power beyond mere flesh and blood, he lay down next to Stella, holding the sweet, precious weight of her close as she succumbed to slumber. And he almost succeeded in convincing his treacherous body that he didn't want anything more than this. Almost, but not quite.

"What do *you* think the prophecy means, Cal? Will the power to rule Otherworld be conferred upon the one who rips my still-beating heart from my body? Or will it be the one I fall in love with? Oh, and let's not forget Moncoya, the one who thinks the way to get what he wants is through my pants." They were sitting at the pool's edge, and Stella trailed her bare feet in the depths, exulting in the cool water playing over her skin. The midday heat was stifling and she had abandoned all her clothing except shorts and a tank top. Even those were starting to cling annoyingly to her skin. Nevertheless, a feeling of well-being pervaded. She put that down to the fact that she had slept so well that the events of the previous night might almost have been a distant dream. That may, or may not, have had something—or everything—to do with the strong arms that had been wrapped around her.

"I hope it means none of those. I prefer to think it means that the triumphant dynasty will be the one upon which you choose to bestow your allegiance." Cal sprawled beside her, half-turned on his side and leaning on one elbow so that he could watch her face.

"Ah. That sounds so much better. But how will I know who to choose? It sounds like they are all as bad as each other. So far you've told me about the faeries, the vampires and the wolves, and I can't see me developing an affinity with any of them."

"Thank God for that. But I've been remiss if I've led you to believe that the only citizens of Otherworld are the ones who want to control it for evil purposes. I've made the comparison with the mortal world many times and I'm going to do it again. There are bad rulers of countries here on earth, politicians and princes who allow their lust for money or power to come before the welfare of their people. We see the consequences of their actions every day in news reports. But the good still outweighs the bad, and it is exactly the same in Otherworld."

Stella turned on her side, mirroring his body position. It felt like an intimate, yet entirely natural, action. *This is how we would lie in bed after we had made love.* The thought sent a flash of heat, one that had nothing to do with the warmth of the day, shimmering through her body. "How will I know who to trust?"

"The same way that you do with mortals. You trust your instincts."

"My instincts were wrong about Moncoya," she pointed out.

"I misjudged that." A slight frown marred his beautiful features and she wanted to reach out a fingertip to smooth it away. "You weren't forewarned. And Moncoya fights dirty."

"When you talk about the others, you do it dispassionately. But you really hate Moncoya, don't you?"

Something shifted and darkened within the lightness of his eyes and, for a moment, she thought he might not answer her question. Instead he gave a brief nod. "Believe me, I have reason. And it's mutual."

"Redress the balance. Tell me something about the good guys. You said the Ghost Lord wasn't seeking to take over. Does that make him okay?"

Cal lay back, tucking his hands behind his head. The movement gave Stella an opportunity to let her gaze linger on the long, lean lines of his body. It was impossible not to let her eyes wander with so much masculine perfection stretched out next to her. She took in every detail, from the sinewy strength of his calf muscles tightening and relaxing as he kicked his legs lazily in the water to the jut of his hip bones just peeking above the waistband of his cutoff jeans. His upper body was all hard ridges and muscles that led her gaze down to the bulge in his jeans. She swallowed hard to clear the sudden dryness that was affecting her throat. Something tightened correspondingly in her stomach, and she fought down a quite overwhelming urge to press her lips to the precise spot where the hair on his chest softened and became a line dipping lower... *Concentrate, Stella, for heaven's sake!* Cal was speaking and she had barely registered what he was saying.

"He is determined to remain neutral at all costs. The ghosts just want to be left alone. They don't want to get involved in Otherworld politics and won't be drawn into any fighting."

"If you had a choice about who to put in charge, who would it be?"

He smiled. "If I was given the role of kingmaker, you mean? Probably the elves. They are the most democratic group I've come across—on Earth or in Otherworld—and, unlike many of the other dynasties within Otherworld, they apply reason to a situation rather than tackling it with aggression. They have a well-defined social structure based on individual freedom, and their laws are fair and well enforced."

"Yet I detect a note of caution."

"You know me too well." The way he said the words made Stella's heart lurch. Could he have guessed how much better she would *like* to get to know him? "The elves are not fighters. If they were placed in charge, I'd give it a week before one of the others—Moncoya, the Vampire

Prince, Nevan the Wolf…you could pick a name out of a hat, but those three would always be contenders—made a bloodthirsty takeover bid. They would probably be successful. Not wanting to be outdone, the others would join the fray and we would descend into mayhem again."

"What is the solution?"

"I have no idea and it tires my brain just thinking about it in this heat."

"Come for a swim instead." Still in her shorts and tank top, Stella slid off the rocks and into the water. The notion of swimming in such a confined space might involve a stretch of the imagination, she conceded. The pool had been formed in a rocky basin, and it was filled from the tumbling flow from a short waterfall. Some ten feet across, it was just deep enough for Cal to stand but Stella was out of her depth in the center.

Cal quirked an eyebrow at her, but, when she began to scoop up handfuls of water and splash him, he followed her into the pool—with a very purposeful look on his face. Laughing, Stella started to back away.

Cal caught up with her as she reached the waterfall. "Not quite so brave close up, are you, Stella?"

"I was trying to be helpful and cool you down," she protested. "You said you were too hot."

"And now I'm returning the favor." Scooping her up into his arms, he walked with her under the fast-pouring water and held her there.

Stella's instinct was to shriek as the freezing water hit her full-on, but opening her mouth proved to be a mistake and she ended up spluttering wildly. Laughing at her shocked expression, Cal released her and she backed away from him.

"That wasn't very nice."

"Oh, I'm sorry." His eyes gleamed as he closed the distance between them. Stella was standing shoulder deep in the water and he stopped in front of her. His eyes still gleamed, but she sensed a shift in his mood. Her breath caught in her throat. "I can be very nice, Stella. If nice is what you want." He ran his hand along her cheek to bury his fingers in her hair. It was a wonderful, feather-light contact that held a world of new promise. The slight tug he gave her scalp sent her heart rate galloping up to a hundred miles a minute. A flutter started in her belly, spreading lower until her whole body felt on fire from that single touch.

He caught her to him, his hands firmly grasping her waist. Stella allowed the movement of the water to hold her tight against his body, her breath hitching harder at the burning look in his eyes. If she'd had any lingering doubts about how much he wanted her, they were swept away under the intensity of that gaze. Her own hands rose, seemingly of their own volition, to grip his shoulders and she shivered as her fingers connected with his skin. Cal leaned closer, his head bending toward hers, and she licked her lips in anticipation. The gesture drew his attention to her mouth, and the way he stared at her lips brought a new quiver to life in her chest. It wasn't nervousness. It was a glorious, exulting acceptance of something that had been inevitable since the first moment she had really looked into those silver eyes. She brushed her fingers up and along the side of his neck. Despite the chill of the water, his flesh was warm and smooth under her fingers. She stroked higher until his hair tickled the back of her hand. Every tiny contact between them imprinted itself into her consciousness.

She closed her eyes in expectation, and Cal's breath was a warm sigh of air against her lips, his mouth a soft caress that made her gasp. His hand twisted farther into her hair, urging her head back. His mouth was slow and steady on hers. He kissed her with a determination and thoroughness that told her clearly he knew exactly what he was doing. He was showing her that his indecision was over. That this was a deliberate choice. The knowledge only made her want him more.

How could he stand to take this so slowly? Not endowed with similar patience or self-control, Stella parted her mouth beneath his with a soft, pleading moan. Instantly, Cal's lips became urgent and relentless in response, as if he wanted to taste and absorb her. One of his hands moved lower to rest on her hip, pulling her to fit into his body. The muscles of his chest were like granite against the softness of her breasts. The brush of his tongue on hers was a wildly welcome invasion, sweeping the inside of her mouth, exploring her with the power of ownership. Even as she decided she had never wanted anything as much as this evidence of his body inside hers, she ached with the need for even more intimacy.

Returning both hands to grip her waist, Cal sank down into the water, bringing his mouth level with her breasts. Hurriedly, Stella tugged her tank over her head. Without hesitation, he drew her nipple deep into his mouth and sucked it, his tongue flicking back and forth over the hardened nub. The warmth of his mouth in contrast to the cool water made Stella cry out, the sounds of her pleasure echoing against the silent rocks. Sparks of pure bliss shimmered from her breast directly to the sensitive spot at her core.

"Off." Cal raised his head long enough to utter the single syllable while tugging at the button on her shorts. With a bit of fumbling, Stella managed to get them undone and kicked them aside. She was about to point out that she was at a definite disadvantage with only her flimsy underwear compared to his jeans, but those magical lips returned to her breast and she lost the power of coherent speech.

When his mouth moved upward to her neck and then back to her lips, she returned the kiss with a need that was close to desperation. Her tongue teased its way past his lips to tangle with his. There was nothing shy or hesitant remaining in her kiss, just her blatant desire for him and an eagerness that sent an answering quiver running through him.

"Cal, if you know everything there is to know about me, you don't need me to tell you it's been a while. Or that I'm careful and I use birth control."

His voice was shaky against her ear. "So your generation really does have these conversations? You say it's been a while. It hasn't been centuries, Stella. That's how long it's been for me."

She rested her head on his shoulder, a slight laugh trembling through her. "Does that mean you've forgotten how?"

He lifted her with his hands on her buttocks, holding her so that she could wrap her legs around his waist and feel the iron-hard length of his erection pressing against her. "I think it's starting to come back to me. Give me a second and I'll have remembered it all."

"Here? In the water?"

His hands slid inside her underwear, cupping the flesh of her buttocks before his fingers moved lower to probe between them. "I don't think I can last a minute longer, Stella. But I warn you now…this time is going to be fast and frenzied."

"Just what I need." The words came out as a hoarse whisper. She moved her own hands down and the button on his jeans popped open. Her fingers found and traced his erection through the wet denim. Cal groaned his appreciation and she switched her attention to his zipper. The metal teeth resisted her first effort to drag them open over the hard bulge. He groaned again as the zipper came down

on the second attempt. Stella's own senses were heightened
by the sound of his arousal and the raw, masculine scent
of him. She freed his cock from the restraining material.
Eagerly she wrapped her fingers around him, exulting in
his length and girth. Her own body was stretched taut with
need. "I need to feel all of this inside me, Cal. Right now."

Removing her underwear and lifting her higher in the
same movement, Cal kept his gaze locked on hers. "Show
me."

She gripped him harder. Beneath the water, their skin
slicked together. His cock pressed hard against her and
then slid inside, in a tight, hot pulse of sensation. "You
feel so good around me, Stella. Like silk gripping me."

Stella had never known emotion like this. It was an
arousal that spiraled higher and wilder each time he pulled
back and then drove back into her. "More." Words she
hardly recognized spilled from her lips as she locked her
legs tighter around him and rocked her hips to meet each
thrust. "Harder."

Release came fast, starting somewhere deep inside
her, an urgent, frantic clamoring for something just out
of reach. Her gasps became moans and then whimpers as
she writhed and rocked against him. Cal's fingers dug into
the tender flesh of her buttocks harder, and the pain intensified her pleasure. His next hard thrust gave her what
she needed and she sank her head onto his shoulder with
a soft cry. Hot, heavy waves burst through her, spreading
out and growing stronger as Cal slammed into her. Stella
cried out again, her voice ragged as her body tightened
around him, spasming wildly with the force of her climax.

Cal's own cry was strained, as his powerful hip thrusts
drove him into her once more. Then he shuddered, his
cock swelling and jerking out his own release deep inside

her. He held her close against him until they both stopped trembling.

When she could finally speak, Stella's voice was husky with the intensity of her feelings. "I'm so glad you remembered what to do."

His own voice was equally shaky. "Some things are worth waiting centuries for."

Chapter 12

"Cal?" He murmured a response. "This can't last, can it?"

They hadn't bothered to use the lamps so the cave was faintly lit by Stella's power. As she lay in his arms, Stella sensed, rather than saw or felt, the tiny shake of Cal's head. "No."

"It's about who you are and the centuries between us. But it's more than that. It's because I have to go to Otherworld and fulfill the prophecy." It was a statement. A final acceptance of who she was.

This time the movement of his head was even smaller. But it was downward. A single, reluctant nod. When he spoke, his voice was bleak. "I wish it didn't have to be this way."

"But it does. So we'd better make the most of the time we do have together." She reached up to seek his lips with hers in the darkness.

It felt wrong to be happy with the world falling apart

around her, but, as she slid her hands into Cal's hair and kissed him hard, she refused to feel anything else. She traced her tongue along his lips and pushed inside, moaning softly as she urged him to reciprocate, begging him to show her that it was enough. That, for the here and now, they could be enough for each other.

Cal groaned, a sound that began somewhere deep in his chest, and he curled his tongue around hers to return her caress. His hand, firm and warm, drifted down her body, coming to rest on her hips. Otherwise, he did nothing but touch his mouth to hers, exploring her with excruciating slowness. Arousal unfurled inside Stella again, slow and patient this time as the heat between them built.

She made a new noise as his tongue circled hers, something that sounded more like a whimper than a moan. Moving his mouth down her body, he captured her nipple between his lips and teased it with his tongue. Edging her legs apart with his knee, he reached his hand down to brush the inside of her thigh. Stella arched up to meet his questing fingers, rocking her hips as he commenced a slow stroking movement.

His fingers brushed a gentle, teasing touch over her clitoris, and she gasped. "Cal!"

One of his fingers slipped inside her. "Yes, Stella?"

Another new sound, this one more of a gurgle, was all she could manage in response. She was developing a whole new repertoire.

Cal coaxed her mouth open, making her lips and tongue tingle, as his hand continued to move against her. When he thrust a second finger in, her arousal spiked out of control. She tore her mouth from his, kissing his jaw and nuzzling his neck. He brought his thumb up to rub tantalizing circles in counterpoint to the thrusts of his fingers.

His teeth nipped her nipple as she arched her hips and

began to buck and writhe beneath his touch. Stella's whole body tightened, hurtling at double speed toward an orgasm that hit her head-on like a freight train. Pleasure swept through her in wave upon scalding wave until her toes curled and her fingers dug into his shoulders. She choked back a scream as, using those skillful fingers and with his mouth still teasing her breast, Cal coaxed the wave to yet another incredible crest. As she shuddered to a stand-still, he kissed her, beautifully, wonderfully, so that she relaxed in his arms.

He lifted his head to study her face, and the look in his eyes caused a sharp flutter deep inside her core, an echo of the climax that had just ripped through her. "I want to make you feel good."

"You just did." Her throat was so tight that the words were barely a whisper.

"I want this to be even better." His mouth sought hers again. As he kissed her passionately, he moved his hand. The contrast between the rough pad of his thumb and the smooth slipperiness of her still-throbbing clitoris was tantalizingly erotic. Stella moved her own hands lower, her fingertips tracking the length of his erection. She pressed her mouth to his neck, tasting his skin and inhaling his scent. He pushed a finger inside her again and her body convulsed, a torrent of sensations charging through her. She began breathing harder as he pumped his finger into her, taking her higher and higher until nothing mattered but the moment and the feelings he was arousing in her. He hooked his fingertip hard up against the sensitive bundle of nerve endings just inside her.

"Oh, dear God, I can't be coming again."

"Are you sure?"

He repeated the movement and she did come, the world exploding with the intensity of another climax. She gripped his arm and held on tight, riding out each wild, glorious wave of pleasure.

"I want to be inside you," Cal whispered. His fingers stroked her inner thighs. The touch was gentle, so intimate and, even though she had just come, instantly arousing.

"Please," she murmured.

As he spread her legs and lifted her so that she could wrap them around his hips, Stella pushed up, desperate to feel him. He leaned over her and his cock pressed against her opening as his mouth found hers. She moved her hips again, offering herself to him. He groaned as she welcomed him into her body, then, in one quick thrust, he pushed all the way into her. Her heartbeat picked up speed as their bodies rocked together, and soon she was lost to everything but Cal. He kissed her and drew her tongue into his mouth. She moaned and pressed her breasts to his chest, wanting the feel of him against her sensitive skin. The difference between his hardness and her softness drove the oxygen from her lungs and what was left of reason from her brain. He began to pound harder, as if he couldn't get deep enough into her. It was as if he was seeking something more from her than his own release. Something was happening between them this time, something beyond their control. She looked into his eyes and the way he gazed back at her told her he felt this new connection between them, as well.

Soft quakes started somewhere deep in her core and rippled upward and outward. Stella couldn't believe that it was possible for her body to endure, let alone crave, a maelstrom of such erotic intensity. She gripped Cal's biceps, holding on to him as she let go, all conscious thought slipping away as searing heat tore through her. A moment later her body splintered into a million tiny pieces. She felt Cal swell and pulse inside her and she clenched her muscles hard around his cock, her body trembling as she held him tight inside her as if she would never let him go.

Her action drew a growl from somewhere deep in Cal's chest. The look of ecstasy in his eyes as he came was enough to make her heart pound even more wildly. He attempted to gasp out a few words. "That was…" The rest of the sentence eluded him and he collapsed onto the bed at her side, drawing her closer.

Stella gave a contented sigh and wrapped her arms tightly around him. "I know what you mean."

"I'm glad one of us does."

Sometime later, Stella propped herself up on one elbow so that she could watch Cal's face in the flickering light of the lamp he had lit. He lay back on the pillows with his hands tucked behind his head. "Tell me about the falcons."

"Every sorcerer has an animal familiar. You know about witches and black cats, right?" She nodded. "My own familiar is the falcon."

"But I thought falcons were associated with evil. I'm sure I've heard of them being a bad omen."

"It's a common mistake. The disposition of the familiar is unimportant. What matters is the intent of the master. So, if we return to the well-known theme of black cats and witches. Black cats are considered to be good omens in many cultures. Celtic superstition would have us believe they bring good luck. If your path is crossed by a black cat you will have great fortune. Those things will only hold true if the master of that black cat wills it so. If the master is evil, no amount of superstition will bring you good luck. When that cat crosses your path, you are doomed. We choose our familiars for other reasons."

"Why did you choose the falcon?" The soothing quality of his voice lulled her.

"They are easily trained, both as guards and messengers. They are loyal to their master and are fiercely protective. As well as being my familiar, the werefalcon is the therianthrope with whom I feel most affinity."

Stella shook her head. "That really is a thing? There are werefalcons as well as werewolves? I keep adding to my vocabulary of beings I never knew existed."

"There can be a hybrid, a were form, of pretty much every animal you can think of. Whether there are any in existence at this time is another matter. Certainly werefalcons are a small but thriving community. Centuries ago, they were known to watch over mortals in isolated areas and warn them of impending attacks. Now, they tend to steer clear of humans."

"Which brings me to the question of how you came to be in falcon form when the werewolf was here. You are not a werefalcon." She studied his face. "Are you?"

He smiled at her questioning expression. "No, I'm not. But I do have the ability to shift into falcon form." He regarded her in surprise as she collapsed back onto the bed, her whole body shaking. "What are you laughing at?"

"You. This. The fact that I am in bed with a gorgeous man who is matter-of-factly telling me he can change into a giant bird whenever the mood takes him."

He pulled her back into his arms, joining in her laughter. "Nobody's perfect, Stella. Not even me."

Ever since the intrusion into the bower by the werewolf, and the new awareness that Nathan had been sent to rip out Stella's heart, Cal had increased the protective barrier around them. Stella was still fascinated by the fact that the spells he cast needed nothing more than the power of his thoughts.

"I always thought a spell involved the mixing of foul-smelling ingredients and chanting of incantations."

"For some it does," he explained. "It depends on what you believe and how strong your ability is."

"And yours is very strong?"

"Yes. As is yours." His face was solemn and she went to him, stepping into the circle of his arms. In a short space of time she had become so dependent on his touch that, if she gave herself a moment to stop and think about it, it frightened her. Cal rested his cheek against the top of her head.

"You have had so many years to learn and practice. I feel as if I know nothing in comparison."

"The prophecy states that you will be ready in your twenty-fifth year. That means your powers are at their peak now."

"I hate that bloody prophecy." Stella burrowed closer into his chest.

Cal's soft laughter ended on a sigh. "I wish…"

Stella never found out what he wished for because the dense branches closest to them parted suddenly and a man strolled into the bower. She gave a gasp of mingled surprise and horror. Cal had assured her that the barrier spell he had used was so strong there was no chance of anyone or anything breaking through it to harm her. Yet, without warning, this stranger had managed to wander into their private world.

Cal was unperturbed at the intrusion. Releasing Stella, but taking her by the hand, he led her forward to where the other man stood. "Stella, this is Lorcan Malone. He's a necromancer, too. He's also a good friend."

Lorcan was tall and lean, with the sort of edgy good looks that made Stella think of hell-raising rock stars or Byronic bad boys. As if eyes the piercing blue of wild cornflowers and dark blond hair that flopped poetically into his view, so that he had to keep pushing it back, were not enough, he was also possessed of a heartbreaking grin.

"I thought you said necromancers were solitary?" Stella was unsure that she wanted to share the peace of the place she had come to think of, albeit bizarrely, as home with another person. Even a friendly one.

"Generally necromancers prefer their own company. They're not hostile to each other, however. And we've even been known to collaborate now and then. Especially on matters such as the future of the world." The three of them went into the cave together and Cal began to make coffee, leaving Stella alone with Lorcan.

"I can't believe I'm meeting you at last." Lorcan's voice was quiet, his Irish accent soft and lilting. "After all these years of waiting for the prophecy to be fulfilled and now... here you are."

"You'll have to excuse me if I'm not similarly enthusiastic." Stella flopped down into a chair. "But this is all new to me. I've only just found out I'm a sorcerer and I don't know much about it. Necromancing has never been high on my list of chosen careers."

Lorcan came to sit on a cushion at her feet. His face was earnest as he spoke. "Those who have heard of it tend to think of necromancy as an evil practice. A dark art. But there is more to this world than what we can see, and necromancy is *not* witchcraft. It is a divine gift. We who have the power can channel the spirit world according to our desire. The responsibility that rests with us is great. We must exercise the choices before us wisely."

"You make it sound like that is not always the case. Have there been evil necromancers?" Stella watched his profile, fascinated by the passion with which he spoke. She was also aware of Cal listening closely to their conversation from a discreet distance.

"God, yes, many of them. Still are. Necromancy can be a lucrative business, particularly now with the increased unrest in Otherworld. Some of our number are happy to sell their skills to the highest bidder."

"You mean like mercenaries?" Stella could feel her eyes growing rounder at the picture that Lorcan was painting.

"That's exactly what I mean." Lorcan accepted the mug of coffee from Cal. "And, on that subject, I have news of our mutual friend. Unless…" He trailed off awkwardly.

"You can speak in front of Stella." Cal came to sit with them.

"Yes, we've reached an agreement. We've decided that the whole 'protecting Stella from the truth' thing isn't going to work. Or one of us has," Stella explained, looking pointedly at Cal. He grinned appreciatively in return.

Lorcan gave them a slightly bemused glance. "Okay. My sources tell me that Jethro has been offering his services to a number of Otherworld leaders. His selling point, apparently, is that he will undertake to outdo the necromancer star of the prophecy."

"And Jethro would be?" Stella looked from one to the other.

"Trouble," Lorcan said.

"Nothing for you to worry about," Cal said at the same time.

"Great. So let me get this straight. Unless I'm very much mistaken, it's a bit like an old-fashioned prizefight. This Jethro—whoever he might be—is offering to step into the ring and beat me to within an inch of my life in return for a bag of cash from the highest bidder?"

Lorcan nodded delightedly. "Do you know what? That's a really good summary." His body jerked sharply and he swiveled round to look at Cal, whose foot had just connected with his ribs. "What was that for?" Stella watched as Lorcan's eyes followed the slight jerk of Cal's head in her direction. "Oh, right."

Stella sighed. Despite the fact that she was the one in the firing line, Cal was obviously going to persist in being protective. She took a moment to examine how that made her feel. It provoked a warm glow that started in the region of her abdomen and spread outward from there. Whatever that feeling was, Stella decided she liked it.

"So do you live in a cave, as well?" she asked Lorcan.

"It's not a prerequisite of being a necromancer," Lorcan said with a laugh.

"I wasn't sure, given that Merlin also seemed to have a preference for caves. Didn't he spend much of his time in one?"

Something changed slightly in the atmosphere in that instant. Stella couldn't pinpoint what it was exactly. Neither Cal nor Lorcan looked at her, nor did they exchange glances with each other. Nevertheless, she sensed something pass between them. An infinitesimal shift in mood, a whisper of caution, a silently raised barrier. No sooner had she felt it than it was gone.

"There are so many stories about Merlin," Cal said. "It's almost impossible to tell which are truth and which are legend."

Stella rose to her feet and stretched, yawning. "You know more about it than I do. Until recently, I wasn't sure whether Merlin was real or a fictional character." There it was again. That *something* flitted swiftly from one man to the other. "I'll leave you to talk. I'm for my bed. No, don't get up." Raising a hand to forestall Cal, she went through into the secondary cave that was their sleeping area.

Their voices had lulled her to sleep earlier as they talked of Lorcan's travels. When she woke sometime later in what she thought must be the early hours of the morning, Stella detected a change in the trend of their conversation.

There was a clink of glasses. *"Sláinte."*

She heard Cal make a choking sound. "Shit, Lorcan. What the hell is that stuff?"

"Poitín. Sure, I brew it myself." There was laughter in the Irishman's tone.

"It's lethal. You could incapacitate armies with that stuff."

"Ah, get it down you, man."

There was silence for a few minutes then Lorcan spoke again. "You should tell her. All of it."

Although Cal spoke in quieter tones, his words also reached Stella's ears. She thought his voice held a trace of regret. "I can't."

"We've been friends for longer than I care to remember, Cal, and I'd like to see you have a chance at happiness. You won't get that if you're not honest with her."

Cal gave a soft laugh. "Since when did you turn out to be the wise one in this friendship? Put yourself in my shoes. Can't you see how impossible it would be to explain it all?"

There was another clink of glasses followed by a brief silence. Frightened of missing something, Stella strained to hear. "Okay. I get it. Looks like you're screwed if you speak, screwed if you don't."

"Thank you for your insightful summary of my life, Lorcan, my friend."

"Anytime. Talking of being screwed, things are spiraling out of control in the other place, Cal. Otherworld is in complete chaos."

When he responded, Cal's voice was solemn. "The situation there is worse than any of us ever imagined. Paranormal activity here in the mortal realm is increasing as a direct result. Evil deeds are on the rise across the globe. The veil between the worlds is thinning."

"It's hard to see a way to resolve it. There are those who do want to see peace restored and who crave a return to the old times when each dynasty had its own independent realm."

"Those halcyon days are gone. There are too many power-hungry leaders who want control of more. The only good thing to be said for Moncoya is that he's up-front. He has stated that he will not rest until he has subdued all the other dynasties and taken control of the whole of Otherworld. And he doesn't care how much blood he sheds in the process." Even from a distance, Stella heard Cal's sigh. "We have to stop him. At least in Stella we now have the means."

"You're not going to like this question." There was a pause before Lorcan spoke again, his words tentative. "Are you quite sure she is the one, Cal?"

"What do you mean?" Stella had never before heard that tone from Cal. It sounded as if he had swallowed liquid ice.

"It's just that throughout all the long years of waiting for the necromancer star to appear, I envisioned a big, powerful presence. I never once pictured a pretty slip of a girl."

"She is the one. I have known it since before her birth." Cal's voice held a trace of the commanding notes she had heard at the airport.

Lorcan's answer was conciliatory. "Your call. After all, you know the prophecy better than anyone."

"I do. And if you think for a minute that Stella is *not* a big, powerful presence—" from the way he spoke, Stella could picture him smiling now "—well, just wait until you know her a bit better. By the way, the fourth choir are on your case. Last time I spoke to the Dominion, he seemed keen to make sure you were doing your bit for the angels."

"Ah, sure, haven't they always had a thistle stuck up their celestial asses where I'm concerned? Just because they persuaded you to join their team they seem to think all other necromancers should turn out for the guys in the white robes."

Cal's laughter was hollow. "Persuaded? Is that what you call it? I don't remember having any choice in the matter."

"To think she still walks free after what she did to you. If I could get my hands around that lily-white throat of hers... Oh, have it your way. I'll shut up, if that's what you wish."

Chapter 13

"Do we have a plan?" Lorcan asked the next morning as they ate breakfast.

Stella was silent. She had wondered if Cal would join her in the bed they had shared for the past few nights or whether the presence of his friend would bring about a change in his behavior. Several hours after she had gone to bed, however, she had felt the mattress sag as he lay down next to her. She had fallen asleep as his arms enclosed her with a hundred questions on her lips. They were still unanswered. Lorcan had just given voice to them.

"The plan is to get Stella to Otherworld, defeat Moncoya and fulfill the prophecy," Cal said in response to Lorcan's question.

"And, as plans go, that one sounds grand. I was wondering if you might have given any thought to the logistics of how those things were going to happen."

Cal's grin was rueful. "No," he admitted.

Lorcan turned to Stella with an exaggerated sigh. "It was always this way. Yer man here—" he jerked a thumb in Cal's direction "—comes up with the big plan. *Let's drive the dark witches out of Fen County. Why do we not assist in the battle of Camlan? The Dryads have a problem with the Satyrs. We should do something to help.* You get the picture?"

Stella nodded. "You're the good guys."

"We are. We're good at righting the wrongs. We ace the rescuing. But we don't do subterfuge. We suck at strategy. Am I right?" He addressed himself to Cal.

Stella could tell that this was a well-worn theme. "We don't need to be subtle." There was a trace of stubbornness about the set of Cal's mouth. "Not when we have the sort of combined power that can realign the planets."

"I'm going to throw a mad idea out here." Lorcan's voice became serious now. "And you can challenge me if you wish. But I think we're going to need something other than brute force this time, Cal."

"We?" Stella looked from one to the other. "I don't understand. I thought the prophecy said I was the one who had to do this."

Cal laid a hand over hers. "Change of plan. I'm coming with you."

Lorcan grinned. "Sure, and I wouldn't be left out of an adventure like this. Not for this world or any other."

Stella swallowed the sudden lump in her throat. "Thank you." The word came out as a croaky whisper.

Cal's hand tightened briefly on hers. "I don't do this very often, but on this occasion I have to admit it. Lorcan is right." His friend made a gesture of mock surprise. "We need a plan that relies on something more than our strength. Otherwise, we will waste all our energy fighting every being we encounter from the first minute we enter Otherworld."

"Can't we just take Grindan and his warriors with us?" Stella asked hopefully.

"We can't be the aggressors." There was a touch of regret in Cal's voice. "To ride in at the head of a vast army would only serve to alienate those elements within Otherworld who might otherwise remain neutral. No, Grindan's role is to be summoned if you are threatened. He must be our defense, not our attack. What we need is to find a way into Otherworld that does not alert Moncoya to our real intention."

There was that coldness again that she had seen before when he spoke of Moncoya. It made Stella shiver. "Remind me. What is our intention?"

"First, to destroy Moncoya. Second, to destroy anyone else who would harm Otherworld."

"And then have lunch?" It was only with humor that Stella felt she could possibly listen to these schemes and retain a grip on her sanity.

"What we need is a plan that will enable us to outcunning the king of cunning," Lorcan said, bringing them back to the point. They all fell silent. "Of course, we could just set fire to his wardrobe. That would finish the vain little..." he broke off, catching himself up on the word that was about to leave his lips "...sidhe off once and for all."

Stella stood up. "Well, I need to bathe, so I'll leave you two to think about it—"

"No!" Lorcan interrupted her excitedly. "I was joking, but that's it. Don't you see? Moncoya's vanity is our way into Otherworld."

"You really do want us to burn his clothes?" Cal regarded him in bewilderment.

Lorcan shook his head. "You said that Moncoya's in-

terpretation of the prophecy is that he has to win Stella's
love. We all know Moncoya. He'll never believe for a minute that he *couldn't* do that."

"I don't see where you're going with this." Cal frowned
in an effort to follow Lorcan's thoughts.

"That's our way in. We give him Stella."

"Have you gone mad?" It was Cal's rugged velvet voice,
the one that Stella imagined him using to pause oceans
and flatten mountains.

"Ah, will you stop being the overprotective hero for
one minute and listen? I mean we pretend to give him
Stella. How do you feel about a spot of amateur dramat-
ics, me darlin' girl?" Lorcan turned his heartbreaking grin
in Stella's direction.

"I have a feeling you don't mean singing and dancing."
Despite her misgivings, Lorcan's smile was irresistible and
his enthusiasm infectious. Stella resumed her seat next to
Cal, feeling some of the tension ooze out of his body as
her thigh connected with his.

"I mean you play the part of Moncoya's besotted girlfriend."

"Like hell she will." Cal's expression was as hard as
granite.

"Have you got any better ideas? Ones that don't involve
storming in and starting a full-scale war?"

"Explain how me pretending to be in love with Moncoya is going to work." Stella's quiet voice cut across the
strained atmosphere between the two men.

Lorcan dragged his eyes away from the staring com-
petition he was having with Cal. "Easy. You'd get yourself into his Otherworld palace. Then you get me and Cal
in there with you."

"You don't seem to be listening to me." There was a
knife edge of danger in Cal's voice.

Stella laid a hand on his arm and he looked down at her. The darkness lurking in the depths of his eyes made her breath hitch. Tactfully, Lorcan rose and moved out of earshot.

"Cal…"

"No, Stella. It's too risky." Stella was shocked at the anguish in Cal's voice.

"Do you think I'll do what Moncoya wants? That I'll become his weapon because I'll be under his spell? Is that what this is all about? You don't trust me to put the safety of Otherworld first."

It was hard to believe that his muted eyes could burn with an inner fire, but Cal's did in that instant. "Believe it or not, those concerns had not crossed my mind. My only thought was that I can't allow you to place yourself in that bastard's power."

He made a jerky movement, as if to rise to his feet, but Stella forestalled him by placing her arms around him and holding on tight. For a few seconds he remained rigid in her embrace. Then, with a shuddering sigh, he relaxed. Stella reached up and, taking his face in her hands, kissed him long and hard. There was a hint of desperation in the way he kissed her back.

"Isn't it better this way? As soon as I leave this bower, Moncoya will be waiting for me. If I am captured by him, then I end up in his power anyway. Lorcan's plan at least ensures we stay one step ahead."

"Whatever Moncoya's other faults may be, he is no fool. And he is fey. His extra sense gives him a greater intuition. He will know if you are pretending."

"You underestimate my acting ability." Stella shook her head in mock sadness. "I was the leading light in many a school play, remember?" A slight reminiscent smile touched his lips. "I'll be shy and a bit scared, confused about all this prophecy nonsense, utterly bewildered by this mad sorcerer who whisked me away from Barcelona against my will. I'll throw myself on the mercy of my kindly employer." The smile widened and Cal finally started to laugh. "Can we at least listen to what Lorcan has to say?"

He looked across at where Lorcan was seated close to the warded edge of the bower. Raising his voice slightly so that the Irishman could hear, he said, "I'll listen, but that doesn't mean I'll agree."

Lorcan strolled back to them. "Sure, aren't you as stubborn as a demon hewn from the fires of Satan himself?"

"Is that meant to be funny?" Cal was on his feet before Stella had seen him move.

"Ah, Cal. I'm sorry." Lorcan held his hands up in an apologetic gesture. "I spoke before I thought about what I was saying. Truly I did."

"Stop being so touchy, Cal." Stella tugged on his hand until he sat back down. "You get offended at me for thinking you're an angel and are insulted when Lorcan compares you to a demon. We get it. There is nothing of heaven or hell about you."

His laughter was shaky. "All this talk of Moncoya must be getting to me."

"I can sympathize with that. A conversation about the faerie folk over breakfast is bad enough, but a man who wears eyeliner? That'll turn your stomach for sure." Lorcan shook his head. "I for one am going to need more coffee before we continue." He lifted the pot from the fire and held it out. When he had replenished all their cups, they drank in companionable silence for a few minutes.

Stella broke the silence. "Supposing we decide to go with Lorcan's plan. How will I contact Moncoya? I can't just stroll back into La Casa Oscura as if nothing had happened."

"Getting in touch with Moncoya won't be a problem. When the falcon came to warn me that danger was on its way, I checked out what was happening in the surrounding area. It wasn't only the wolf-man who was seeking you. There are sidhes here in Carmarthen, just waiting for the chance to get you away from me." Cal's lips thinned. "Even Moncoya himself has been seen close by."

Instinctively, Stella glanced over her shoulder. "You said yourself he's no fool. He knows I've been with you all this time, so he will be aware that you've told me all about him. I know what his motives are. I know exactly what he wants from me. Do I come across to either of you as the sort of power-crazed megalomaniac who would marry the faerie king so that she can rule over Otherworld as his necromancer consort?"

The two men studied her thoughtfully for a minute. She tried to see herself through their eyes. Short, slender and clad in one of Cal's shirt's that came almost to her knees. She had not yet washed her unruly dark hair, so it would be standing up in various directions. Her eyes would be greener than ever as they absorbed the colors of the surrounding forest. She knew they dominated her small, delicate-featured face. She didn't think she was anyone's idea of a delusional obsessive dictator. As if reading her mind, Cal and Lorcan shook their heads in unison.

"So how do I convince Moncoya that I am?"

"What you have to convince him of is that you love him so much you are prepared to do anything, even become that person for his sake. Throw yourself on his mercy." Lorcan paused, casting a wary glance at Cal, who had clenched his fist hard on his thigh and drawn a hissing inward breath. When Cal didn't speak, Lorcan continued. "That's where we use the little feller's vanity against him. Sure, doesn't he love that sort of thing?"

"He does think he's irresistible." Stella nodded. To be fair to Moncoya, he had every reason to believe that. His allure was fairly potent. She didn't voice that thought aloud. The look on Cal's face told her it would be wise not to.

"So, having given it some thought, you've decided you can no longer resist him," Lorcan said encouragingly.

"Do you really think he'll fall for it?"

"Even if he doesn't—even if he suspects it's a trick—he gets his hands on what he wants." Lorcan's glance flicked across to Cal again then back to Stella. It was to her he spoke. "You." The word hammered his point home.

"Since I seem to be outvoted on this, can someone explain to me how Stella acting like Moncoya's besotted dupe enables us to achieve our objective?" It would not be fair to say Cal's tone was resigned. It was just that he seemed to have more of a grip on his rage.

"Firstly, we don't know who Moncoya's allies are. Or even if he has any. If I'm right, some of our usual suspects will have jumped on the faerie bandwagon, but they may be biding their time in preparation for an attempt to get Stella onto their own side. This buys us time to find out what alliances Moncoya has made. It also gives Stella protection."

"I am Stella's protection." There was nothing subdued about Cal's fury this time. "It's what I do."

"And you can continue to do that in the way you have always done," Stella assured him. "I think what Lorcan means is that, if I have Moncoya's protection, I will be safe from rogue attacks like the one the wolf-man tried."

Lorcan nodded. "You have to admit it. For a short, cosmetic-wearing fashion plate yon faerie feller has a fearsome reputation. Not many are brave enough to cross him. Once it's known Stella is to be his bride…"

"Stop right there! No one said anything about marriage." The mutinous thundercloud had descended on Cal's face once more.

Lorcan backtracked quickly. "Once Stella's sham engagement to Moncoya gets out, is what I meant. He's told everyone the necromancer star will be his bride. He's not going to settle for a bit of coy hand-holding and a promise to think about it. He will want to parade his prize before the great and good—or bad—of Otherworld. That's where we come in."

"Because you'll be my guests," Stella said, taking up the thread. "That's how we'll get the two of you openly into Moncoya's palace."

Cal's beautiful mouth twisted into a scornful sneer. "There's just one problem with this plan that hasn't occurred to either of you." They both turned to look at him. "Whether Stella invites me or not, Moncoya would rather wear an unfashionable shade of nail color than allow me within a ten-mile exclusion zone around his home."

Chapter 14

"But I don't want to fight with Cal," Stella protested as she followed Lorcan toward Carmarthen.

"You two are made for each other, do you know that? Both as stubborn as all hell and neither of you prepared to listen to good Irish sense when you hear it." Lorcan's expression was long-suffering.

Stella cast a longing look back in the direction of the bower. If it wasn't for that blasted prophecy, maybe she and Cal could stay there, shielded in their own bubble. What was so great about bloody Merlin anyway? Why did everyone immediately assume a long-dead sorcerer had to be right? It wasn't a subject she had ever felt she could broach with Cal. She cast a speculative sidelong glance in Lorcan's direction.

"Did Merlin ever get it wrong?"

He made a curious choking sound. "Get what wrong?"

"The whole prophecy thing. I thought I'd ask. You know, since my life depends on it."

"Oh, that." She thought he sounded relieved. "No, he never got a prophecy wrong."

Interesting. The implication was that the great sorcerer may have got other things wrong. She stored that piece of information away for a later date. "There has to be a first time for everything, right? What if this is it?"

He shook his head. "It isn't. Cal would not put you in the firing line if there was any margin for error."

She decided not to pursue it. Lorcan was clearly as devoted to the memory of Merlin and the great man's legacy as Cal. She supposed they thought of the legendary sorcerer as some sort of founding father of their modern-day-equivalent guild. She might be persuaded to think of him in the same way over time. As long as there were no other cataclysmic predictions with her name on them lurking in the ether. Anyway, she was more interested in Lorcan's comment that she and Cal were made for each other. It might have been a facetious, throwaway remark, but it had been made by the man who knew Cal better than anyone. She allowed herself a brief daydream in which it was true. In which Cal had no dark, centuries-old secrets that invaded his dreams and shadowed his eyes. In which he didn't mutter that hateful word *Darnantes* and murmur disjointed, pain-filled phrases in a language she didn't understand. And, if he was free of his past, perhaps she could find it in her to trust him with her heart the way she trusted him with her body. Too many ifs. Too many obstacles. Even if the obstacles had been of this century or this world...

"Is that clear?"

Stella came back to reality with the realization that she had not been listening to Lorcan. They were on the outskirts of the town now and he had been giving her some sort of instructions. "Run it by me once more," she said, regarding the bustle of market day with misgivings. "Just so I'm clear about what we're doing."

"We're going to browse the market stalls for a while. Once we're sure there are sidhes about, you'll wander away from me slightly. I'll keep you in my sights, but you need to make it look like you are deliberately trying to get away from me. Then Cal will turn up and play the high-handed protector. He's getting really good at that." Lorcan grinned at her and Stella returned the smile. "You'll have bit of a squabble so that the sidhes think there's trouble between the two of you and then he'll drag you away back to the bower. It'll get back to Moncoya faster than you can say 'evil faerie.'"

"What if they try to snatch me?" They were approaching the town square now and, although it was only midmorning, there was a throng of people heading for the market. Stella scanned the faces of those approaching them. So far, she had not noticed anyone who appeared to be extraordinarily beautiful.

Lorcan regarded her thoughtfully. "It's understandable to be nervous, but I'm here and Cal isn't far away. This is a bit of scene setting. We're whetting Moncoya's appetite. Letting him see there might be a way in so that he can get you on his side. I hope to God it goes okay. It took long enough to persuade the big feller, I doubt he'll agree to a repeat performance if this one goes awry."

Stella supposed it was a hierarchical thing that made Lorcan refer to his friend as "the big feller." He and Cal were of similar height and build, although on close inspection Cal might be considered more muscular. Lorcan seemed naturally to defer to Cal's authority, and it was obvious that Cal was the stronger of the two in terms of his magical ability. *Where do I fit into the ranks? Or am I the one in the firing line?*

They reached the entrance to the indoor market now. "Carmarthen is the oldest town in Wales and, as long as there has been a settlement here, people have gathered to trade," Lorcan said as they followed the flow of people inside. "They rebuilt the market hall recently, but I preferred it as it used to be centuries past."

Stella didn't have time to ask him what he meant by that since they were immediately swallowed up into the press of shoppers who wandered the narrow aisles. On each side of them traders offered a dizzying array of foodstuffs, antiques, jewelry and crafts. Lorcan's long strides took them into the center of the thoroughfare, and Stella hurried to keep up with the rapid pace he was setting.

She became aware of Cal on the periphery of her vision, and the sensation conjured up conflicting emotions within her. As always, it was comforting to know he was there. He had been right when he said to Lorcan that protecting Stella was what he did. As far as Stella was concerned, it was what he had always done. But things between them had changed and she didn't want to go back to a time when he was just a shadowy image halfway between her imagination and reality. She wished she knew what Cal was thinking. Could he bear for their relationship to go back to the way it had been? Was that his intention when this was all over? Or would he move on and be someone else's protector once he had seen the prophecy through to its end? Something hard and hurtful lodged in her throat at the thought and she swallowed hard to get rid of it.

They paused in front of a craft stall and Stella made a cursory inspection of the handmade cards and bookmarks that were on display. Lorcan lounged beside her, arms folded across his chest, back to the stall and his eyes on the people around them.

"Showtime." His voice was close to her ear. "And you are honored. We are in the presence of sidhe royalty."

Stella glanced around to see what he meant. The two young women who stood at the nearby stall that was across the market aisle would have been remarkable in any setting. In this everyday scene, they were breathtaking. With their graceful, elfin beauty, they were strikingly similar and yet uniquely individual. Each was about Stella's own height—which, based on her admittedly limited experience, she imagined was tall for a sidhe. Both were possessed of the sort of lily-pale, flawless complexion that would have cosmetics firms gnashing their teeth. They were blondes, but, while the one who stood slightly closer to Stella and Lorcan had her dark gold hair cut in a short, spiky style, the other wore her long locks in an intricate plait hanging almost to her waist. Stella couldn't see their eye color, but she was willing to bet they had the familiar sidhe ring of fire around their irises. The girl with the short hair wore a serviceable outfit of leggings, boots and thigh-length tunic. Her clothes were an indication she meant business, Stella decided with a shudder. The other was clothed in a gauzy, layered dress that would not have looked out of place at a 1920s dinner party. Stella was torn between incredulity and a brief pang of envy. Even so, she sensed that the vibe from this girl was more dangerous than from the other. It was a powerful statement. *I can look this good and still take you.*

"Who are they?" Stella whispered to Lorcan.

"Tanzi and Vashti. Moncoya's twin daughters." He grinned. "If Daddy gets his way, you'll be their new stepmom."

"Don't even think about making jokes in connection with this situation."

"Believe me, Stella, those two are no laughing matter.

Vashti tries to look tough while Tanzi, as you can see, prefers the 'butter wouldn't melt approach.' In reality they are both highly skilled and equally deadly warriors. Moncoya sent them to train with Valkyries when they were just six years old. Either one of them would be a match for me in hand-to-hand combat." At Stella's look of alarm, he added reassuringly, "I don't think they'll try a full-on attack while they don't know where Cal is. He's the one they fear."

The short-haired sidhe stared directly at Stella and addressed a few words to her companion. The other girl turned to look, as well. It was like being caught in the twin glare of two very powerful sets of headlights. "I know that should make me feel a whole lot better. I'm not sure why it doesn't. What now?"

Lorcan had been scanning the market stalls around them. "I can't see any other sidhes. Mind you, those two are powerful enough not to need any support. Just wander off but try to make it look furtive, like you're trying to sneak away from me. Don't worry. Even though I'll look like I'm not aware of what you're doing, I've got your back."

Stella didn't answer. Instead, in an attempt to get into character, she gave him a dirty look and hunched her shoulder before turning her back on him. She caught the very faint sound of Cal's whispered words, "Well done. Go for it." Requiring no further encouragement, she edged away from Lorcan along the front of the craft stall.

Following Lorcan's instructions by casting a few surreptitious glances over her shoulder in his direction, she made her way to the next stall. She was conscious of the two sidhe princesses moving closer. It made her feel claustrophobic. The stall sold secondhand books and she picked one or two up, flipping absentmindedly through the pages. Suddenly, her gaze became fixed. All thought of sidhes and prophecies were briefly forgotten. The book she held in her hand was a very old, tattered volume. Embossed in worn gold lettering on the front cover were the words *Merlin—The Man behind the Legend*.

"How much is this?" She held the book out to the vendor, cursing the fact that she had only coins in her pocket. Her strange new lifestyle didn't include much need for cash.

The man squinted over the top of his glasses at the book and then at Stella. "That old thing? Been lying here gathering dust for as long as I can remember. Tell you what. You buy a couple of these old thrillers for a quid and I'll throw in that book and a carrier bag for nothing. Can't say fairer than that, can I?"

Stella scrabbled around for the right change among the coins in her pocket. How had she managed to lose the ability to count out money in such a short space of time? She could no longer sense Cal on the edge of her vision and that troubled her. What she could see instead was that there was now only one stall between her and Tanzi and Vashti. Thrusting the money into the vendor's outstretched hand and grabbing the bag containing the books in exchange, she muttered a word of thanks and moved on.

Casting one of her fake covert glances over her shoulder in Lorcan's direction, she saw him bearing down on her with a frown on his face. The two sidhes were only feet away now. Close enough to hear everything they said? Lorcan obviously thought so.

"I thought we agreed you'd stick with me?"

"No, you ordered me to stay with you. I don't remember *agreeing* to anything. I don't remember having a choice. In any of this." Stella spat the words at him, forcing herself to speak louder than she would normally and to enunciate clearly. It really was like being back on the stage at school.

Close by, Tanzi pretended to show Vashti a knitted tea cozy. Somehow Stella couldn't picture Moncoya's daughters using such a mundane domestic item. Vashti, on the other hand, gave up any pretense and ignored her sister as she openly watched the byplay between Stella and Lorcan.

"Look, Stella, if you want to get yourself killed that's your choice. But I promised I'd watch out for you and I'm not going to risk the big feller's temper just because you decide to take your bad mood out on me by going off on your own."

"I'm tired of telling you, and him, that I don't need either of you."

Other people were starting to look at them now. They'd discussed this eventuality. Cal didn't want any innocent bystanders caught in the middle if the sidhes decided to attack. Even worse would be the possibility of Cal or Stella being identified as the couple the police were still looking for in connection with the airport incident. As they had rehearsed, Stella turned on her heel and stomped away from Lorcan. He followed her as she stormed out of the market hall and into the bright sunlight of the street outside. Making sure that Lorcan was close behind her, Stella swung sharply right and into a narrow lane of Tudor-style buildings.

"Stella, wait!"

She ignored him, but glanced behind her to check on the whereabouts of Tanzi and Vashti. Walking purposefully now, the two sidhes came around the corner close behind Lorcan. They would be upon him within the minute.

"Now, Cal," she murmured and it was as if he heard her. No sooner had she spoken than he was approaching her from the opposite end of the lane.

To an onlooker, Stella was effectively trapped between the two men. The sidhe princesses shrank back against the wall of a house, apparently having discovered something riveting on Vashti's phone. The loathing and fury emanating from them in Cal's direction was tangible. It was tempered only slightly by a single measuring glance of fear that Tanzi gave him as she looked up once from her sister's screen. *Enjoy the show, ladies. It's all for your benefit.* Stella had time for that single thought before she was caught back up in the carefully staged performance.

"What the hell do you think you're doing out here on your own?" Cal played his part to perfection. Eyes narrowed, shoulders back, nostrils flaring. The picture of enraged alpha maleness.

"Trying to get a few minutes of peace and quiet away from the babysitter," Stella said, jerking her thumb over her shoulder to indicate Lorcan. She hoped she had managed to infuse enough bitterness into her tone. "It didn't work."

"Sorry, Cal." Lorcan joined them. "She got away from me."

"Which speaks volumes about your usefulness." Cal dismissed Lorcan with a single phrase and turned back to Stella. "I wouldn't have let you come out today if I'd known you were going to throw your toys out of the baby carriage."

"You wouldn't have *let* me out? Am I your prisoner now, is that it?" Stella decided to go for the full hands-on-hips effect. Even though she had to throw her head back to look up at Cal, she wanted to give the sidhes the impression that she was standing up to him. Giving him a hard time.

"Stella, we've been through this. Over and over. You know what the danger is…"

"I know what you *tell* me the danger is, Cal. In reality, the only times I've been in any peril are when I'm with you. Until I met you I had a good job, a roof over my head and none of this prophecy crap. Now I'm living in a cave with you watching my every move and I can't even go out without the nursemaid here following me everywhere." She drew in a deep breath. "Well, you know what? I've had enough. Find yourself some other birdbrain and convince her she's the one who's going to save the world."

Stella made a movement as if to whirl away from him, but Cal caught her by her upper arms and pulled her hard against his chest. Her eyes opened wide at the reminder of his incredible strength, and he relaxed his hold slightly.

"I can't let you do that. Like it or not, you're staying with me."

Lorcan came up on Stella's other side and the two men took an arm each. Stella dug her heels in slightly, like a puppy trying to resist the leash. She did a quick check that the sidhes were still in earshot. "You might be able to force me to go with you this time, but I'll get away from you the first chance I get."

Cal and Lorcan propelled her up the lane. A final check as they rounded a corner revealed that Tanzi and Vashti had already gone.

Chapter 15

"Nursemaid, is it? Babysitter?" Lorcan's blue eyes were alight with laughter. "You've got yourself a feisty one here, Cal my friend, and no mistake."

Lorcan was preparing to go and apprehension hung heavy in the atmosphere. The Irishman's departure signaled the unspoken reality that Stella and Cal must soon leave the bower in his wake.

Cal grasped Lorcan's hand. "We can count on you? You'll be there?"

"You know it." Lorcan turned to Stella, drawing her into a brief hug that Cal feared might crush her ribs. "See you in Otherworld, me darlin' girl."

The words made her shiver and, as she watched Lorcan walk through the trees until he was out of sight, Cal could see her mood lowering. She was holding a plastic bag and she placed it on the ground near the cave entrance. Its bright colors made a garish splash against the natural forest shades, and Cal raised a brow at her.

"I didn't realize you'd actually had time to indulge in some retail therapy today as well as street theater."

She smiled. "Books. You know, in case I have nothing better to do with my time while I'm in Otherworld."

He went to sit on a flat rock close to the fire and held out a hand to her. "Come here."

When Stella came to him, he drew her down to sit on his lap and she melted into him. Her lips were warm as they brushed his. Just before rational thought deserted him, Cal decided that moments like this should be allowed to last forever. And forever meant more to him than it did to anyone else. The world should not be able to intrude. Stella shifted position so that she could press herself closer against him. His mouth became more insistent, but Stella needed no persuasion. Her lips parted beneath his instantly, urgently. The first touch of her tongue exploring his mouth sent a jolt pulsing through him that was halfway to orgasm. A hungry moan escaped him. Cal slid his hands inside her shirt and traced the ridges of her spine with the tips of his fingers.

Dark clouds above the trees were draining the sunlight from the sky and the first big splatters of rain penetrated the leafy canopy. Cal ignored the downpour, his lips continuing to claim Stella's. His hands possessed her body, moving to stroke her neck and breasts, teasing her nipples with a featherlight touch, dipping behind and into her jeans to trace the cleft of her buttocks.

"Cal?" Stella was quivering desperately.

"Hmm?" He had undone the top buttons of her shirt and was holding it open so that he could run his tongue along her collarbone.

"Can we go inside now?"

He rose and pulled her to her feet. "You're shivering. Let's get you out of the rain."

"What rain?" She grabbed his hand and dragged him with her into the cave, lighting their way as she went. "I want to see you," she explained. "I don't want to miss a second."

Even through the fog of his own desire, Cal sensed the desperation behind her words and knew it was because the time for parting was near. Their clothes, torn off along the way, littered a path along the cave floor to the bed. Falling together onto the soft mattress, they teased and stroked and fanned the fires of wanting and needing until they were both panting.

Cal couldn't get enough of watching Stella in the heat of their passion. Her mouth was parted, her lips slightly swollen from the intensity of their kisses. She returned his gaze, her eyes bright with the urgency of her need for him. There were other emotions as well in their emerald depths. He could see the raw depth of her feelings for him and knew how complete her trust in him was. For once he did not shy away from the reality of her need. How could he? Her eyes were a mirror of his own.

He closed his eyes and pressed his lips to hers. The firmness of his mouth just grazing the softness of Stella's caused his whole body to stiffen. She turned her head and fitted herself to him, and he pressed his lips harder to hers with a low growl of satisfaction. Stella sighed as their tongues danced in time together. Unable to wait any longer, Cal moved between her legs and hooked his hands under her knees, pulling her closer to him.

Bringing her legs up over his shoulders, he positioned himself so that the head of his cock was just grazing her entrance. It was all Cal could do to stay in control and stop himself from plunging into her. Because he wanted this to be slow, he didn't follow his raging desire to ram straight into her welcoming warmth. Instead, he slid slowly forward, penetrating her inch by inch. As he began to move, his thick shaft opened her farther. It was like sliding into molten heat. His hips moved between her legs, pushing her thighs wider apart. Stella gripped his shoulders, throwing her head back. Her soft cries spurred him on and he began to thrust faster. Stella's hips slammed up from the mattress in response. She was so hot and wet, gripping him so tightly.

Cal kept up the new rhythm of steady, fast thrusts. Stella slid her hands down to grip his buttocks, urging him on. Their bodies slammed hard together, both of them gasping now, staring into each other's eyes as they neared their peak. His cock felt like granite as he drove into her. Stella gave a cry as she met each forward movement, and Cal felt his body begin to spiral into tightly wound ecstasy.

The first hot, thick spurt shot high up inside Stella. That sensation sent her over the edge as well, and she clenched her inner muscles even tighter around him, deepening his explosion. Cal groaned, his cock jerking wildly. Stella's hands locked onto his shoulders, as her back arched and her breasts pressed into his chest. She wedged her body tight against his so that every part of them from groin to neck was welded together. They both writhed and trembled and were left limp in the wake of the enormity of the climax that ripped through them.

Stella's eyes were closed, her breathing still ragged, when Cal pulled out of her and lowered her to the bed. Lying next to her, he drew a hand over her breasts, delighting in the way her indrawn breath signaled her pleasure at his touch. It was the answering tug within his chest that rocked him to the core. It was an affirmation of something he already knew.

He was in love with her.

He had known that his feelings for Stella went deeper than anything he had ever known for a woman, but it was only now that the true magnitude of this new awareness hit him. After all these centuries of aloneness, of being the world's great protector, of guarding his heart because his mission came first. He had finally found someone who meant more than any of those things. In his case, love was a luxury in which he could not indulge. Whole worlds, lives without number, depended on his ability to keep his heart neutral. A thought, frightening in its unfamiliarity, coursed through him. He had never needed anyone until now. In the face of that new awareness, could he maintain his impartiality?

Despite his thoughts, he was unable to resist the temptation to touch Stella. He leaned over, brushing her hair back from her face. Stella's eyes opened and she smiled. She had no idea how that smile tested the limits of his heart. Reaching up, she hooked her hand behind his head, pulling him down to her. His mouth urged her lips apart so he could slide his tongue inside. No matter how dangerous it was, he could never get enough of her. Winding her arms around his neck, Stella mimicked the gentle thrusting motion of Cal's tongue.

"Dim the lights." The tightness in his chest was heightened to the point of pain. "We need to get some sleep."

"I had other plans," she whispered, pressing closer. "I thought after a brief rest we could go for a repeat performance. But if you're too tired…"

"It's not that. You need to be ready to face Moncoya tomorrow."

Cal thought he could hold her and still ride the wave of emotion that wanted to crush him. He truly believed he could rise above it. Until Stella spoke again just before she drifted off to sleep.

"All those years, when I knew you but didn't know

you? Even though you weren't real, you were the only real thing in my life."

That was when he knew that human hearts really could be broken. And he wasn't immune just because his own heart was only half human.

Stella came awake slowly, her eyes adjusting gradually to the gloom of the lamp-lit cave. The strong arms around her and muscular chest beneath her cheek filled her with a sense of well-being and she allowed herself to revel in its comforting warmth for a few brief moments. Then reality intruded and her happiness oozed away like honey poured back into its jar.

Cal was awake, his eyes on her face. She wondered if he had slept at all. "I need to bathe." She rested her chin on his chest. God, she would never get tired of gazing at that beautiful face. But she'd like to have the chance to keep trying.

His arms tightened possessively. "I don't want to let you go." It sounded as if the words were being choked from him.

"Then I'll make it easier for you." She slid from the bed, reveling in the way Cal's eyes hungrily raked her body. "Moncoya won't come while I'm in the pool, will he?"

Cal shook his head. "He won't be able to get through at all until I lower the barrier spell I placed around the bower. I won't remove it completely. It will just be weaker. He'll be able to talk to you but he won't be able to touch you, and none of his sidhes, not even Tanzi or Vashti, will be able to breach the barrier."

"Will you be there?" Stella threw on a shirt and grabbed up her towel and toiletries.

"I'll be nearby." His face hardened. "If he knows I'm close, he may sense a trap."

She couldn't stand to know she was the cause of the pain on his face, even if it was unintentional. "Come with me."

When he rose from the bed, her breath caught in her throat at the perfection of his body. Nobody said life was fair. She got that. It had thrown some pretty spectacularly unfair things her way. But to taunt her with Cal and the knowledge that this couldn't be forever? That was downright cruel. Cal wrapped a towel around his waist and came to take her hand.

The pool water was crisp and Stella shivered slightly as she undressed and stepped into its chilly depths. Strangely enough, she would miss this early morning ritual. Hot water had its attractions, but this had become a refreshing way to start her day. She ducked under the water, immersing herself fully and allowing it to cleanse away the last traces of sleep. When she emerged, she reached for the rock where she had placed her toiletries and opened her shampoo bottle.

"Let me do that."

She hadn't noticed Cal removing his own towel and joining her in the water, and she started slightly when he came up behind her and took the shampoo from her. His hands were gentle but firm as he massaged the perfumed liquid into her scalp. Stella closed her eyes and relaxed into the moment, willing her thoughts to remain at bay. When he'd finished, she ducked back under the water and rinsed her hair.

"Your turn now. But you're taller than me so you'll need to sit down."

Cal obligingly sat on a rock so that she could stand to one side of him and shampoo his hair. It was thick and springy as she ran her fingers through its length. Cal closed his eyes, and tilted his head back so that she could complete her task.

"Rinse this off now."

He leaned farther back so that his head was under the water, keeping his eyes on Stella's the whole time, snaring her in the silver beam of his gaze. When he sat up again, he dragged both hands through his hair, slicking it back. Droplets of water clung to his eyelashes and dripped down onto the hair on his chest.

"Can you pass me the soap?" Stella indicated the bag containing her toiletries that sat on a rocky ledge behind Cal. When he handed her the sweet-scented bar, she stood before him waist deep in the water. Two could play at this staring game. Locking her gaze onto his, she began to soap up her arms to her shoulders and then down across her breasts. Wordlessly, she held the soap out to Cal. Seizing her invitation, he rose to his feet, taking the sudsy bar from her. Following the same movement Stella had used, his hands smoothed the slippery bubbles across her breasts. Her nipples, already hard from a combination of cold water and anticipation, tightened painfully.

Moving around her in a circle, Cal took his time, covering her entire upper body in soap. His hands lingered on her flesh, smoothing and massaging. As he stood behind her and ran his soapy fingers up and down her neck, his iron-hard erection pressed into her back.

When he faced her again, Stella took the soap out of his hand and slid it across his chest and stomach. His sharp hiss of indrawn breath told her exactly what her actions were doing to his self-control. She paused to slowly trace gentle circles in the bubbles around his nipples.

"Stella…" It was a mixture of pleading and warning.

Ignoring him, she copied his actions of minutes earlier, moving around to soap his back. Dipping her hand lower, she kneaded the firm muscles of his buttocks.

"Give me that." It was a growl of command and, standing in front of him, Stella obeyed. Cal moved his hands below the water, down between her legs. She opened them slightly, and he ran the bar of soap up her thighs. Gently, he caressed her outer lips with the tips of his fingers, slowly opening her. Spreading her wider and massaging the soap into her flesh, he worked one finger inside her.

His cock was throbbing and pulsing against Stella's stomach, and she encircled it, her grip tightening as she lightly and slowly ran her hand up and down his shaft. She started with soft caresses, her movements becoming bolder as her fingers moved up to stroke the head of his cock before gliding back down again. As Cal began to move his thumb in a relentless circle around her clitoris while pumping his finger in and out of her, Stella's own movements became faster.

"You do know I will never be able to take a bath again without remembering this and getting aroused, don't you?" she murmured, leaning forward to trace his nipple with her tongue.

"Good." Cal's voice rasped in her ear. "When we are apart I want to know you are thinking about me. About this." He punctuated his words with harder strokes, driving her on and joining her in a shuddering climax.

When they finally emerged from the pool sometime later, Cal scanned the patch of blue above the treetops. After a few minutes, Stella heard the familiar sound of a falcon's wings.

"Moncoya is close." Cal's expression made her think of thunderclouds racing across an already stormy sky.

Chapter 16

When Stella finally faced Moncoya from a few feet away, it was as if she was viewing him through a thin sheet of translucent glass. He was almost, but not quite, clear. There was no sign of Cal in either human or falcon form, yet she sensed his nearness. She paused to examine the effect Moncoya had on her. No. Nothing. She almost smiled. It was such a relief. One of her biggest fears had been that he would still have that strange fey hold over her. She had been unaware of its potency until she was removed from his presence. Of course, it could be the barrier spell between them that reduced his powers. Stella preferred to think it was because she knew what he was. Or perhaps it was because she was in love with Cal.

"Ezra…" She had spent so long anticipating this moment that, now that it was finally here, she had no idea what to say to him.

"My little star." The words were a caress and there was

a hint of laughter in his voice. "A cave dweller? This is what has become of you?"

She glanced swiftly around, hoping to convince Moncoya of her nervousness. "Cal will be back soon."

"Cal? Is that what he is calling himself these days? He hasn't used that one in a while."

Stella wanted to ask what he meant. What did he know of Cal? And what was at the root of this world-destroying animosity between the two of them?

"Ezra, you really shouldn't be here. He will be angry if he knows I've spoken to you."

"You think I am afraid of a sorcerer? Oh, Stella." He shook his head, his multicolored mane of hair flying wildly about his face. "Has he succeeded in convincing you that he is all-powerful? That he cannot be beaten? When you are free of this madness, my little one, I will tell you more of this would-be protector of yours. He is not all he seems."

"I can't get free of the barriers he has put up around this place. Believe me, I've tried. And even if I get away from here, where could I go?"

"To me, of course. I will care for you."

"You are very kind…"

"I am not offering you my kindness, my star. You must know that. When you ran from me, you wounded me deeply. I thought you knew how I felt about you. I want you."

Stella resisted the impulse to shiver. Everything depended on her ability to play this part. "I didn't want to leave you. He… Cal told me the most fantastic story. I was confused, scared. He told me he would care for me. We came here, but now he wants me to do everything he says. It's like I'm his slave."

"What is this story he has told you?"

She hung her head. "It's too foolish."

"Look at me."

He still had some power over her. Although she could resist him, she felt the pull of his words. She would have to watch that. Once away from the barrier spell, it might be even stronger. She didn't want to find herself commanded to do things she was unable to resist. Lifting her head, she looked directly at him. "He told me that I am the great sorcerer the world has been waiting for, the necromancer star of Merlin's prophecy. That he who claims my heart will rule Otherworld."

"He has been busy. Is that all he told you?"

"All?" Stella reeled slightly. What more could there possibly be? "Isn't that enough?"

He laughed. "Maybe for him. So you do not believe that you are the necromancer star?"

"I don't know what to believe. But I do know being cooped up in a cave is sending me batty. If you'll pardon the pun."

"Come to me." There it was again, that compelling note. Stronger now. It would take all of her own powers to resist it.

"I can't get through this barrier he has placed around me."

"I am your king. You are my subject. I command you."

Hold on a minute. "Rewind a bit, Ezra. I am your subject? How did that happen?"

"It may have suited the sorcerer not to tell you the truth about yourself, but I will not lie to you, Stella. Why should I? You are a faerie. That makes you my subject."

The world tilted slightly off its axis. Then it began to spin out of control. Stella sat down abruptly on a rock, closing her eyes until the wild movement around her subsided. "No." The word was a croak.

"I could be offended by your dismay, my star."

"My parents died when I was three. I knew them. They were mortal." She conjured up a hazy mental image of them. It was difficult because it was so long ago and she had been so young. The picture in her mind was her last memory of them. Her mother, so like Stella herself in looks, had been clinging to her father's arm, laughing up at him. He, much taller than her mother, had been smiling down at her in return.

"Your father was mortal, that is true. But your mother was a sidhe princess, of the purest bloodline." Some of the charm slipped from his face. His voice hardened and became cruel. "She shamed her royal name when she fell in love with a mere human. She compounded that disgrace by running away and choosing to live a mortal life with him."

"No." Even as Stella repeated the word, she knew it was true. It explained so much. The way Moncoya had tracked her down. His assurance that she, the necromancer star, would be his to command. Her own ambivalent feelings about the faeries. Did it also explain Cal's reluctance to talk about the sidhes? Had he known this all along?

"But yes. I am offering you my heart, Stella. I could command you to give me yours in return. Instead, I ask it of you. Come to me. I will await you at La Casa Oscura. It is fitting that our triumphal entry into Otherworld should commence in Barcelona."

"Why is Barcelona so important?" With so many thoughts jostling for supremacy inside her head, it seemed an odd one to force its way to the surface.

"Our ancestors, the Fair Folk, known in the Celtic language as the *daoine sidhe*, hailed from Ireland. Long ago, we were defeated in battle by an invading horde from Iberia and driven out of Otherworld. Although we fought and regained our beloved homeland, Iberia is the place where I have chosen to live among mortals. It is my reminder to all who question me that I will fight for what is mine. No doubt the sorcerer told you I have blood on my hands."

"He told me you killed the last king and massacred his people. He also said that you rule through fear."

His laughter shattered the stillness. "Didn't he tell you anything bad about me?" The caressing note returned to his voice. "I await your answer, my star."

Stella needed to call on all her acting skills in order to dredge up something approaching a convincing response. It was also an effort to keep her newfound hatred of him out of her voice. She now knew exactly how Cal felt. "I will see you in Barcelona before the week is out, Ezra."

Waiting while Stella faced Moncoya alone was the worst torture Cal had ever endured. There was no other word for the range of emotions he endured in that agonizing half hour. Even Darnantes paled in comparison. When a falcon eventually landed close to where he sat on the hillside and flapped its wings in a prearranged signal, he knew that Moncoya had gone. Rising to his feet, he made his way back to the bower, unsure of what he would find. Cal had no doubts about where Stella's allegiance lay. He knew she loved him. He should wish she didn't, but the thought made his heart lurch with pleasure. Even if that had not been the case, she could be relied upon to do the right thing. It was who she was. But Moncoya was unpredictable. There was no knowing what tactics he would employ to get his own way.

There was no sign of Stella in the bower or at the pool. He found her in the cave, curled up in a ball on the bed. There was a single lamp lighting the gloom. When he placed a hand on Stella's shoulder, she flinched and the movement caused a knife-sharp pain to rip through his gut.

"What happened?"

She answered him with another question. "Did you know?"

"Stella, look at me." After a moment's hesitation, she uncurled and turned to face him. The green of her eyes was so dark it appeared black. "Know what? What has Moncoya said to you?"

"He told me I am a sidhe."

Cal thought he had prepared himself for anything she might say. Perhaps Moncoya had threatened an atrocity a week until she came to him. Or offered her a celebrity lifestyle. There was a strong possibility he might have threatened to harm Cal himself. He believed that threat, more than anything else, would have elicited a response from Stella. Not even his wildest imaginings had made him ready for this.

"Is that why we can't be together, Cal?" Stella sat up abruptly, hugging her knees to her chest. "All this time I thought it was because of a dark secret in your past." The little laugh she gave was hollow. "I never imagined it might be because of a dark secret in *my* past."

Cal was stunned into silence. His initial reaction was to laugh the idea off, and yet... Becoming aware of those huge, hurt eyes fixed on his face, he focused his attention on the most important task. Reassuring Stella.

"This is the first I've heard of it." Her face told him it was an inadequate response to the enormity of her pain. "Stella, I would not have kept something like this from you. You have to believe me."

Her eyes raked his face. He could see the battle taking place inside her. Then she gave a shuddering sigh and nodded. The soft cushion of her lower lip trembled pitifully and tears shone in her eyes. "If you say it, then I believe it. If I don't have you, I don't have anything."

Cal drew her into his arms, holding her shivering form

close and running his hands up and down her back. Gradually, the quivering of her limbs subsided and she sat up straighter. "At first, I thought he was lying."

"He could be," Cal said.

She shook her head. "Look at me, Cal. I mean look at me properly. I look like one of them."

"You don't have the ring of fire." It was clutching at straws. Not all sidhes had that telltale fiery brand. He should know. Even as he tried to reason Moncoya's words away, part of him was accepting them. Stella was the necromancer star, but she was also so much more. If she was indeed a faerie, that would explain some of her additional powers.

"Moncoya said my father was mortal. Which means I'm only half sidhe. Oh, I have so many questions and no one I can ask!"

"That's where you're wrong." Cal stood up. "Come on."

"Where are we going?"

"To see an angel."

Cal had only ever traveled across dimensions alone. Attempting to do so with a companion would be a first, but Stella had powers to match his own. All she had to do was stay with him. He doubted the Dominion would be happy if he turned up with a friend in tow. Good. Because he was in just the right mood for a fight with an angel.

"Think with me, Stella." He drew her close, holding her so that they stood face-to-face, their hands clasped. Stella's eyelids fluttered closed. He felt the intensity of her thoughts lock onto his. Her power grew stronger every time. His might be the experience of centuries, but the prophecy was right. She was the star.

Cal cleared his mind of everything but their destination. Familiar sensations took over, sweeping him up and out of the cave, transporting Stella with him so that they were floating and flying into the cloudy sky. On and on they soared, higher and higher, through inky, impenetrable darkness and cold so thick and raw it hurt until at last the movement slowed and they began to glide down.

When their feet touched solid ground once more, Stella opened her eyes. She blinked once in surprise. The Dominion favored a businesslike approach. His appointed meeting place resembled an old-fashioned office with an elaborate walnut desk in the center and high bookshelves stacked with leather-bound volumes. The room didn't have any walls and beyond the few square meters where they stood lay a vast expanse of nothing.

"Is this heaven?" Stella whispered.

"More like a waiting room before you go in."

The Dominion rose from behind his desk, his billowing robes, snowy wings and benign expression perfectly in keeping with his role. "I do not remember granting permission for this audience." There was gentle reproach in his tone.

"I don't remember agreeing to put Stella's life in danger while you kept us both in the dark. Now, do you mind telling us what the hell is going on?" The Dominion winced at his use of the word *hell*. Cal held up a hand in an apologetic gesture. "Sorry. Do you mind telling us whether this story of Moncoya's about Stella's parents has any grain of truth in it?"

The Dominion tented his fingers beneath his chin and appeared to consider the matter. Then, with a brisk nod, he held out his hand to Stella, who, with an expression of vague disbelief, took it. "It is my great pleasure to meet you. Your involvement and your help in the events in Otherworld have been much anticipated." He indicated two chairs and then returned to his own seat. "So the king of the faeries has been telling you about your parents? No doubt he did so in order to convince you that, as one of his subjects, you are obliged to obey him?"

"Yes." Stella seemed to have found her voice at last. "He said he could command me to give my heart to him, but he would rather I gave it willingly."

"He was being somewhat economical with the truth. Not a first for him. Even under Moncoya's rule the faeries retain free choice about whom they choose to love. He cannot command your heart, Stella, any more than he could command your mother's. He is simply trying another tactic to get you to give it to him."

"He tried to command my mother to love him?"

"I see he has not told you the full story about your parents." Although Cal wanted to tell the Dominion to get on with it, he couldn't help noticing that the angel's voice was having a soothing effect on Stella. With an effort, he controlled his impatience.

"He told me that my mother was a sidhe princess who disgraced her royal name by eloping and choosing to live a mortal life with my father."

"A short, rather biased account of some of the facts. Thalia, your mother, was *not* a sidhe princess. She was a princess, that much is true. She was of the true faerie bloodline, a direct descendant of King Ivo, the ruler Moncoya overthrew. Moncoya has always been wary of those remaining relatives, mainly because King Ivo was greatly loved by the faeries. Moncoya is a sidhe and not of the true bloodline. It is a fact that has always rankled with him. Since the massacre and Moncoya's ascent, many of Ivo's descendants have died in mysterious circumstances. Moncoya would not be foolish enough to bring the wrath of the faeries down upon his own head by openly harming them. Your mother was an exception. From the moment Moncoya set eyes on Thalia, he was devoted to her."

Stella shivered slightly. "Moncoya was in love with my mother?"

"Wildly. Beyond all reason. And he saw marriage with her as a way of finally securing his throne. Because there have always been rumors that a true heir exists, a direct male descendant of Ivo. It is said that he was a baby who was smuggled out of the palace on the night of the massacre. Marriage to your mother would have laid the rumors to rest. With Thalia, another of Ivo's descendants, at his side, Moncoya's new dynasty would have been secure."

"But my mother didn't return his love?"

The Dominion shook his head. "Thalia was true to her line. She hated Moncoya, as all of Ivo's descendants do… and she had already met and fallen in love with your father."

"Who was my father? I remember very little of him. Just that he was big and gentle and he made me laugh."

"Your father was a great man, Stella. And a noble necromancer. One of the greatest and a descendant of a long and ancient line. It is from him that you have inherited your power over the dead and the undead."

"Did you know him?" Stella turned to address her question to Cal.

"No, I know most necromancers so he must have kept his identity well hidden."

The Dominion nodded. "He preferred a quiet life. On occasion, when we called on him, he would assist us. Most of the time, he lived a quiet, human existence. It was on one of his missions for us that he met Thalia. When Moncoya learned of their love, his rage knew no bounds. Thalia fled Otherworld and lived happily with your father until they were killed."

"Why didn't you tell me any of this when you gave me the task of protecting Stella?" Cal asked incredulously.

"It was felt that, given the strength of your existing feelings toward Moncoya, it might be best if you knew nothing of Stella's background. We felt it might have clouded your judgment."

"Either that or I would not have taken an assignment in the first place that brought me further evidence of what that black-hearted bastard is capable of."

The Dominion inclined his head in acknowledgment.

"I have a birth certificate, a passport. I exist legally in the mortal world. How did that happen if my mother wasn't mortal?" Stella had been lost in thought but she roused herself again now.

"You parents could not go through a marriage ceremony because your mother did not have any proof of her mortal existence, but your father insisted that he wanted you to live a normal life. He was able to register your birth and provide proof of his identity. That was all that was needed."

Stella's brow wrinkled as if the weight of her thoughts was too great. "How long will I live? I mean, will I have a mortal life span or am I immortal?"

"You are a necromancer. That will be your choice."

She gave a shaky laugh. "That's quite a choice."

The Dominion glanced from her to Cal, his expression bland. "And one you should exercise wisely. There is one more thing you should know."

"I'm not sure I can take one more thing."

"You must, for it is very important. When Thalia left Otherworld, Moncoya swore he would be revenged."

There was silence as Cal and Stella digested the meaning behind this information. Cal spoke first. "You said Stella's parents were killed."

"I did. They were murdered by Moncoya."

Stella raised a shaky hand to her lips. "Has it always been his intention to have me in place of my mother?"

"I believe so. For him, Stella, you are the embodiment of two dreams. You are the necromancer star of Merlin's great prophecy. And you are Thalia's daughter. Through you, Moncoya gets to rule Otherworld and finally take his revenge against the woman who broke his heart. He may also want you because of *you*." The Dominion smiled his beatific smile. "You are very like your mother, you know." He became suddenly businesslike. "Now, if you will excuse me. We did not schedule this meeting and I do have others waiting…"

Cal rose and took Stella's hands again. She looked up at him with a slight smile in her eyes. "So I'm not half sidhe. What was that word you used for an illegitimate hybrid? *Dóc*. That's what I am."

He returned the smile. "That makes two of us. But, unlike you, I *am* half sidhe."

Chapter 17

Even though the news reports about the suspected terrorist attack seemed to have gone quiet, Cal had decided that Stella should avoid Manchester airport. As a result, she had made the journey alone by train to Liverpool and boarded a budget airlines flight to Barcelona from there.

"It's killing me that I can't come with you." Cal had held her tightly in his arms as she made ready to leave him behind.

"You don't need me to tell you that Moncoya will have me watched every step of the way. Besides, you will be with me. Just not openly."

"That's not good enough anymore. Not for me." His lips had been hungry on her throat and she had been forced to pull reluctantly away before the caress became something hotter and more demanding. She was on a schedule that didn't allow for what Cal's mouth was asking of her. No matter how much she ached for him. "And, even invisible, I will never get inside his palace where you'll need me most."

"Why didn't he stop you from protecting me for all those years?"

"Simple. He didn't know about me. Oh, he may have been aware that you had a protector. But he didn't know who it was. If he'd found out it was me, he'd have moved heaven and earth—literally—to get rid of me." His grin had been heartbreakingly mischievous. "You'd have had an even more eventful childhood."

It was frightening how much she already missed him, how quickly she had come to depend on his nearness. It wasn't possible, she told herself severely, as she buckled herself into her seat on the plane, to pine for someone after just a few hours apart.

"You been to Barcelona before?" The man next to Stella leaned a little too close to view the city they were leaving behind as he asked the question.

"I worked there for a few weeks not long ago." She noticed the game on his iPad. It was one of Moncoya Enterprises' bestselling titles. Her eyes flickered warily up to his face. He was nondescript looking. Not pretty enough to be a sidhe nor ugly enough to be a gargoyle. She relaxed a little.

"Cool."

You have no idea. She felt a brief impulse to shock him by telling him the whole story. *Yeah, I had to flee because it turns out I'm the powerful necromancer Otherworld has been waiting for and my former boss, the king of the faeries, wants to use me as a weapon to win the war to gain control over all supernatural beings. Oh, and guess what? The man I've been seeing is an influential sorcerer and I'm descended from faerie royalty. I'm on my way back to*

Barcelona right now to trick Moncoya into thinking I'm in love with him. So, yeah. "Cool" about sums it up.

He looked as if he'd be impressed. He looked like a keeper...and a stalker. Bad combination. She drew her book out of her backpack. Her companion returned to his iPad. The book she'd hurriedly shoved into her bag was the old volume about Merlin that she'd found in the market at Carmarthen. This was the first chance she'd had to look at it and she opened it, frowning as she concentrated on the archaic language in the text.

Now that she was away from Cal, an idea about his identity insinuated itself into her mind and refused to be dislodged. *Too far-fetched,* she told herself. *So many crazy things have happened, you are allowing your mind to run away and invent new ones.* Nevertheless, she attempted to search the ancient book for clues to prove or disprove her fantastic theory.

They'd been in the air for about twenty minutes when she became aware that her fellow passenger was watching her as she read. He had paused his iPad and she saw he had been watching an episode of the latest Merlin-related TV series. Her heart gave an interested little jump. He nodded from his screen to her book.

"You a fan, too?"

Stella nodded, feigning eagerness. She even managed a flutter of her eyelashes. He went an interesting shade of pink. "I missed that one," she sighed, nodding at the screen.

Half an hour later, her book was firmly closed and her new friend, whose name was Ged, was in midflow offering his own version of the legend behind the story and why the screenwriters had got it all so hopelessly wrong. Stella's face was starting to ache from maintaining an enraptured expression. She would have to interrupt him soon or she wouldn't be able to ask her questions before they landed in Barcelona. They had only two and half hours.

"Are you connected to the in-flight Wi-Fi?" she asked when Ged finally paused to take a sip of his cola.

He nodded. "Wouldn't be without it, even though it's a rip-off."

"Can we search for something about Merlin? I've always wanted to know what other names he used." *Why not push her theory a little further? Prove to herself once and for all just how foolish she was being.*

"Oh, I can help you with that," Ged boasted proudly and Stella resisted the temptation to gnash her teeth. "The name Merlin came from the Welsh name Myrddin. The great wizard was known as Merlin Ambrosius in Latin, Merlin Emrys in Welsh—"

"What did you just say?" Stella sat up a bit straighter.

"Merlin Emrys was his Welsh name. Why?"

"Oh, nothing." She could hardly tell Ged that she had used a credit card of Cal's in the name of Emrys Jones, could she? Emrys wasn't exactly common, but it was a Welsh name and they had been heading to Wales. It must be a coincidence.

There was nothing coincidental about Ged's next words. "And in Scotland he was Caledonius."

"He was *what*?" Aware that her voice had become an undignified screech, she battled her emotions back under control.

"Merlin Caledonius. That was his Scots name."

Or Cal for short? Maybe I should have asked Lorcan the all-important question. "Have you ever seen Cal and Merlin in the same room?"

"Wait till I get my hands on you." She became aware that she'd spoken aloud and grabbed up her water bottle, taking a long calming gulp to give her something distracting to do.

"Are you okay?" Ged watched her with concern written all over his face.

"I'm fine," Stella told him with a bright smile. And she was. Because it was all starting to make sense now. Either that or her sanity was unraveling.

"Ged, you are clearly a Merlin expert." He preened himself delightedly. "What do you know about Darnantes?"

He shook his head. "Nope. You've lost me there."

"Niniane?"

"Ah, she was the sorceress who Merlin fell in love with." Stella felt her hands curl into claws and quickly straightened them. "She made him teach her everything he knew and then used his own magic against him to entomb Merlin in a rock in an enchanted forest. That's the story anyway. I'm not so sure. I'd have expected Merlin to be smarter than that." His expression was sad, as though he had been personally let down by Merlin.

"What was the name of the forest where he was imprisoned?"

"No idea." He looked a bit put out.

Stella was willing to bet the forest was called Darnantes. "Is that how Merlin died?" she asked casually, knowing full well that, if her admittedly wild suspicions were correct, Merlin was very much alive and well. In fact he had kissed her goodbye that morning and would be awaiting her in Barcelona. Where he was going to get the shock of his long, wizardly life.

"No one really knows. He was never seen again after that. I go on lots of Merlin forums and opinions vary about whether he died, if he still lives buried deep in the rock or whether he escaped. If he escaped, it's safe to assume he emerged with a different identity."

"Maybe he went into a sort of wizard protection scheme?" Stella suggested. He looked mildly offended and she realized he was far too serious about the subject to appreciate jokes. "Sorry."

"Why don't we meet up in Barcelona and talk about it some more over a few drinks?" He pushed his glasses up his nose nervously. He wasn't a stalker. He was just a harmless geek. Stella had met more than a few of them in her time. If only letting Ged down gently was the sum total of her current problems.

"That would be nice. My boyfriend would enjoy meeting you." *And you have no idea how much you'd love to meet* him.

Ged seemed to lose interest in her after that and Stella gazed out the window, not seeing the snowy peaks of the Pyrenees or the vast beautiful city of Barcelona unfolding far below the plane's wings. Instead, she allowed her mind to dwell on the unthinkable. If she did that, if she admitted—just to herself, just for now—that what she suspected was true, that Cal and Merlin really were the same person, then so many other things made sense.

She heard Lorcan's lilting Irish tones calling him "the big feller." It was no longer a description of Cal's height. Instead the description signaled Lorcan's acknowledgment of Cal's presence, his status as the greatest sorcerer the world had ever known. Then there were those silent looks the two men exchanged whenever Merlin was mentioned. She thought of the changes she had witnessed herself, the way Cal could, in an instant, assume a commanding, powerful aura that dominated everything around him. Her mind took her back to Moncoya's mocking voice. *Cal? Is that what he is calling himself these days? He hasn't used that one in a while.*

Then there were Cal's nightmares. That muttered word

Darnantes so full of fear and torment. His words about a sorceress called Niniane…

The plane screeched onto the tarmac. *Either way, you have yourself quite a problem,* she told herself. *Because if you haven't fallen in love with Merlin, you've lost your mind.*

As she strode through the Barcelona airport, Stella was reminded of the last time she had walked through the vast, brightly lit corridors. Her hopes of the job with Moncoya had been high, her thoughts firmly earthbound. How much had changed in that short time! Now she had discovered that she was not mortal. More than that, she was the necromancer star the world had been waiting for since Merlin—or maybe she should get used to saying Cal?—had first prophesied her arrival. She had learned that Moncoya was an evil despot who, among the many atrocities he had committed, had murdered her parents. Now she was back to seek revenge and to save Otherworld. Yes, it was safe to say the past month had been an eventful one.

When she came out of the arrivals hall, a tall figure was lounging near the exit watching the crowds. Her heart gave an upward thud and then a downward lurch as the excitement of recognition was replaced by disappointment when she realized he was alone. She shrugged the feeling of discontent aside. It might not be Cal, but Lorcan was the next-best thing.

"Is this safe?" Stella asked when she finally emerged from the suffocating bear hug Lorcan wrapped around her.

"Sure, why wouldn't I be meeting my good friend at the airport when I'm in the area? Anyway, I can't see any of the little people about." His grin was full of mischief. "Except you, that is."

Stella dug him sharply in the ribs with her elbow, then sighed. "Cal told you about that."

"He did indeed. Don't worry. I'm Irish. We have a peculiar fondness for the faerie folk."

"Where is Cal? I haven't sensed him around since I left the cave."

"He's waiting for you in a safe house near the Ramblas."

"It's like being in Paris during World War II." Lorcan swung Stella's backpack onto his shoulder and she followed him onto the escalator that led to the underground station. "Who are the resistance?"

"The Iberian sidhes. They'll offer sanctuary to anyone who is prepared to fight Moncoya."

Stella glanced around at the crowds on the platform. "I thought Moncoya would be tracking my movements every step of the way."

"He has no reason not to take your word when you said you'd meet him at La Casa Oscura this week. I'd be willing to bet there are a couple of pairs of gold-ringed eyes on us right now just to be sure. They won't be feeling the need to do more than watch, since their boss is feeling pretty sure of you right now. As long as you're not seen with Cal, we've no problem."

"What about you?"

Lorcan smiled down at her as they stepped onto the train. "Sure, aren't I just a harmless wanderer? Nobody ever sees me as a threat."

Barcelona was a city full of beautiful art and architecture, but, like all big cities, it had its seedy side. This was something Stella hadn't seen on her last visit. She glanced around nervously as Lorcan led her away from the wide avenues around the Ramblas and into streets so narrow that the fading afternoon sunlight could barely penetrate through to ground level.

"This is the red-light district," Lorcan informed her cheerfully. "Grim, isn't it?"

It got grimmer. They took an alley between two tall buildings that was so narrow Stella felt she might have to turn sideways to walk down it. Lorcan stepped over a mattress on the cobbles and held out his hand to help Stella do the same. It was only when the bundle of rags piled on top of the mattress moved that she realized she was disturbing a sleeping man. Lorcan paused before a flight of stone steps. A woman in a grubby flamenco costume was seated on the bottom step rolling a cigarette and drinking brandy straight from the bottle. She looked up at Lorcan and licked her lips, murmuring something in Spanish and winking.

"She keeps doing that," he told Stella as they skirted around the woman and made their way up the steps.

"I think she's after your body."

"That's what worries me. I'm terribly shy around women." He regarded Stella, who was laughing, with a hurt expression. "It's the God's honest truth, so it is."

Stella glanced around. "If Moncoya's spies have followed us, we'll have given away this location."

Lorcan shook his head. "You wouldn't believe the spells we have around this place. If you don't know your way in you'd be like a monkey up a monkey puzzle tree, running around and meeting yourself coming back."

The door to the building looked as if it was being held together only by several layers of peeling paint. Lorcan knocked and it was opened after a few minutes by a small man who was clearly a sidhe. He greeted Lorcan with guarded pleasure and regarded Stella with interest.

"This is Pedro. He doesn't speak English. We've told him you're a friend of Cal's, nothing more." Lorcan led Stella along a gloomy corridor to a staircase. "They love Cal because Moncoya hates him so much. The Iberian sidhes don't have much of a resistance left, but don't tell them I said that. Over time, most of their number have joined Moncoya. It's always more fun on the winning side."

"Why do they need a safe house in the mortal realm?"

"La Casa Oscura may have seemed innocuous to you, but that was because Moncoya wished it to be so while you were there. Over the years it has become a portal to the darker side of Otherworld. Mortals or hybrids who are escaping need somewhere to hide. And it is not just those who are on the run from Moncoya who need this place." They climbed the stairs, passing several closed doors on each landing. "The people who seek sanctuary here may be on the run from vampires, werewolves, satyrs…who knows what stories are behind each of these doors?"

"Do your wanderings bring you here often?" Stella had a feeling there was much more behind the artless Irish charm that Lorcan presented publicly than he would like the world to believe.

"They might." His blue eyes twinkled. They had reached the top of the stairs now and there was only one door facing them. Lorcan nodded at it. "The big feller is inside. I've some business to attend to downstairs so I'll leave you alone for now. We can speak again later."

Stella paused a moment with her hand on the doorknob. Her pulse fluttered nervously. Alongside her desperate longing to see Cal again, even though it had been only hours since they parted, was a burning apprehension. She would have to confront him about his identity. But what if her suspicions were wrong? They must surely be wrong. It was too ridiculous to even think about it…

As she stood there hesitating, the door opened and Cal stood framed in the opening. One look into those silver eyes was enough to convince her. It was true. Of course it was. He was Merlin. How had she missed all those signs? Because he had duped her, that was how.

Cal tried to draw her into his arms but she evaded him. A worried frown dawned in his eyes as he watched her face. "Is there something wrong?"

She stepped into the room, closing the door behind her. Even through the slow burn of her anger, she had time to note that the attic room was small, with barely enough room for the old-fashioned brass bed that almost filled it. "Yes, as a matter of fact, there is. When I asked you if Cal was your real name, you told me it was."

"Ah." He sat down on the bed and it creaked alarmingly. "Cal is my real name. Well, it's one of my names."

Stella stood in front of him, still unable to believe she was about to ask her next question. "Are you Merlin?"

He tilted his head back to look up at her. The light from his eyes was pure silver. "Yes."

Stella hit him so hard on the shoulder with the heel of her hand that he toppled backward onto the bed. Before he had time to spring back up, she was on top of him, straddling him with her knees on each side of his hips so that he was pinned to the mattress by her weight. He could have thrown her off at any time he chose, but from the gleam in his eyes she suspected he might be enjoying himself. She intended to put a stop to that.

"You lied to me."

"I didn't. This is the first time you've asked me that question and I've answered you truthfully."

"Stop being logical when I'm angry at you."

He held up his hands in a gesture of surrender and lay back, watching her face. The warm light in his eyes did something to her insides. Something that felt suspiciously as if he was deliberately melting them. Stella did her best to remain aloof. "Are you *the* Merlin?"

"I am. Although, while we're talking about names, I prefer Cal. Emrys at a push. Never Ambrosius. That one is just too pretentious. Merlin is what the medieval writers who told the story of King Arthur went with. It sort of stuck, but I've never liked it."

Stella shook her head. "You are unbelievable."

He adopted a mock-hurt expression. "It's the truth. Ask Lorcan if you don't believe me."

She leaned forward so that she was bent over him and prodded him in the chest with one fingertip. "The whole world thinks you died in a tomb in some forest centuries ago and all the while you're alive and well and going around tricking people into—" She bit her lip just in time to stop the words from spilling out. She'd been about to say "falling in love with you" but instead finished with "—bed with you."

"You got me." She made an enraged sound and, laughing, he pulled her down on top of him, his breath tickling her ear. "Did I trick you, Stella? I agree it is magical between us…every time, but there's no sorcery involved. Unless *you* have cast a spell on me?"

His laughter infuriated her further and she squirmed to get out of his hold. "I can't believe you think this is funny!"

He turned then so that they were lying on their sides. Keeping his hands on her waist, he held her so that their bodies were just in contact. "I'm sorry. I shouldn't have laughed. I suppose I'm just relieved that it's finally out in the open. Can't you see how hard it would have been for me to tell you who I am? At what point in our relationship could I have said 'By the way…' and not risked you running away screaming because you thought I was a madman? It's the same with anyone I meet."

"So I'm just anyone?" Stella felt her anger slide away only to be replaced by hurt.

"No, you're not." There was no trace of laughter left now. On the contrary, the look in his eyes scorched her face with its intensity. "You were always special, but I didn't know at first just how special you would become. By the time I did, it always seemed to be the wrong moment to tell you. And being me carries so many other complications along with it."

Stella weighed her options. Keep her hurt and anger going, or let it go? She was lying in the arms of the beautiful man she loved on the eve of leaving him to go into the enemy's den, not knowing if she would ever see him again after that. It was the biggest no-brainer of her life.

Pressing herself closer against him, she reached up and drew his head down to hers. "No more secrets. And, if we get out of this alive, you are going to tell me every last detail."

His lips brushed hers. "It's a long story."

"If I choose immortality, we'll have plenty of time."

Chapter 18

"Haven't either of you ever played a computer game? What have you been doing with your lives?" Stella regarded the two men with a combination of amusement and frustration. "Anyone would think you'd been busy saving the world."

She was seated on the bed with her back to the brass frame. It creaked every time she moved, reminding her of the previous night. Blushing, she recalled that she and Cal had been forced to use every ounce of ingenuity they possessed to avoid disturbing the whole household. It had resulted in some very interesting positions. Lorcan was perched on the end of the bed while Cal paced up and down in the limited space between the end of the bed and the attic window. The sun was just making an appearance over the rooftops.

"We don't have much time for gaming just now, me darlin' girl. Not with yon faerie feller bustin' a gut to get at you."

She shook her head. "I'm not suggesting we sit down and play, Lorcan. What I'm saying is, you are going at this all wrong. When the time comes, the two of you are planning to throw everything you have at Moncoya from the start. Instead of that, you should take the measured approach of a computer game. Make him work through different levels."

"Go on." Cal stopped pacing and turned to look at her.

"Who are the weakest group on our side?"

"Probably the Iberian sidhes. Although they have the same natural powers as Moncoya's sidhes, they are a small group and they are not battle ready. Moncoya's army is a huge, powerful, well-trained fighting force."

"So the Iberian sidhes are Level One. We bring them on first. Next?"

Cal regarded her in fascination. "The werefalcons. Their natural role is to watch and protect. They are messengers. Fighting is not their remit, although they can be vicious when provoked."

"The werefalcons are Level Two then. The three of us will be involved throughout. The third level will be the corpse army, those of the dead who are willing to fight for us. Then we bring on the elves and finally Grindan and his warriors. We make Moncoya work through our levels one at a time."

"Like in a computer game." Lorcan nodded his agreement. "You should have been a general, so you should."

"Exactly like in a computer game. The only problem is, we don't know Moncoya's levels. We'll be playing his game at the same time. It's frustrating because we are starting a whole new game that we've never played before. When you buy a game in the shops or online, you at least have an idea of what you're getting. Do we know anything about his strengths, other than the sidhes? Any whispers about who else he has on his side?"

"You'll get a better idea of that once you are inside his palace," Cal said. "He will want to show you off, let the world know that he has achieved what he promised and won the heart of the necromancer star. I'm guessing there will be quite a lineup there waiting to meet you. It should be easy to figure out who his allies are." It was the first time he had managed to speak of Stella's forthcoming deception without bitterness sounding in his voice. He didn't quite succeed in keeping it out of his eyes.

"Which brings us to the question of when and where the fight will take place," Lorcan said. "We want to be in control of the timing and venue for the battle so that we can have our own allies ready."

Cal came and sat next to Stella, slipping his arm around her and hugging her close against his side. "It has to be at the wedding. That is the time when everyone will be assembled in one place."

Stella made a choking noise. "Well, you'd better get your timing spot-on, boys, because if you don't I'll end up being Mrs. Moncoya."

"Won't the wedding take place inside the palace? Not the best place for a battle," Lorcan pointed out.

"If I remember the layout of the building correctly, there are formal gardens with a lake beyond. The gardens are the only place large enough to gather that many people together. That will be our battleground."

"What'll I do if Moncoya wants to take things slowly and suggests a long engagement?"

"He won't. He'll be desperate to make you his queen. But if he did suggest it, I'm sure you could persuade him to hurry things along. We want the wedding to take place within a day or two." Cal dropped a kiss onto the top of her head. "I want this over and you away from him as soon as we can do it."

Stella didn't need to tell him that she wanted that, too. It went without saying, but she couldn't add the other thought that came close on its heels. *What's next for us, Cal? If we walk away from this, where do we walk to? And do we go there together?* Solving the riddle of who he was had only added to her list of questions. It didn't seem to bother Cal unduly that she knew he was Merlin. Which meant that his identity was not the dark secret that was going to keep them apart. He had promised no more secrets once the battle for Otherworld was won. Could she trust him to keep that promise?

"Stella will insist on me being there to give her away." Lorcan grinned. "Sure, I'll have to get my best suit pressed. But we still have one final problem…" Stella said the next words with him. "How are we going to get Cal inside Moncoya's palace?"

"There is only one way I can think of." Cal's voice was expressionless.

"What's that?" Stella lifted her face so that she could look at his profile. His jaw was rigid with tension.

"I have to let him capture me."

Stella barely noticed the panoramic view of Barcelona in front of her or the enchanting creations of the Park Güell behind her. Lorcan held a pair of binoculars to his eyes and was engrossed in training these on one particular property situated above and to the right of the park. This was the only angle from which La Casa Oscura was not completely hidden by trees.

"What will Moncoya do to Cal when he captures him?"

"Imprison him." Lorcan's attention didn't waver from Moncoya's home.

"Is that all?"

"The dungeons under the faerie king's palace are not exactly the Ritz, me darlin' girl."

"He won't hurt Cal, will he?" Stella gave his sleeve an insistent tug and Lorcan reluctantly lowered the binoculars.

His eyes softened slightly as they scanned her face. "Cal's not an easy man to hurt."

Stella chewed her thumbnail. "Maybe not, but he'll be placing himself in the power of his worst enemy. Moncoya hates him."

"I'm thinking it's a feeling that's reciprocated. If I was a betting man, I'd be putting my own money on Cal to come off best. Now stop your fretting and concentrate."

"What am I focusing on exactly?"

"That." He pointed up the hillside at La Casa Oscura.

"I've been there before, remember? I worked for Moncoya before all this madness kicked off."

"But, back then, you thought it was a house. You didn't know what it really was."

"And what is it, exactly?"

"A dark house."

"It's in the name. La Casa Oscura means 'dark house,'" Stella pointed out.

"Yes, and isn't it just like that little shit Moncoya to flaunt it in that way? A dark house is a portal to Otherworld. Not just any portal, a very specific opening into the very worst that Otherworld has to offer. Yon casa there is unique. It can be a portal to Moncoya's splendid royal palace or it can take you right into Otherworld's dark underbelly, the place where Moncoya and his friends carry out their nasty business."

Stella turned her back on the iconic view, leaning against the tiled parapet so that she could keep Lorcan and La Casa Oscura in her sights. She had a feeling she really didn't want to know exactly what sort of nasty business Moncoya got up to.

"I didn't notice anything of the things you describe when I was working there. Surely, given that I am the necromancer star, I should have."

Lorcan smiled. "You didn't know who you were back then. I guarantee it will feel different this time."

"I still don't fully understand Otherworld," Stella confessed. "How it exists and how you and Cal travel between here and there with seeming ease, yet most mortals remain unaware of it."

"Otherworld is no less real just because, most of the time, we can't see it. Centuries ago, people were more accepting of other beings and of what they believed to be magic. They took great pains not to anger the spirits and gave offerings to their pagan deities. They knew the truth...that the curtain between the worlds is a thin one. Sometimes, it becomes invisible." He glanced up at the late afternoon sky. "The worlds are closest at dusk and dawn."

"That's the sort of thing I can't get my head around. One minute you say Otherworld is all around us and the next you speak about it as a physical place."

"Sure, isn't that because you're trying to think about it logically? All mythologies—Roman, Greek, Norse, Indian—vary about the original location of Otherworld. My own ancestors, the ancient Celts, believed it was a series of islands set far out in the Atlantic. Even now, there are stories that it appears magically now and then to Irish sailors, only to disappear when they get closer. Some portals, like yon casa, are the dark ones, recently created and well guarded. Others, like the stone circles of the Druids, have existed for thousands of years. Getting in? Easy. All you have to do is believe it exists." He grinned. "It's once you're in that things get tough."

"And on that note—" Stella pushed herself away from the wall and hauled her backpack onto her shoulder. Gathering up the bags that contained items she had purchased that morning in the Plaça de Catalunya, she squared her shoulders. "Time to go."

"I'll be seeing you in less than a day. Look after yourself in the meantime." Lorcan raised his hand in a curiously formal salute as she walked away from him in the direction of La Casa Oscura. Stella comforted herself with the thought that she was getting better at leaving people. Or maybe it was just because he wasn't Cal.

Twenty minutes later, after getting slightly lost among the narrow streets, Stella paused, studying what little she could see of La Casa Oscura from the exact point where she had first viewed it. She tried to recapture her initial impression of the house. How different life would have been if she'd trusted her inner, warning voice that night. It was no good telling herself bewitchment was what Moncoya did best, that it was his faerie trademark. This was where it had all begun, and Stella felt now that she had somehow failed by not knowing that she was walking into a trap. Yet, if she had not stepped through these wrought-iron gates that night, would anything have been different? According to the prophecy, this was her fate. So even if she had turned tail and run, she would still have arrived at this point in her life. And the journey had not been all bad. Parts of it—a smile touched her lips at the thought of Cal—had been quite amazing.

"Oh, just get on with it," she muttered under her breath.

The words galvanized her and she marched decisively through the gates. It seemed she was expected. As she approached the steps leading to the entrance, the front doors opened. She couldn't see anyone in the gloom beyond. Decision deserted her. *Flight, fight or freeze.* Her brain offered her body those options and refused to accept a fourth. *Smile and keep walking.* Although she willed her feet and her face into action, nothing happened. *Come on, Stella.* Eventually, just as she was starting to resemble a statue—fixed forever in midstride on the gravel drive—her brain unfroze and she managed to put one foot in front of the other. The smile remained beyond her capabilities.

The interior of the casa was delightfully cool after the heat of a Barcelona evening. The huge room was exactly as she remembered it, complete with several electronics geeks lounging around on cushions, chatting and playing games. Even though it looked the same, Lorcan was right. It *felt* different. The crawling sensation up her spine warned her of danger.

"Stella!" It was Diego, struggling to untangle his limbs from the depths of a cushion. He glanced at her backpack and bags. "You been away for a few days?"

"Something like that."

She gazed around her. It was a surreal feeling, as if she really had been away for only a day or two. Was Moncoya playing mind games? Stella stared at the glass window that had been shattered by the Valkyries. The repair job was flawless. "Was anything damaged when the window broke?" she asked Diego.

"Which window would that be?" Diego appeared mildly interested.

Stella waved him back to his friends. "I'm going upstairs to unpack."

This was not how she had imagined her return to the casa would unfold. No welcome party. No sidhes. No Moncoya. The feeling of unreality—or too much reality—lasted as long as it took her to climb the spiral staircase and open the door of her room.

Moncoya was lounging on her bed eating an apple. He

wore the trousers and waistcoat from a pin-striped suit over a flawless ruffled shirt. Two-tone spats on his feet and a gray felt trilby on his head completed the look. Beneath the hat, his wild mane had been tied back into a ponytail. Anyone else would have looked ridiculous. Moncoya looked as if he was ready for a photo shoot.

When Stella paused just inside the door, Moncoya sat up, throwing the apple across the room without looking. It landed, with unerring precision, in the waste bin.

"Your flight from England landed thirty hours ago." He rose and came toward her with his unique fluid grace. "I hope you did not get lost, my star."

Stella held up her bags. "Prewedding shopping. Bride-to-be's perks, Ezra. I'm sure your spies have told you which shops I visited on the Plaça de Catalunya this morning. I didn't think you'd begrudge me a little retail therapy before we tie the knot."

His eyes narrowed, then he laughed, showing very white, very even teeth. "You are good, Stella. Very good. Not entirely convincing, but at least you are here. Where does Lorcan Malone fit into your schemes?"

"He's my friend." Now or never. "And he'll be at our wedding, giving me away."

"I think not."

"Think again."

They faced each other like a pair of wary cats. Stella could feel him testing her. His power rippled through her whole body. It was an unwelcome, invasive but not entirely unpleasant sensation. Stella remained stock-still and tried to shut him out. She didn't know how much he could discover from his probing. Let him think she was weaker than she was. She didn't want to reveal her true strength to him. Not yet.

Moncoya shrugged. "If you insist. Although he has been

known to consort with the other one, Lorcan Malone can hardly be considered a threat."

"Thank you." She inhaled, recognizing only in that moment that she had been holding her breath at all. She had rehearsed her next little speech. "No matter how strong my feelings for you may be, I'm not sure I wish to marry you, Ezra. It's all happened so fast. But you are right. I have no other choice."

"You are very wise to choose me, my star. It will be my privilege to protect you from those who would harm you because of their flawed interpretation of the prophecy."

"And in return you'd like me to slaughter your enemies."

His smile was all charm. "But of course."

"What now?" Stella glanced around the familiar room as if seeing it for the first time. *I am discussing my wedding to the faerie king as if it is the most normal thing in the world.*

"Tomorrow there will be a betrothal feast at my home in Otherworld. You will love my beautiful palace when you see it." Stella remembered Cal's prediction that Moncoya would want to show her off. "The following day the marriage ceremony will take place."

"Talk about sweeping a girl off her feet."

"You have admitted that you are not sure you wish to marry me. I am not entirely convinced that your presence here is not some sort of elaborate pretense, although I don't yet know what you hope to gain from it. Once you are my queen, you will be in my power, Stella. Your motives are unimportant. You have delivered yourself up to me. The end result will be the same."

Stella shivered, no longer caring if he saw her fear. "You have a unique—and rather scary—wooing technique, Ezra."

He bowed slightly from the waist as if she had paid him

a compliment. "I will leave you to prepare. We will depart
for Otherworld within the hour."

"Some see the world with the inner eye, while others
remain stubbornly determined to cling only to their outer
vision," Moncoya spoke softly in Stella's ear as they stood
in the garden of La Casa Oscura just as the final rays of
day faded from the sky. "With the inner eye, nothing is
invisible. Look around you, Stella. Tell me what you see."

As pointless questions went, that one had to be the most
infuriating she had heard in a long time. Stella felt as if
she was back in school and reading a passage from a book
that was spoiled when a teacher insisted on overanalyz-
ing it until it lost all meaning. She had already spent long
evenings here drinking in the beauty of the casa's location. The views across the city were second to none. The
city itself was breathtaking. She had no idea why Moncoya
had brought her out here to look at it again, but she had no
doubt it was one of his games. It felt as if he was wasting
time, but Moncoya never did anything without a good reason. Why did she feel like a mouse trapped between the
paws of a very dangerous, very well-groomed cat?

"Ezra, when do we go to Otherworld?" She made no
attempt to keep the impatience out of her voice.

"Look with your inner eye, Stella. Then tell me."

Sighing, she stepped up to the balustrade. *Right, my
inner eye. Whatever that might be. Because I've really
got time for this.* The lights of the city flickered below
her. She closed her eyes, putting on a show for Moncoya.
What had Lorcan said about Otherworld? It was closest
at dawn and dusk. If Moncoya persisted in this nonsense,
they would miss their opportunity to get there today. Lorcan had also said you must believe it existed. That part was
easy. *I have to believe it. When my entire future, and that*

of the whole world, depends on it, how can I disbelieve?
Deciding she had played this game for long enough, Stella
opened her eyes.

The sensation of unreality as she did made her feel
giddy. She was standing on a different terrace, high on
a rocky cliff. Far below her the lights of Barcelona were
gone. The evening sunlight illuminated a chain of tiny
green islands clinging to a turquoise-and-gold coastline.
She turned her head, gazing upward in disbelief. La Casa
Oscura was gone, too. In its place was a soaring white
marble fairy-tale palace of endless turrets and towers.

"Welcome to your new home." They were the exact
words he had spoken to her when she first arrived at La
Casa Oscura. "What do you think of Otherworld, my star?"

Aware that her mouth was gaping open slightly in
shock, Stella closed it with an audible click. She had not
actually given any thought, prior to this moment, to what
Otherworld might look like. She supposed now that, in
her mind at least, she had made it into a dark, frightening
place with horrors lurking around every shadowy corner.
Nothing had prepared her for the breathtaking beauty of
the reality that was Otherworld. The air was lush with the
mingled scents of pine and lavender, and she could hear
the sounds of the waves far below and the gulls overhead.

"It's amazing." Stella leaned far out over the rail so that
she could see the water churning onto the rocks below.

"Do you see now why it is fought over?"

"No. I don't understand how you could bear to spoil
so much beauty with violence. Why can't you be content
to share?"

"Your youth and lack of familiarity with Otherworld
history dictates your prosaic approach. My feelings are
born of blood, passion and poetry. I hope in time to edu-
cate you into my ways."

There was a message in the words that was about more than the legends and politics of Otherworld. The gleam in Moncoya's eye was lascivious, and he made a move to place his hand on the bare flesh of Stella's forearm. She moved slightly, so that his fingertips connected with thin air. The frown that descended over his features drove away any trace of geniality and, in that instant, his expression was truly terrifying.

Although Cal had said that, even invisible, he would never be able to break through Moncoya's barriers, Stella kept hoping to see that trick-of-light movement at the edge of her vision. *I need you, Cal.* There was nothing. Even though she couldn't feel his shadowy presence, she sensed he was on his way. The thought comforted and alarmed her at the same time.

Moncoya interrupted her thoughts. "Let us go inside. I wish to present you to my family."

That could mean only one thing. It was time to be formally introduced to Moncoya's formidable daughters. Tanzi and Vashti. Valkyrie-trained warrior princesses. Being a stepmother was never an easy job. This was going to be a nightmare.

Dragging her feet slightly, Stella followed Moncoya through a high-arched doorway and into the opulent interior of the palace.

Chapter 19

"The banquet hall is the palace's finest room." Moncoya's voice echoed with pride as he escorted Stella into a space the approximate size of an aircraft hangar. It was encircled at first-floor height by galleries and its magnificent walls were decorated in extravagant murals of dazzling gold and blue.

At one end, set on a raised dais in front of three arched, stained glass windows, there were two elaborately carved high-backed thrones. Vashti lounged sideways on one of these with her legs swinging casually over the side. She was dressed in combat fatigues, which seemed to be a very specific statement about her approach to meeting her father's new bride. Tanzi was standing beneath the windows. The light from a wall sconce gave her golden hair an extra sheen and illuminated her ethereal, unearthly beauty. She looked up as Moncoya brought Stella forward, her eyes dark and unreadable. Vashti did not glance their way, but instead she carried on talking, finishing what she had been saying to her sister.

"...nothing more insufferable than keeping people waiting." She glanced up, as though surprised to see them. "Oh, good evening, Father Dear. Tanzi and I were just saying that of all the things we hate most, unpunctuality must rate among the highest." She turned the fire-ringed beam of her gaze onto Stella. "We were expecting *you* an hour ago."

Stella detected bitter jealousy dripping through Vashti's words. She had heard that note before when, as a child, she had gone to foster homes where the family already had children. Then, it had been hurtful, but understandable. Vashti was an adult. A grown woman and a spoiled brat. And one who was trained in combat by the Valkyries. Possibly not the best person to cross. *Thank God I'm not in this for the long haul.*

"What a pity no one informed me of the schedule," Stella replied in her sweetest voice. "It's nice to meet you, too."

A slight hissing noise emanated from between Vashti's clenched teeth and she sat up straighter, tension coiling through her frame. Stella stiffened, anticipating an attack.

"You will remember your manners, my daughter." Despite the coolness of Moncoya's voice, the threat was unmistakable. Vashti subsided again, her lovely face sulky. "You will both—" he turned so that his words encompassed Tanzi "—treat Stella with courtesy or know my wrath."

Silence hung thick and heavy in the vast room. It was like a child's staring contest to see who would break it. Mildly amused by a situation that felt as if it was happening to someone else, Stella took the opportunity to gaze around the room. There was a definite swan theme going on. The middle, and larger, of the three stained glass windows depicted the story of the god Zeus seducing Leda in the guise of a swan. The window panels on each side were pictures of goddesses with female forms adorned with the white wings of a swan. Some of the murals featured chariots drawn through the skies by swans in flight. Beautiful, but a little obsessive.

Tired of the game, Stella spoke first. "Well, this has been nice and I'd love to stay and chat for longer. But I'd like to go to my room now, please."

"I will take her." Tanzi spoke for the first time, moving swift and sylphlike to Stella's side before Moncoya or Vashti could move. "Which room?"

"The queen's chambers, of course."

"No, not my mother's rooms." The venom was back on Vashti's face.

"Since she is to be my wife, where else would she go?" Moncoya was beginning to sound bored.

"Anywhere else. *She*—" the look she threw at Stella could have stripped the gold paint from the walls "—is not worthy to occupy my mother's rooms."

"You do not make the decisions here, Vashti." Moncoya turned his frown from her to Tanzi. "Take Stella to the queen's chambers."

"Look, if it's a big deal I can just as easily have another room…" Stella broke off as the thread of Moncoya's temper snapped.

"I will not be questioned!"

Tanzi gestured for Stella to follow her. "It is wise to do as my father wishes," she said as they followed a long, scarlet-carpeted corridor.

"What happens when you don't?"

Although Tanzi's eyes were blue they were so dark that, at times, they appeared black. She turned their full magnetic force on Stella now. "Bad things," she said quietly and, without elaborating further, continued along the passage.

Throughout the building Moncoya had intertwined his nostalgia for the medieval with his knowledge of the very latest technology so that the whole palace was a combination of ancient and modern. Tanzi led Stella up a flight of stairs and past sleeping quarters that showed a strong Gothic influence and through more corridors embellished with paintings and frescoes of Otherworld women. Valkyries, sidhes, nymphs and vampires in various states of undress gazed down at them from pale pastel walls.

The queen's chambers occupied one of the turrets and were decorated in a style that made Stella wonder what sort of woman Moncoya's first queen had been. She clearly was not one who compromised when it came to her own comfort. In addition to a bedroom bigger than Stella's entire studio back in London, there was a sitting room, dressing room and bathroom. Stella waded across a carpet so rich and thick it seemed to swallow her feet up to her ankles to place her bags near a mirrored wardrobe that lined one wall. She would have to be careful not to lose her belongings inside it.

The room had a swan-shaped dressing table and the tiles in the luxurious bathroom formed a swan mosaic. A beautiful robe made of white silk edged with white feathers was draped over the end of a bed so vast it could have easily accommodated five people.

"Swans seem to be a popular motif around here. Is there a reason for that?"

"Our mother, mine and Vashti's, was a Valkyrie."

Stella dredged up what little she knew of Valkyries from her limited knowledge of Norse legends. The fabled Viking goddesses were not only famous for their fighting skills, they could also transform themselves into swans.

A tough act to follow. It seemed to be yet another reason for Stella to be glad she wasn't sticking around for the actual ceremony. She touched the swan-feather robe and wondered if Moncoya liked his sexual partners to dress up. The thought made her shudder and she quickly withdrew her touch.

"You must miss her very much. How old were you when she died?"

Tanzi's laugh sounded like a silver bell ringing in an empty room. "She is not dead. Vashti and I were babies when she left because she could stand to live with my father no longer. Does that sound like a warning? It should."

It did. Stella stared at the closed door after Tanzi had gone. The highly polished wood looked expensive, like something out of a glossy home-decor magazine. It also looked a lot like a prison door.

Going out onto the balcony, she gazed down onto a grotto, where little waterfalls and colored lighting created the impression of a mysterious cave. Her chest tightened at the memory of Cal's cave. The only place she had ever thought of as home. It wasn't that she liked living like a Neanderthal enough to make her miss the cave. It had felt like home because of Cal. She wondered where he was and if she would see him before Moncoya captured him. There could be no doubt about his ability to escape a prison cell. But Moncoya would know that. If he had Cal in his power, would he allow him to live? The thought of Cal putting himself in danger for her was unbearably painful.

What did you wear for your own betrothal feast when you didn't really want to be there? Wardrobe decisions didn't get much tougher than this. Stella suspected that between them, Moncoya and Tanzi would raise the glamour stakes of the occasion through the roof. And who knew what the other guests would wear? None of it mattered, of course. But if she turned up in the shorts, black tights, ballet pumps and striped jumper she had been wearing when she arrived, Moncoya would smell a rat. A bigger rat. The faerie king already had the scent of rodent in his perfectly carved nostrils.

Stella flipped a hand through the items she had purchased the day before in the Plaça de Catalunya. The only reason for the shopping trip had been to provide an excuse for delaying her arrival at La Casa Oscura. Limited time and funds meant she had selected a few random items that were within her price range. She gave the results a final despairing look. There was only one item that was remotely suitable. It was a simple, black shift dress that hugged her slim figure and came to rest just above her knee. Viewing herself in this garment in the mirror, Stella had to admit that it looked good. She suspected that "good" was likely to be a long way from dressy enough on this occasion.

Her shoe choices were even more limited. The well-worn ballet pumps or her trusty Doc Martens. Neither said "bride-to-be hoping to make a good impression on the groom's family and friends." In fairness, she had never envisioned a situation in which she planned to kill her fiancé. Who knew getting the wardrobe details right in advance would matter so much? If the situation arose again, she would be forewarned. In desperation, Stella opened the mirrored doors. There was an eye-watering array of shoes inside, but weren't the Valkyries of Amazonian build? It seemed not. To her surprise, she found a pair of understated black heels that fitted her perfectly. Having helped herself to these, Stella also selected a crimson cashmere wrap to lighten the funereal tone of her outfit.

A final glance in the mirror told her that her hair, which had grown and was slightly longer than her usual style, was behaving itself. On the outside she looked okay. On the inside she knew how the Christian slaves felt just before they were thrown to the lions. She had never needed Cal as badly as she did now.

Moncoya was waiting for her at the foot of the stairs. He wore a white silk suit—the jacket of which had red-and-black embroidery in a Japanese design over one shoulder—and his trademark frilled shirt. Diamonds glittered in his ears and on his fingers. His makeup was flawless, his mane of hair wilder than ever.

He smiled appreciatively at Stella's own understated outfit. "We complement each other perfectly."

She resisted the impulse to run upstairs and change back into her shorts. A familiar, and very welcome, voice stiffened her resolve.

"Sure, me darlin' girl, why did you not send me the dress code? I knew nothing about the black, white and red theme."

Lorcan strode through the castle doors with all his usual nonchalance. It took every ounce of Stella's resolve not to hurl herself at him and demand that he should get her out of there right now and take her straight to Cal. His blue eyes quizzed her face as he approached, and she guessed he knew exactly what she was thinking. His eyelid drooped into a quick wink before he turned to Moncoya.

"Your Majesty." Moncoya inclined his head, acknowledging the deferential greeting. "I am honored to be invited to this gathering and delighted to be able to support my friend at her wedding. As her supporter, it will be my pleasure to be at Stella's left hand throughout this feast."

Stella could see Moncoya mentally reviewing the seating arrangements. "I am happy to welcome you into my home." He didn't look happy. With a nod, he walked away.

"His hairdresser earns every penny, don't you think?

You bearing up okay?" Lorcan asked as they prepared to follow Moncoya into the banquet hall.

"I've been better."

"You'll be just fine." He lowered his voice. "The big feller is on his way."

Those words acted like a shot of steel injected straight into Stella's backbone. Gripping Lorcan's arm tightly, she walked with him into the banquet hall. The room was full and the party chatter that had filled it prior to their entrance ceased instantly as they walked through the double doors. Stella felt the force of every single eye as she made her way into the center of the room.

"Have we just walked into the party scene from *The Great Gatsby*?" Stella murmured, taking in the old-fashioned glitz and glamour of the assembled company. Her attention was caught by the orchestra, who were seated on a podium at the far end of the room.

Lorcan followed her gaze. "The greatest musicians of the past five centuries. All dead, of course."

"Ghosts?" Stella whispered.

"Yes, you could say they play a haunting tune."

She groaned in response. The conversations around the room had started up again. She no longer felt as though she was being assessed from every angle. Although to say she was relaxed would have been an exaggeration. "So whom should we be looking out for? Who are Moncoya's allies?"

"It's difficult to tell just yet. There are a few leaders here I wouldn't want to get on the wrong side of, but that doesn't mean they have thrown in their lot with Moncoya. I hope not for all our sakes. There are some alliances no one wants to see."

Before Stella could ask what he meant, her attention was claimed by a man who was so good-looking she decided he could only be a model. Then she remembered they were in Otherworld, a place where physical beauty was almost obligatory. Even so, this man was striking. There was no trace of a fiery ring around his unusual ice-blue irises so she assumed he was not a sidhe. Yet there was definitely something otherworldly about him. His features seemed to have been hewn from granite, resulting in razor-sharp cheekbones and a square, sculpted jaw. His white-blond hair had been shaved so that the stubble on his head was the same length as that framing his surprisingly full lips and, in contrast to his Scandinavian coloring, his skin was lightly tanned. Add in a lean, hard body in a perfectly fitting dark suit, and it was no wonder every woman in the room was casting envious glances in Stella's direction. Lorcan, on the other hand, was frowning slightly as he moved closer to Stella.

"It is a great honor to meet the necromancer star of whom we have all heard so much." His accent was unusual and he bowed low with old-fashioned courtesy, raising Stella's hand to his lips. He was accompanied by another man who appeared to be a bodyguard. It didn't seem odd that he should have such protection. In addition to his looks and impeccable manners, there was something imperial or presidential about the man, who was stroking her hand with his mouth. It was an oddly sensual caress. Stella got the distinct impression that he wanted to taste her flesh.

"Stella, allow me to introduce Prince Tibor." From his expression, Lorcan might have been a disapproving parent greeting his daughter's unsuitable prom date. Did he think she was going to forget Cal over a pretty face? Surely Lorcan knew her feelings for his friend went deeper than that.

Prince Tibor bowed again and made his way over to Moncoya. Side by side, Moncoya and the newcomer certainly made a striking pair.

"Well, he seemed nice," Stella said.

"Don't be fooled by those old-school manners. You were lucky to get that hand back intact. Let's just say, in Tibor's case, it's safe to say his bite is worse than his bark."

Stella actually heard the gulping noise her throat made as she swallowed. "I take it he is the vampire prince Cal warned me about?"

"Yes, and that—" he nodded to where Moncoya and Prince Tibor were deep in conversation "—is exactly what I meant when I said there are some alliances none of us want."

"He doesn't have fangs." As soon as the statement left her lips it seemed an inane comment. What she meant was that Prince Tibor did not look like the vampires she had read about in books or seen in films. But then Moncoya bore no resemblance to the faeries who were supposed to dwell at the bottom of the garden and Cal was nothing like the white-bearded, robed wizard of Arthurian legend. So she didn't know why she should be surprised that Tibor didn't fit the vampire stereotype.

"Be thankful for that. When he does you will need every ounce of your power to keep him under control. And don't ever turn your back on Dimitar, his human servant." He nodded in the direction of the bodyguard.

"I might be getting a bit ahead of myself here, but surely we don't need to worry about vampires. They are undead. We can control them."

"True, but just as Prince Tibor has Dimitar, every other vampire also has a human servant. We can exert absolute control over the vampires, and nothing over the human servants. They will obey their master's orders no matter what we do."

"So they have a substitute army in place?" Lorcan nodded, his face grim. "This just gets better. Now, *he* is more my idea of what a real vampire should look like. Tall, dark and dangerous." Stella nodded to a man who had paused just inside the door. His height allowed him to scan to room. Lorcan followed her gaze and groaned, his expression clouding further. "Who is he?"

"Trouble. That is Jethro de Loix, one of the few bad necromancers I've met."

Stella looked again. With his swept-back wavy hair and hawk-like profile, Jethro had a look that belonged to another era. He should have been a riverboat gambler, a smuggler or at the helm of his own pirate ship. He looked like a man who thrived on danger. "And he's the one who has offered to fight me for money?"

"The very same."

"This day just keeps getting better. What about the werewolf leader—what's his name? Nevan? Is he here as well just waiting for a chance to tear out my heart?" Stella cast a fearful glance around for anyone who looked—or perhaps didn't look—like a werewolf.

"I can't see him, but it wouldn't surprise me if Moncoya still had a few tricks up his sleeve."

Chapter 20

The guests began to make their way to the tables and Moncoya returned to Stella's side to offer her his arm with an old-fashioned bow. The scene became a bustle of activity as the first course was served and wine was poured. Stella was conscious that she was once again the object of considerable scrutiny and gossip. The glances sent her way ranged from the speculative to the frankly incredulous. She hid a smile. *I'm not what they expected. Good. Let's hope I can surprise them some more.*

Moncoya made a great performance of taking a sip of wine from his own goblet and then offering it to Stella to drink from. It seemed to symbolize something important to him. When, to humor him, she took a sip, a ripple of applause went around the room.

"We have shared food. In the faerie tradition that is a commitment even greater than the marriage ceremony." Moncoya's eyes blazed fire into Stella's.

Stella thought of all the times she and Cal had companionably eaten from the same bowl or drunk from the same cup back at the cave. Somehow, it comforted her that, even though she had known nothing of the tradition until this moment, Moncoya's attempt to ensnare her had been thwarted by her prior attachment to Cal.

Her status as the main attraction didn't last long. Even above the noise within the banquet hall, it was impossible to ignore the fact that there was a commotion taking place in the corridor outside. Heads began to turn away from Stella and toward whatever was going on.

Lorcan paused in the act of devouring an elegant fish dish. "Sounds like the big feller has arrived."

Stella's heart began to pound wildly. Her appetite had deserted her anyway, even though the food looked delicious. Placing her knife and fork down, she clasped her hands together beneath the table. Pressing her nails into her palms until it hurt seemed to be the only way to stop the desperate trembling that had seized her limbs.

"I don't care what's going on. I have to speak to her... now!" The door burst open and Cal erupted into the room just ahead of a group of pursuing sidhes. He halted, glancing swiftly around. Seeing Stella, he launched himself across the space between them. It cost Stella every ounce of self-control she possessed not to meet him halfway and hurl herself into his arms. Instead, she remained stock-still, conscious of Moncoya's gaze burning into her profile. *Play your part,* she reminded herself.

"I'm afraid you are mistaken. Admittance to this party is by invitation only," Moncoya said when Cal was mere inches away.

Cal ignored him. "Stella, this is madness. Don't do this."

He reached across the table for her hand, but before their fingers could connect there was a flash of movement and Vashti had pounced upon him, her broadsword poised between his shoulder blades. Stella sprang to her feet, aware of Lorcan doing the same at her side. Dozens of sidhes poured into the room and surrounded Cal, who now lay sprawled facedown on the floor. *This is what he planned,* Stella told herself. *He can get away from Vashti anytime he wants.* Even so, she wished he didn't have to make it look quite so convincing.

"Well, my father? Shall I finish him here and now?" Vashti gripped Cal's hair and raised the sword higher.

"Ezra, please. You cannot allow this…" Stella encountered a venom-laden glare from Vashti.

Muttering rolled around the room as the guests began to voice their opinions on the matter. "Silence." Moncoya held up a hand. "My bride wishes to speak." He turned to Stella. "Well, my star? What will be the fate of he who was your captor?"

Could she look into those silver eyes and not betray her feelings to the hundreds of people who were watching her? She had to try. Stella drew in a deep breath and looked directly at Cal. Just when she thought she couldn't possibly love him more, one corner of his mouth lifted slightly. Her heart expanded to a point just short of rupture.

"I do not wish for any blood to be shed during our wedding celebrations." She could feel Cal willing her on. "Let him be imprisoned instead."

"What nonsense is this?" Vashti's voice rang out above the disgruntled rumbling all around them. "This is a trick. There is no prison cell that can hold one such as he. The only way to stop this sorcerer is to kill him."

Moncoya raised a hand and the clamor stilled. He turned to Stella. "Vashti is right, of course. But, as my wedding gift to you, I will give you his life. If he breaks free of his cell, however, I will hunt him down and tear him apart with my bare hands." He lifted his glass and dashed off the remaining liquid before speaking directly to Cal. "Besides, I have a little surprise for you. One which will ensure you cannot escape. You may wish Stella had chosen death for you by the time I am done."

With an exclamation of disgust, Vashti sheathed her sword and stomped away. Cal's sidhe captors made a move to drag him to his feet.

"Not so fast." It was Jethro de Loix's deep tones that halted them. "Why not allow him to stay and watch the entertainment, Your Majesty?"

Stella cast a swift sideways glance at Lorcan, who shrugged his own lack of understanding. "Ah, yes. In all the excitement, I had almost forgotten." Moncoya turned his most charming smile on to Stella. "Jethro here has offered you a challenge, my star. His pride is hurt at the suggestion that there is one who might be a greater sorcerer than he. He wishes to pit his own skills against yours."

Stella cast a swift glance around her. Every face seemed to be turned in her direction once more. Was it her imagination, or was there a distinctly feral look in each and every one of those eyes? She forced a laugh. "I'm being challenged to a fight? At my betrothal feast? Surely I am not obliged to accept this, Ezra?"

"Not obliged, no. But it occurs to me that none of us, not even I, have seen any true evidence of who you are and what you can do." He lowered his voice slightly. "And you will not shame me in front of my guests with a refusal." The words were light but the threat contained within them was heavyweight.

Stella stared defiantly back at him, her chin raised. "Refuse? Not a chance."

He laughed. "A wise choice." He clapped his hands.

"Fetch a chair so that the prisoner may sit next to his friend."

Stella risked a glance in Cal's direction. "Don't." He mouthed the word and gave an infinitesimal shake of his head.

She shrugged, turning her palms upward in a gesture that indicated she had no choice. His look of resignation said it all. Taking no chances, six sidhes grabbed Cal and manhandled him into a chair to the left of Lorcan. He slumped into it with a show of reluctance. A small army of guards lined up behind him.

"Hold my wrap, would you?" Stella passed the garment to Lorcan, who seemed unmoved by the events unfolding before him.

He grinned up at her. "You can take this guy, me darlin' girl. I've been hearing a rumor that he has a glass jaw."

Stella swallowed hard as she watched Jethro take up a combative position in the center of the hall. "I'm not even sure I can reach his jaw."

Lorcan's face became serious. "Jethro doesn't fight fair so don't feel you have to. Use your size to your advantage, take him by surprise."

Slipping off her heels, Stella stepped down from the dais and went to face her opponent.

Cal and Lorcan were both tall and muscular but there was something about the sheer width and power of Jethro de Loix that dwarfed everything and everyone around him. Stella didn't just look small in comparison, she looked unbelievably fragile. As if one touch from Jethro would snap her delicate frame in two. It was obvious, by the way his eyes widened in disbelief as he looked down at her, that Jethro himself believed that would be the case.

Ignoring the disapproval of his captors, Cal turned to

Lorcan. "I can't keep up this pretense. There's no way I can let her face him alone."

"Look around you, my friend. Unless you want this war right here, right now, I don't think you've much choice. And she's something special, remember? Give her a chance to prove it on her own. If it looks like she's in trouble, then we can step in, not before."

It was sound advice. Nevertheless, it took all of Cal's willpower to listen to his friend and not rush to Stella's side.

Jethro looked Stella up and down once more as they faced each other a few feet apart, before calling across to Moncoya, "*This* is your star?"

Moncoya was lounging in his chair, clearly enjoying himself. "It is indeed."

Jethro threw him a look of intense dislike. "Then the deal is off. I will not fight a *girl*, no matter how large the purse."

"When and where did he dredge himself up a few morals? Last time I saw him he was running contraband between Otherworld and the mortal realm and the Dominion wanted his guts on a platter." Cal's nerves were stretched too tight to respond to his friend's murmured question, and Lorcan subsided into silence.

"It seems the great Jethro is afraid of being worsted by a girl, my friends." Moncoya's voice was jeering.

Jethro, who had been about to stalk away, turned back to face Stella at that. "Sorry, but if you are stupid enough to marry that shit you deserve everything you get." His face had darkened with anger.

"Do your worst." She smiled sweetly up at him. "Or even your best."

Cal almost groaned aloud. *Don't provoke him, Stella. He's dangerous enough already.*

Without warning, Jethro lifted one hand and sent a ball of fire flying through the air in her direction. Stella didn't move. Cal could only watch nervously as the flames paused in midair mere inches before her face. Then, to a gasp of delight from the guests, the fireball began an intricate dance before returning the way it had come and exploding above Jethro's head in a shimmer of sparks. Stella looked unconcerned, as though the mind control it took to perform a trick like that was simple. For her, of course, it was. She might have only recently discovered her powers, but magic came as easily to Stella as breathing. Until he got to know what she could do, Cal had never encountered anyone else who was his equal in that respect.

Jethro threw another, larger fireball at her and Stella batted it back as if she was playing a lazy summer's day game of tennis. The rage on Jethro's face intensified. Wave upon wave of fireballs rolled toward Stella and each was swatted back to him with the same unerring ease. Not once did she lift a finger. Her calm expression didn't falter. Jethro was beginning to sweat. He tried to take a step closer to Stella and was brought up short, thwarted by an invisible barrier.

"Show my guests what you can do, my star." Moncoya's voice throbbed with pride. "Bring him to his knees."

"Yon faerie feller is starting to seriously annoy me now," Lorcan muttered.

From the glare Jethro gave his host, it seemed he was sharing Lorcan's emotions toward Moncoya. Jethro muttered something that Cal couldn't hear, but whatever it was brought a slight smile to Stella's lips. Cal's chest expanded with pride. She was amazing! Even now, when she was facing such extreme danger, her undaunted spirit shone through.

"Arise." Stella spoke the Old English command quietly.

"What the hell is she doing?" Lorcan murmured.

"Exerting her power over the undead. Watch."

All around the room, guests began to rise to their feet. Their expressions ranged from confusion through annoyance to fury. Vampires, werewolves and ghosts, unable to resist the call of the greatest necromancer the world had ever known, were powerless to resist Stella's summons. Prince Tibor looked as though he wished to protest, but no words left his sensual lips. Jethro gazed around him. Although Jethro was not the sort of man to show nervousness, Cal decided it was fair to say the mercenary no longer looked confident.

"Hidercyme."

Like puppets with Stella as their master, the gorgeously attired, undead group left their places and moved into the middle of the room, surrounding Stella and Jethro. Cal clenched his fist on his thigh. If Stella made one small mistake now, or if Jethro really was stronger than her, she would be torn apart.

"Oflinnan." The group froze at the word, becoming statue-like in their instant stillness. Cal spared a brief glance around him at the other guests. Those who were alive or never living had not been affected by Stella's commands. They remained in their seats, watching the scene unfolding before them with fascination. Stella could not have chosen a better way to demonstrate her powers and put to rest any lingering doubts about who she was.

Moncoya leaned forward in his chair, his expression orgasmic. "What are we waiting for? Finish this."

The silence that followed his words was so absolute that Cal was able to hear Stella's words as she spoke to Jethro. "What do you say? Shall we do as he says and finish it?"

He looked down at her in some bemusement, testing the barrier between them again with his hand. For a man facing certain death, he was surprisingly calm. "Your call. I seem to be yours to command."

She smiled. "*Swinsian*. Play for us." The ghostly musicians picked up their instruments and an appropriately eerie melody filled the air. "*Fríce*. Dance."

In one single, concerted movement, the vampires, ghosts and werewolves unfroze and took up their places on the dance floor. Instantly the room became a whirl of brightly colored waltzing figures. The seated guests seemed to heave a collective sigh. All except Moncoya, who looked furious. Cal kept his gaze on Stella and Jethro, who were still in the center of the room, the dancers swirling around them. Perhaps because he was concentrating so hard, he could still hear what they were saying, even from a few feet away.

Jethro had begun to laugh. "Shall we join them?"

Stella stepped into the circle of his outstretched arms. They waltzed a few circuits of the room and, despite Jethro's height, Cal had difficulty following their progress among the other dancers. Many of the seated guests had risen now and joined in the dance. The waiters who were attempting to serve the next course were seriously impeded in their efforts to cross the room.

Moncoya remained slumped in his seat, playing with the blade of his upended fish knife. His expression was murderous.

"I'd not want to be in Stella's shoes right now." Lorcan kept his voice low.

"Stella is too valuable to him for him to do her any harm. For now. She's not the one who needs to take care," Cal murmured. If he knew anything about Moncoya, it would be Jethro who would pay the price for what had just happened. His keen eyes scoured the room, locating Stella and Jethro again close to the door. He kept his gaze fixed on them. They were talking conspiratorially. Was he the only one who noticed the moment when Jethro slipped out of the room? He hoped so.

A few minutes later, Stella made her way through the dancers and back to her seat. "Looks like the party is getting started at last."

Moncoya's slow-burning scowl deepened. "Where is your new mercenary friend?"

"Jethro? He had to leave." She gave Moncoya a bright smile, for all the world as if this was an everyday conversation, a normal party.

For a second, as he glared back at her, Moncoya made no attempt to hide the full force of his fury. The mask dropped to reveal his true nature. His eyes blazed pure sidhe fire and his lips were drawn back in a snarl. Cal saw Stella recoil slightly as she realized exactly what she was dealing with. Without speaking, Moncoya rose from his seat, brushing past the dancers as he stormed from the room.

"Was it something I said?" The words might have been flippant, but Stella's voice wobbled slightly. "Should we be doing something to stop him? It wasn't Jethro's fault I turned the tables on him."

"Jethro is an adventurer. And, even for a sorcerer, he leads a surprisingly charmed life," Cal said. "He usually manages to keep himself out of trouble."

One of the sidhes whose job it was to stand guard over him snapped at him to stop talking. With a slight shrug and a grin in Stella's direction, Cal sat back in his seat, parodying acquiescence. His mind was racing. Had they fooled Moncoya at all? The faerie king would know better than anyone that Cal could not be contained by a prison cell. Only in Darnantes had he ever been confined, and then not by walls of stone or iron bars. Cal was not about to make the mistake of underestimating his greatest enemy at this late stage. If this was a double bluff, they could be in deep trouble. Moncoya had mentioned a surprise. Cal had a feeling any surprises planned by Moncoya were not going to be pleasant ones.

Something else occurred to him and he turned back to Stella. "When Moncoya told you to bring him to his knees, what did Jethro say to make you smile?"

"He asked me why I was throwing myself away on a simpering faerie." Her green eyes sparkled as she leaned across Lorcan to speak softly to Cal. "He said I should find myself a real man. I didn't tell him I already had."

Cal's shoulders shook with silent laughter. Unable to help himself, he ignored his guards and angled closer to her. Moncoya, entering the room again with his genial expression restored, could not have heard what they were saying. Pausing in the doorway, his eyes narrowed as he observed the exchange taking place between his bride-to-be and the man he hated more than any other. A smile that touched his lips but did not reach his eyes appeared and he clapped his hands together. The musicians halted their playing instantly.

"The mercenary has been captured. Take the bastard sorcerer to the dungeons to join him and see that he is guarded round-the-clock. Should he escape, it will be death to those who are on guard at the time."

The sidhes converged on Cal's chair, pulling him roughly to his feet. He kept his gaze fixed on Stella's up-turned countenance, trying desperately in those seconds before he was dragged away to convey the strength of his feelings to her. He didn't know if he succeeded. As the crowd of dancers parted and he craned his neck for a final glimpse of her, he took his own measure of comfort from the answering glow in the green depths of her eyes.

Chapter 21

"Come, my friends. Let us continue our feast. There will be time enough for dancing later." Moncoya's voice rang out around the hall and his guests obediently returned to their seats.

Lorcan bent closer to Stella. "Don't worry. He'll sit quiet in his cell. Let them think they have him trapped. Then, when the time is right, he'll come and join us." The whispered words went some way toward restoring her composure.

"Is the food not to your liking, my star?" Moncoya leaned uncomfortably nearer to her, his shoulder almost touching hers. "You have eaten nothing. My cook will be most perturbed."

"I'm not very hungry. I find being challenged to a gladiatorial contest in the middle of a meal tends to drive away my appetite." Stella kept her gaze on his. No matter how much she wanted to look away. Actually, she wanted to run away. All the way to the dungeons below the palace and into Cal's arms.

"The victory was yours." His expression darkened. "Even if your method of achieving it was not my preference."

"You'd rather I'd had your guests rip him limb from limb?"

"But of course. And, after tomorrow, you will do as I say. Always." A smile—one that was really a warning—gleamed before he turned back to his plate.

Stella toyed with her own untouched food, consoling herself with the reminder that he was wrong. Tomorrow she would be free of Moncoya, the prophecy and the huge burden placed upon her. She just had to keep telling herself that instead of focusing on the members of this glittering gathering. There was Tanzi looking like a 1930s movie icon in floor-length, shimmering silver, Vashti combining elegance and functionality in a figure-hugging black catsuit, Prince Tibor and his faithful companion, Dimitar, sitting still and watchful with their food untouched. And, of course, there were the beautiful party people. The flaming eyes of Moncoya's sidhes followed Stella's every move. It was an oppressive feeling, as if their stares were driving the air from her lungs. *How did we think we could do this and come out alive?* She tried to tell herself fatalistic thoughts were crowding in on her because it was all so real, so close. In her heart she knew the real reason. It was because Cal wasn't there.

"Will you do one small thing to perk up my Irish spirits, me darlin' girl?" She turned to look at Lorcan, a question forming on her lips. She never got to ask it. Lorcan's attention was fixed on the entrance to the banquet hall, his expression of incredulity almost comical.

The woman who stood poised just inside the door was

tall and willow slender with hair as white as snow and an equally pale complexion. In contrast, her eyes were so dark that, like black holes in the emptiness of space, they reflected no light. Her features were sharply hewn and, while the overall impression was of beauty, it was also of ice. She wore a floating gown in shades of blue and green that made Stella think of seaweed stirred by ocean waves.

"My God, what a striking-looking woman. Who is she?" Stella whispered.

"Niniane. Known as the Lady of the Lake," Lorcan whispered back. "The most powerful sorceress in Otherworld. The vainest being that ever walked either world. The woman who, centuries ago, seduced Merlin, cast a spell on him and trapped him in a prison made of rock in the French forest of Brocéliande, or, as it was better known at that time, Darnantes."

"You could have just said she's Cal's ex. I'd have known who you meant." Stella tried to keep the huffiness out of her voice. She didn't think her efforts worked.

"Ah, so you know all about that." With difficulty, Lorcan dragged his eyes away from Niniane, who was making her way across the room toward Moncoya. "Look, Stella, we all have that one ex we don't want to talk about. In my case she was a sweet girl who made me all my favorite meals and then tried to run me down with her car when she caught me talking to her best friend. Cal's ex just happens to be Niniane…the woman who nearly destroyed the whole universe when he attempted to end it with her."

Moncoya had risen from his seat and gone to greet Niniane with his hands outstretched. At the same time, Prince Tibor joined them and the threesome stood together, hands clasped. It was a powerful statement to all those assembled. A triumvirate you wouldn't want to mess with. *But we've got no choice. We have to take them on.* Stella felt an icy finger prod her spine.

The implication of Niniane's presence hit Stella with the force of a rampaging bull. She clutched Lorcan's arm so hard that he let out a yelp. "She's what Moncoya was talking about."

"I've lost all feeling in that arm now."

"Lorcan, we have to get down to the dungeons and get Cal out. Right now."

"Sure, it may have escaped your attention, but we are right in the middle of your engagement party. And, in case you hadn't noticed, your other half has some nasty friends lined up on his side."

"Don't you see?" Impatience was making Stella almost incoherent. She jabbed a finger in the direction of the threesome in the middle of the room. "Moncoya said he had a surprise for Cal. One that meant Cal wouldn't be able to escape from his cell."

Realization dawned on Lorcan's face. "Oh, shit, Stella. It's her, isn't it? Niniane is Moncoya's surprise. She incarcerated Cal at Darnantes and she's been biding her time waiting to get him ever since he escaped. Now she's back so they can imprison him indefinitely again."

"You cannot leave your own betrothal feast." Moncoya's face was a mask of suspicion. "What will our guests think?"

"I don't care what they think. If I don't get some fresh air, I'll throw up all over your chef's spectacular dessert."

"I don't believe you."

"Try me." Stella challenged him with her eyes. "It's your own fault I feel like shit. You shouldn't have made me fight Jethro."

To the accompaniment of much "ooh-ing" and "aahing," four waiters were staggering into the banquet hall, weighed down by a platter upon which was an elaborate cake in the shape of a swan. Stella spared a moment to register an incongruous thought. *If I really was in love with him, the swan fetish would send me running screaming for the hills.*

"Very well. I will escort you out to the gardens for a few minutes."

Lorcan rose to his feet. "No need for both of you to leave your guests, Your Majesty. I'll take Stella for a walk around the gardens."

Moncoya's eyes narrowed. He glanced from Stella to Lorcan and back again. "Get back here soon."

"He'll have us followed," Lorcan muttered, grabbing Stella's elbow as they hurried out of the hall.

"We can take out a few sidhes." Once out into the long hallway, Stella broke into a run, propelling Lorcan along with her toward the building's grand entrance.

"You're starting to sound like Cal. Next thing you'll be telling me it would be a good idea to go in search of the Holy Grail. And anyway, it's not the sidhes I'm worried about. Before we even start on the subject of Moncoya, Niniane and Prince Tibor have each got the devil's own temper on them."

They stepped out into the sunlight. There was no one around. So far so good. "We'll worry about them if we need to. For now let's concentrate on the important stuff. How do we get to the dungeons from here?"

Lorcan glanced around. "Probably best if we go around to the back of the palace. I think there are steps down into the cellars and the dungeons are beyond those."

After teetering and stumbling for a few yards in the unfamiliar heels, Stella removed her shoes and, after throwing them into a laurel bush, followed Lorcan along the pool-table-perfect grass borders. Twice they were forced to press themselves back against nooks and crannies within the pale stone walls as patrolling sidhe guards passed uncomfortably close.

Lorcan rolled his eyes. "This reminds me of my cousin's wedding in Ballycasheen when I sneaked out to meet one of the bridesmaids. It was only when I'd had half the village after me with pickax handles did she think to mention she was to be married herself the next week."

"I thought you were terribly shy around women?" Stella whispered back as they tiptoed around a corner.

"That was the start of my shyness."

If the front of the castle was decorative, the rear, in contrast, was businesslike. Steep stone steps led down from the gardens to the basement level, and Stella immediately started to descend these. Lorcan, after a swift glance around, trailed after her. There was a nondescript door at the bottom of the stairs and Stella reached out a hand to open it.

Lorcan forestalled her. "Let me. We don't know what's inside."

Almost hopping with impatience, Stella let him go first. When Lorcan was fully inside the cellar, she peered around him into the pervading darkness. There was a musty smell of old sackcloth, candle wax and silver polish.

"This isn't a dungeon." Although she had whispered, her voice sounded unnaturally loud, as though she had yelled the words.

"Beyond the cellars, that's what I've heard said about Moncoya's dungeons. But it's too dark to see anything down here. We could be stumbling around all day, and Moncoya has us on the clock."

Stella could feel bitter frustration burning the back of her throat. *Focus.* Getting overemotional was not going to help Cal. She raised her arm and swept her hand in a wide arc around the cellar. Instantly, the darkened space was filled with golden light. It looked just like a cellar should. Piled high with the sort of household necessities a property as vast as Moncoya's palace would need to function.

Lorcan whistled. "Would've taken me ten minutes or more to get the place lit and I'd never have got it this bright."

Stella prowled around, becoming increasingly despondent. "I don't see anything that looks like it would lead to a dungeon."

"Not unless you count that massive trapdoor you're about to step onto."

It took only seconds for them to haul the wooden door up by pulling on the iron ring in its center. The wooden panels fell back against the stone floor with a loud thunk and Stella gazed into the depths below. Roughly hewn stone steps led down, but it was so dark that she could see only the top two. It would be like stepping into nothing. This was for Cal. She placed her bare foot on the top step.

"Do you not think this is all a bit too easy, Stella?" Lorcan's question made her pause half in and half out of the opening. "If yon faerie feller really has Cal down there, would he not have a better guard around him than this? Can we be sure we are not walking straight into a trap?"

"No. But if there's even the slightest chance he's down here, I'm going anyway. With or without you."

Lorcan's sigh followed her into the murk. "You two really are made for each other, do you know that?"

I do. I'm just not sure if Cal agrees, Stella thought, as she felt her way gingerly into what felt like a rocky pit. But that was a problem for another time. Although she could no longer see her hand in front of her face, she was reluctant to use her powers to light their way. If there were any sidhes down here—and surely there must be?—it would be foolish to give them advance warning of their arrival. Lorcan was right. It felt like a trap. Using her right hand to guide her along the jagged wall, she held her left hand out in front of her. Beneath her feet the rocky floor was uneven and slimy. Water dripped onto her head and shoulders, and an ominous scurrying sound ahead signaled that they were not alone. Although it seemed the company might be of the rodent rather than the faerie variety.

"Ow! Shit…" Lorcan's yelp of pain echoed in emptiness. "Banged my head," he explained as Stella reached for him in the blackness.

"Who's there?" Another voice rang out in response, coming to them as though along a tunnel. It wasn't Cal, but Stella's heart leaped hopefully in her chest as she recognized it.

"Jethro?" Stella moved on again.

"Stella! Thank God! There are rats down here the size of mountain dogs."

Since their voices had not brought any sidhe guards screeching down upon them, Stella took the opportunity to cast a faint light ahead of her. As she had pictured, they were in a narrow tunnel. She could stand with an inch or two to spare. Behind her, Lorcan was uncomfortably hunched over. Up ahead the passage widened. Hurrying along to that point, she was faced with another channel. This one formed a T shape with the first and was much wider and higher. Along one side it was divided into a series of small cells, each of which had iron bars across the front. Jethro was standing inside one of these. He looked considerably less well-groomed than the last time Stella had seen him.

Stella didn't waste time. "Where's Cal?"

"They took him to the end cell. I've tried talking to

him, but he hasn't been answering me. Not since Niniane came down to see him."

Cold terror seized her. "She has already been down here?"

"Yes, only minutes after they brought him…"

Not waiting to hear any more, she ran to the end of the line of cells. Lorcan was hard at her heels. The last cell in the row looked different from the others. In place of iron bars, there were slabs of white granite. It had been bricked up. Lorcan ran a finger along the joint between two stones, bringing it away to show Stella that the mortar was still drying.

"Fresh." His voice was neutral, but his expression was raw. "That's why it was so easy for us to get in here. They don't need guards. That bitch Niniane got to him before we could."

Chapter 22

"There must be a way to get through it. Why can't the three of us working together even make a dent in it?" Tired and dejected, Stella slumped against the granite wall. She no longer cared that she had been missing from the party for over an hour, or that her dress was covered in a combination of dust and slime, her shoes gone and her fingernails broken from scrabbling at the marble slabs. She only cared that Cal was behind those bricks. Her head was aching with the fierceness of concentration, but her efforts had been to no avail. Nothing she did, even combining her own powers with those of Lorcan and Jethro—whom they had freed from behind his bars—had made any difference.

"Stella, even if we could get past the wall, she's bespelled him. It's what she did at Darnantes. The only person who can get to Cal now is Niniane herself."

"No." She shook her head. "The Dominions got him out last time. They will have to do it again."

Lorcan sat down next to her. "Sure, and didn't it take them centuries?" His voice was gentle. "And don't we have a big battle to prepare for tomorrow?"

She looked up at him, tears blurring her vision. "I can't do it without him."

"You're not without him. He's given you the strength to be ready for this by teaching you everything he knows."

Jethro cleared his throat. "I know I can't replace Cal, but you can count me in. I'm with Team Stella from now on."

"Come on." Lorcan rose to his feet, reaching down a hand and pulling Stella up. "I'll tell Moncoya you're feeling no better and you've taken to your bed. Go to your room and get some rest." He eyed Jethro thoughtfully. "I suppose you'll be wanting somewhere to hide out until the fun starts tomorrow?"

"Does that mean we're going to be roommates?"

"Let me tell you now, Jethro my friend, any snoring and it's the balcony where you'll be spending the night."

Even their banter couldn't raise a smile from Stella as, with a final backward glance at the walled-up cell, she trailed behind them out of the tunnel. How could she explain to Lorcan that her feelings of utter defeat weren't just about facing Moncoya on the following day? The only thing that mattered anymore was the yawning chasm of awfulness that was the prospect of never seeing Cal again.

Closing and locking the door to the queen's chambers behind her, Stella waded across the cloying carpet of the sitting room, grimacing as she stripped off her ruined dress. She halted as she stepped out of the offending garment, a frown creasing her forehead. The door to the bedroom was open. She was certain she had closed that door behind her when she left to go down to the feast. More than certain. She remembered it clearly because the beautiful crimson wrap had caught on the handle.

Someone had been in these rooms in her absence. A sound from the bedroom—so slight it might almost have been her imagination—caught her attention. Whoever had broken in was still there.

Stella's exhaustion vanished and a tremor of fear and anticipation thrilled through her veins as she peered into the darkened bedroom. Who had a reason to break into her room? There were a few possibilities. Was it Vashti still harboring a grudge that Stella was occupying her sainted mother's chambers? Moncoya feeling amorous? Prince Tibor seeking revenge for being forced to be part of Stella's undead puppet show? Niniane seeking her out in jealousy over Cal? Or another Otherworld power looking to claim the heart of the necromancer star?

The voice that came from the gloom from beyond the bedroom door was unexpected and familiar. And beloved. "After the cave, I'm not sure I can get used to a bed this size. But I'm willing to give it a try as long as you hurry up and join me."

"Cal?" The word came out as a squeak.

"Were you expecting someone else?"

In reply, she ran into the bedroom, forgetting her powers as her fingers groped wildly for the light switch. Cal laughed and turned on a lamp beside the bed. Stella stood still for a moment, drinking in the sight of him sitting on the bed, propped against the bank of pillows with his hands hooked behind his head and his long legs stretched in front of him. When she finally grasped that it was true—it really *was* him and not some wild trick of her imagination—she flew across the distance between them, throwing herself onto the bed and into his arms.

Between covering every available part of him with kisses, Stella fired a series of increasingly incoherent questions at him. After submitting to this onslaught for some time, Cal eventually caught hold of her and held her still, smoothing her hair with one hand. "Stella, look at me. Speak slowly."

She subsided against him, her limbs still trembling. "How can you be here? Jethro told me Niniane had been to see you and I saw the bricked-up cell for myself."

Cal frowned. "You've been down to the dungeons?"

She held up a hand to show him her ragged nails. "I tried to tear the wall down with my bare hands."

Catching her hand up to his lips, he kept it there as his eyes darkened to the gray of a storm-laden sky. "I wouldn't have put you through that for the world. But I never imagined you'd leave the party before it finished. When you came in just now, I thought you'd come straight up here from the banquet hall. My God, I feel like such a louse."

Stella took his face in her hands and very slowly pressed her lips to his. She touched the tip of her tongue to his luscious lower lip, tracing its perfect line. Cal angled his mouth to deepen the kiss, cradling her head with his hand. Until that precise moment as his touch unthawed her, Stella hadn't even been aware that she was cold. Now she knew that the instant she had seen that granite wall the blood in her veins had turned to ice. "I still don't understand how you are here. I saw the bricks with my own eyes. How did you escape?"

"I've had centuries to prepare for this. I knew Niniane would come for me again one day so I made ready for her. It was a case of letting her believe she'd trapped me again while making sure I kept my own, more powerful, barrier spell around me." His arms tightened around her. "Her magic never touched me this time, Stella. It never came close and she didn't suspect a thing. She went away laughing, telling me she would be back to see me later. As soon as she'd gone, I left the cell and came up here to wait for you. Even so, I can't be sure I could fool her twice."

"Tell me about Niniane. Why does she hate you so much?"

"Niniane doesn't hate me. That's the problem. But I don't want to hold you in my arms and have to think about her at the same time."

Stella rested her chin on his chest. "Just lately, I've read some of the stories about what is supposed to have happened between you and her. Now I need to hear the truth from you."

He sighed. "There has been a lot of nonsense written about what went on between us. Only Niniane and I know what really happened and her version would be...distorted. The Dominion knows some of it. Lorcan knows a little more. The things you have read are part of the folklore that has built up around me over the centuries." His smile was self-deprecating. "The modern world thinks it invented the cult of celebrity, Stella, but I am living proof that it has existed for thousands of years. What I'm trying to say is, it's very unlikely you've read anything with even a grain of truth about me and Niniane. Oh, we had a relationship. I was dazzled by her...at first. Niniane is a chameleon. She was able to make me believe she was something she was not. Good, kind, pure of heart. It wasn't long before I began to see through her. She is the most malevolent being I have ever encountered." He stopped, appearing to consider the matter. "And, yes, I am including Moncoya in that. Moncoya's evil stems from his out-of-control ambition. Niniane simply enjoys poisoning everything around her."

"You mean it's her hobby?"

He laughed, pulling her down so that he could kiss her again. "It's exactly like a vile hobby. When I realized what she was, I tried to end it. That was when things went from bad to worse."

"She didn't go gracefully?" Stella squirmed with pleasure as he ran his hand down the curve of her waist and over her hip.

"She didn't go at all. She simply refused to listen to what I was saying. From then on, wherever I went Niniane was there. She behaved as though we were still together, clinging to me, telling me that I was just afraid to admit my true feelings for her. When I tried to avoid her, she started sending me endless poems about how she wanted me to share her pain."

"Like the medieval equivalent of posting sad song lyrics on your Facebook page so your ex knows how much you're hurting."

He looked perplexed. "Are you trying to remind me of the chasm between you and me?"

Stella shook her head. "Just the opposite. I'm pointing out that the entity of the mad ex has always been there. It's only the technology that's evolved."

"It was frightening. She went quiet for a while and I thought she'd got the message. Then the threats started."

"She threatened you?"

"No. She's not stupid. She knew I wouldn't respond to threats against myself, so she directed her menace to others instead. 'We need to talk. Meet me at the lakeside. Be there or a fire will engulf the village of Mickle Bunby.' That was just the start."

His expression was bleak and Stella knew that the memory was painful. She pressed a kiss to the corner of his mouth and he turned on his side, propping himself on one elbow so that he could look at her. "Did you go?"

"I had to. I knew she would carry out her threats if I didn't. Each meeting was the same. She was convinced I

loved her. I just couldn't see it. Why was I fighting the inevitable? The same questions and pleas, then ultimately
threats of revenge. Over and over. It culminated in her
threatening to bring about the end of the mortal world if
I didn't swear my undying love."

"Did you do it?"

"I asked her for some time to think. I couldn't see a way
out. I knew she would carry out her threat but I couldn't
bear the thought of spending eternity with Niniane. I hid
myself away in a cave deep in the ancient forest of Brocéliande in the Bretan region of France."

"Darnantes." Stella said the word in the same doom-
laden tone that Cal used in his dreams.

"Yes, it was one of my favorite places. Then. Not now.
Not anymore. Unknown to me, Niniane had tracked me
down and was watching me. Stalking me, people would
no doubt say these days. The elders of a village in the area
close to the forest appealed for my help with a minor problem and, while I was there, I happened to have a conversation with a young girl. I didn't even remember talking
to her afterward."

"Let me guess. Niniane remembered it," Stella said.

"Not only did she remember, she also convinced herself I had fallen in love with this girl. She became like a
woman possessed. Or—more dangerously—like a sorceress possessed. That night I fell asleep in my cave. The
next day, when I awoke, I found I couldn't leave. The only
person who could get in to see me was Niniane. Her rea-
soning was that if she couldn't have me then no one else
could either. She brought me food and water—when she
remembered—and taunted me with the stories she was
telling the world."

"How did you escape?"

"It took a long time. In the end, it was Lorcan who brought

about my release. He tried repeatedly to get into the cave, and he knew better than to believe Niniane's tales that she had been forced to imprison me to protect herself. He went to the Dominions and asked for their intervention. At first they refused. Their role is to oversee, not to become actively involved. But I was too valuable for them to lose. And events were shaping in Otherworld that would lead to this looming confrontation. Eventually, they agreed to release me. There were conditions attached."

Stella swallowed hard. "Am I a condition?"

"You were once. You stopped being that a long time ago. In return for my release the Dominions put me to work as a protector of the barrier between Otherworld and the mortal realm. Guarding you was part of that because of the prophecy."

"And Niniane has been waiting for a chance to get you back in her clutches all this time."

"Yes. I don't think the words *forgive* or *forget* are in her vocabulary."

"There are stories out there that she was an innocent young girl until you pursued and then seduced her. Then you taught her magic, which she eventually managed to use against you by entombing you in a rock. She had to do it because your sexual demands were so insatiable."

"Niniane was always good at propaganda. Believe me, she was about as innocent as sin, and if there was any pursuing being done it was by her." He gave a rueful grin. "Insatiable? Is that really what is being said?"

"Yep. Merlin the sex pest," Stella teased, sliding her hands under his T-shirt and lifting it over his head.

He groaned. "That bad?"

"Not at all." Stella gave a chuckle, moving on to undo his jeans. "On the contrary, it's very good. I should know."

Cal shrugged out of the rest of his clothes quickly,

catching hold of Stella and pulling her hard against his chest. "You have a wicked sense of humor. I think we need to do something about that. I have this plan…"

Before he could put any plan into action, there was an almighty pounding on the door and Moncoya's voice almost took the wood from its hinges. "The mercenary has escaped. Open up at once!"

Stella scrabbled for some clothes, dragging on shorts and a vest over her underwear. "Quickly, Cal, find somewhere to hide." The words were unnecessary. He was gone.

She opened the door, feigning sleepiness and bewilderment. Moncoya almost bowled her over as he burst through into the room, his eyes darting wildly into every corner.

"Has he been here?"

"Who?" Stella yawned and stretched for a bit of added effect.

"Jethro the mercenary, of course. The other bastard mongrel son of a mortal bitch will never be free again."

"Ezra, you are going to have to be a little more specific about whom you are cursing. And maybe you could come back and do it at a more reasonable hour?"

He grabbed her by the shoulders and pushed her hard against the wall so that the breath left her lungs in a gasp. "Stop playing games with me!"

Stella caught a glimpse of familiar movement on the edge of her vision and raised a hand to forestall Cal. If he stepped in to help her now, Moncoya would know he was free and all would be lost. They were so close. Moncoya was unraveling before their eyes. Cal had said he couldn't be sure he could fool Niniane twice. If the sorceress got her way and Cal really was rendered ineffective, Stella and Lorcan would be weakened to the point of helplessness even with Jethro on their side. Niniane was Cal's kryptonite. They had to keep him secret and keep her away from him until the final confrontation. She sensed the shadowy figure calming as if Cal's own thoughts echoed hers.

Finding her breath, and with it her voice, Stella whirled herself away from Moncoya. "If this is a taste of married life, you are not selling it to me."

Moncoya ran a hand through his hair, ruffling its careful disorder. *Things must be bad.* Stella bit the inside of her cheek to stop herself from smiling at the incongruous thought. "Jethro may seek revenge. You cannot be alone tonight."

"Call me old-fashioned, but no way are we spending the night before our wedding together."

Moncoya looked as if he could cheerfully have strangled her. Maintaining control of his temper with an obvious effort, he nodded. "Very well. I will send guards to stay here with you."

"They can sit outside the door. I'll call them if I need them." Stella forestalled his protest. "I need my sleep, Ezra. After all, a girl wants to look her best for her wedding day."

He turned on his heel and stalked out without a response. Stella hurried to lock the door after him.

"If I didn't know better, I'd say he might be regretting his decision to marry me, after all. What do you think?"

Cal materialized just behind her. Still naked. And gloriously erect, from what she could feel as his hands gripped her hips and he drew her back against his body. "I think the faerie king may well have met his match in the necromancer star. I'm also wondering why the hell we're wasting valuable time talking about him."

Chapter 23

"I don't think my bridegroom would approve of this as my wedding day alarm call," Stella murmured as Cal's lips traced a line up her neck and along her jaw. "Not that *I'm* complaining, you understand."

He took her face between his palms, catching the soft moan that escaped her with his mouth when he moved his lips across hers and his tongue swept inside. Stella moved closer, fitting the contours of her body to his like two parts of an interlocking puzzle. The long, thick length of his erection pressed insistently against her stomach. He ravished her mouth slowly, stroking, licking and sucking until she was gasping and whimpering with need.

"I want you all the time. Every minute," he whispered.

"That's good, because I want you all the time, too." Her voice was husky in response.

Cal sucked in a deep, ragged breath. He should go. Instead, his fingers strayed to her breast. He was playing with fire by staying here while the palace bustled into life. But those mewling sounds Stella was making were driving him wild with desire. And this was the kind of fire he liked playing with.

Moving between Stella's thighs, he nudged her knees apart. The broad head of his cock stroked her opening and Stella surged against him.

"Please…"

Slowly, he pushed inside her, stretching her sensitized muscles. He began to move gently, working just the tip of his cock in and out, going only a fraction deeper with each movement. Stella ground her pelvis upward. Cal ignored the mute invitation to thrust deeper, continuing to tease her, rocking in and out in a slow, tormenting rhythm that was delicious agony for both of them.

Stella dug her nails into his shoulder. "Cal, if you don't stop torturing me I'll scream."

"You can't. There are sidhes just outside the door." He smiled into her eyes.

In answer, Stella curved her legs around his hips so that he sank into her, stretching her tight flesh and penetrating deep as she yielded and opened to him. She lifted her hips, meeting his lunge with a gasp. Cal ground his hips in a circle, delighting in the expression on Stella's face as she closed her eyes and let her head fall back.

"You like that?"

Her response was a muffled sound that he took to be a sign of approval. Her muscles gripped him tight, embedding him deep within her as he thrust slowly and purposefully. They strained together, finding the rhythm they had already made uniquely theirs. Stella's nails dug deep into his shoulders, urging him to go harder and faster until, with a sharp high cry, she shattered with pleasure around him. Cal's own climax followed seconds later, starting at the base of his cock and radiating out until his whole body shook and trembled with the force of it.

Sometime later, the world was restored to normality and Cal lay on his side, studying Stella's face. "You look troubled." As soon as he uttered the words, he winced. She had every reason to be worried, after all. He was about to send her into battle against some of the most powerful forces Otherworld had ever known.

Stella leaned on one elbow so that she could look at the clock. The hands seemed to have speeded up all of a sudden. "Moncoya will have more surprises in store for us later, won't he?"

"You can count on it." To hell with the time. Cal drew her back into his arms. "The only thing that is predictable about Moncoya is his unpredictability."

"How do you know so much about him?"

There it was. The question upon which everything, including Cal's own identity and very being, hinged. The only question that mattered. The one question he could never answer. Because if Stella found out the truth, the look he saw now in her eyes would vanish. That warm glow that told him how much she loved and trusted him would be gone forever and in its place he would see hard, cold disgust. It was something he couldn't risk. Not today. He had promised her the truth and he would keep that promise…once the battle for Otherworld was over. He would tell her and then he would walk away from her. Forever. Even if it cost him his very soul, he would not stay to see the expression in those green eyes change.

"Know thy enemy. They are wise words," he said.

Sliding from the bed and tugging on his jeans, he held out a hand. Stella wrapped a sheet around her and went to him. Cal led her to the balcony, standing back so that they could survey the scene below, without being seen themselves.

It didn't look like a battleground. From the balcony of the queen's chambers, it looked like a celebrity wedding venue in an exotic location. The Italian Riviera or a privately owned island.

Chairs were set in rows on squares of green velvet lawn, facing a flower-laden arch. The scent of lemon and orange trees vied with the sharp tang of pine forests covering the steeply sloping hillsides. Lush formal gardens rolled away to the edge of a vast shimmering lake. Behind the gathering guests, the fairy-tale palace glimmered white in the afternoon sunlight, and beyond that soaring cliffs resembled the jagged teeth of an ancient slumbering dragon.

Silently, Stella took all of this in, her eyes solemn. Cal kept his own gaze fixed on her face. When she spoke at last, her words were unexpected. "That was only half of the quote."

"Pardon?"

"You said 'know thy enemy.' That's only half of the quote." Her green gaze was very direct. "Know thyself, know thy enemy. That's the full quote, Cal."

"Aren't you a sight for Irish eyes?" Lorcan lounged in the doorway of Stella's room, looking her up and down. "Tell me this and tell me true, do you have the big feller hidden away somewhere safe?"

"How did you guess?" She glanced into the corridor to check that no one was around before closing the door.

"Sure, and what else could have brought that smile to your face on a day like today?"

Stella gave him a quick précis of Cal's escape from the dungeons. "He's gone to find Jethro. Then the two of them will be waiting on the hillside for our signal."

"And what will that be?"

"When you place my hand in Moncoya's."

The thought made her shiver. There was no going back now. Stella cast a final glance at her reflection in the mirror. All credit to Moncoya. For an evil, murdering bastard, he had impeccable taste in clothes. Stella had been reluctant to wear a dress of his choosing, but she had nothing else that was suitable. The dress, flowers and shoes that were delivered to her room that morning were exquisite in their bohemian beauty. She didn't like to dwell on how closely Moncoya must have observed her to get it so absolutely right. The whole outfit had been chosen to complement her delicate, elfin looks. The sleeveless dress, which fastened up the back with tiny pearl buttons, was made from vintage ivory lace. It was perfectly fitted over her upper body, skimming her hips and ending in handkerchief points at midcalf. On her feet were sandals in the same ivory color, adorned with more pearls. A circle of tiny white rosebuds nestled in the glossy darkness of her hair. She grimaced. It was going to be hell getting blood out of the lace.

"Ready?" Lorcan held out his arm.

"As I'll ever be." Gathering up a bouquet of rosebuds tied with ribbons, she slid her hand into the crook of his elbow. Lorcan didn't scrub up too badly himself. He looked rakishly smart in a pale gray suit and blue shirt.

When they stepped out into the sunlight, Stella could almost have believed she had been transported into the mortal realm and someone else's celebrity lifestyle. The champagne-sipping guests were seated and, as she and Lorcan walked slowly down the aisle between their chairs, they craned their heads to get a glimpse of the bride. Just as if this was a normal wedding. As if she was not walking to meet the faerie king. As if everyone didn't know this was a crazy charade in which all were waiting to see who would make the first move.

Moncoya was standing beneath the arch of flowers with Prince Tibor at his side. In front of them was Niniane. Of course. This was the sort of ceremony that was crying out to be performed by a mad sorceress.

Moncoya was jaunty in a faintly military three-piece suit with epaulettes and gold braid edging. Prince Tibor looked as if he had taken time out from a photo shoot for a men's fashion magazine. Floating robes of gray green enhanced Niniane's witchy remoteness. They all turned to watch Stella and Lorcan as they approached. Moncoya's eyes blazed sidhe fire and triumph. Niniane's gaze could have frozen the pit of hell itself. The prince smiled. Still no hint of fangs, Stella noted, her mind determined to dwell on the smallest detail.

Soon, she told herself, *this ridiculous pretense will be over and we can all get on with trying to slaughter each other. And when that happens*—she looked directly at Niniane with a bright smile—*you are all mine, lady.* Showing a flicker of emotion for the first time, the sorceress recoiled slightly as though she could sense the trend of Stella's thoughts.

"You look beautiful, my star." Moncoya came toward her. For a moment Stella thought he was going to kiss her. Although it was a perfectly natural gesture for a bride-groom, she wasn't sure she would be able to stop herself from pulling away. Fortunately, he simply moved to take her other arm so that he and Lorcan escorted her the last few steps together.

When they stood before Niniane, with their backs to the assembled guests, Stella drew a steadying breath. This was it. Everything seemed to slow to half speed. Lorcan withdrew her hand from his arm. His eye closed in an infinitesimal wink.

"Showtime."

He placed Stella's hand in Moncoya's and, the instant their fingertips touched, an explosion ripped through the eastern wing of the palace. The uppermost part of the turret exploded in flames while chunks of white marble rained down onto the gardens and the wedding party. Chaos ensued as the guests scurried from their seats, screaming and seeking cover. Instinct prompted them to run away from the scene of the explosion, but the only shelter offered was the dense forest on the hillside. As soon as the first partygoers moved in that direction, a pack of Iberian sidhes burst out of the foliage and stormed toward the open ground.

Without releasing Stella's hand, Moncoya barked a command to Prince Tibor. "Deal with this. You—" he modified his tone slightly as he addressed Niniane "—may begin the ceremony." His hand was like iron closing around Stella's wrist. "This is a formality. We shared food. You are already mine."

Prince Tibor whirled away, issuing commands to Dimitar in a guttural Germanic language. Stella risked a glance over her shoulder. Within seconds, all around the prince, ebbing and flowing as if drawn to him on currents of air, the vampire hordes were massing. It was clear that his powers, although very different from Stella's, were equal to her own. The Iberian sidhes would be outnumbered in minutes.

It was time to stop pretending. Stella tugged her hand free. "Sorry, Ezra, I hate to disillusion you, but I've been cheating on you. I've shared food with another man." She dropped her bouquet at Niniane's feet.

"Cavalry's here." Lorcan nodded to where Cal and Jethro were advancing with the Iberian sidhes.

"I can't tell what's happening down here. I need to be able to see what's going on." Stella looked around.

"What you need is a command post."

"Exactly. That'll do." She pointed to an ornate pagoda on top of an incline. "Tell Cal I'll be up there."

When she reached the vantage point, the scene below her had changed beyond recognition from the wedding party of minutes earlier. The battle lines were drawn. Moncoya's sidhes, the vampires and their accompanying human servants were facing the hopelessly outnumbered Iberian sidhes, led by Cal, Lorcan and Jethro. Several guests, injured by flying debris from the explosion, scurried—bloodied and covered in white dust—out of the way. Bright flames and black smoke pouring from its eastern wing marred the storybook perfection of the palace.

"You?" Stella's attention was drawn to Niniane as she heard her speak for the first time. The sorceress was staring at Cal with a mixture of loathing and longing on her face. "How can this be?"

"Sometimes you're only as good as your last trick," he told her, walking away. So much for kryptonite. It seemed Cal really had managed to break free of her at last. Stella winced as Niniane's desperate howls followed him. Someone really needed to sit Niniane down—bottle of wine in one hand, tissues in the other—and talk to her about handling a breakup with dignity.

Moncoya's attention had been fixed on his beautiful palace. When he finally dragged his gaze away, the air around him shimmered with the force of his fury. "Get on with this."

Obedient to his command, Moncoya's sidhes rushed forward. Bravely, the Iberian sidhes prepared for their onslaught. Stella tried to follow the action as fierce hand-to-hand fighting ensued. There was nothing she could do about this. Sidhes were not dead or undead. They had never been mortal. Her powers would be useless against them.

Prince Tibor issued a command and lightning fast, the vampires moved as one flowing mass to join the fray. Stella braced herself. This was something she could control. At least she could stop the vampires from harming the Iberian sidhes.

"Oflinnan." Stella issued the halt command from her vantage point at the same time that Cal's compelling tone rang out below her. Their combined power was such that they halted the vampires in their tracks instantly.

All around the vampires—frozen in place now like beautiful, monstrous statues—the fighting between the two opposing sidhe factions raged fast and vicious. Dirty tricks seemed to be compulsory. Across the distance between them, Stella had trouble locating Prince Tibor amid all the biting, gouging, kicking and scratching. Scanning the melee, she spotted him standing obediently stock-still in the midst of a particularly frenzied exchange. Nearby, Vashti punched one of the Iberian sidhes in the face before driving the full force of her elbow into his windpipe. Her prey fell to the ground and a pack of Moncoya's sidhes fell on him like ravening dogs. Stella looked away as they systematically ripped him apart. Unmoved, Vashti advanced toward her next victim.

Stella focused her full attention on the vampire prince. She needed him and his followers out of the way even though their human servants would continue fighting on behalf of their masters. She needed an uncluttered view of what was going on.

"Swactrian."

Although Stella spoke the Anglo-Saxon order to retreat

softly, the word reached the prince, acting like a charm to rouse him from his trance. Prince Tibor and his followers were gone with the swift flash and sway of movement that was unique to vampires. She breathed a sigh of relief. It was short-lived.

"You dare to give orders to my master, necromancer? You will pay for this impertinence."

Turning, she found herself confronted by the ice-carving features of Dimitar, Prince Tibor's human servant. Dimitar's smile deepened to a point beyond malevolence. His hand flashed out, grabbing her around the throat.

"Let go of me." Stella's words came out on a croak as his grip tightened, compressing her windpipe.

"I am not undead. I still live and breathe. You cannot command me, necromancer bitch."

"While that might be true, it doesn't mean a good kick in the balls won't make your eyes water." Coming up behind him, Jethro lifted Dimitar off his feet and away from Stella by the scruff of his neck. "What do you reckon, shall I throw this piece of shit into the lake?"

Massaging her bruised neck, Stella didn't answer. Before she could take stock of what was happening in the gardens below, a rumbling noise from the direction of the forest drew her attention. Even Dimitar stopped struggling in Jethro's hold and craned his head in that direction. It sounded like looming thunder or the first tremors of an earthquake. Stella looked down on where Moncoya was directing his followers to finish off the heavily outnumbered resistance fighters. Despite the yards between them, he was staring directly back at her. Her intuition told her his expression blazed pure exultation. The noise from the woodland grew louder and more distinct. It was a regular, rhythmic thud. Like giant footsteps looming ever nearer.

It was only when Cal appeared at her side, sliding a protective arm about her shoulders and staring at the hillside with a mixture of anticipation and dread, that Stella knew for sure they were in deep trouble.

Chapter 24

"I need to go to Stella." Cal shouted the words to Lorcan above the chaos around them. "Sooner or later Moncoya will try to get to her."

Lorcan nodded a response. "Keep our star safe."

"That's my job."

And even if it wasn't, he knew that keeping Stella safe would always come first with him from now on. That was how much she had changed him, changed his priorities. His life. As Cal was closing the ground between the raging battle and the pagoda where he could see Stella's slender, white-clad figure, two questions troubled him. First, where the hell were the werefalcons and elves? When he and Jethro had left the forest they had been hiding in the foliage, ready to come to the aid of the Iberian sidhes. Moncoya's sidhes were systematically destroying their resistance counterparts, yet, despite Cal signaling frantically, there was still no sign of the next wave of good guys. The second question was becoming increasingly bothersome. What the bloody hell *was* that noise?

"Ogres," he said as he slid an arm around Stella's shoulders, drawing her close against him.

"Oh. That doesn't sound good…"

He had no need to explain exactly how far from good it was. Before Stella had finished speaking, the hillside appeared to break apart as dozens of giant figures erupted from the trees. That explained what had happened to the werefalcons and elves. Cal hoped they had managed to get away before the cannibalistic ogres arrived. The thought of any of his friends ending up as a prebattle snack for an ogre was not one he relished.

"Tell me you have a plan." Jethro kept his eyes fixed on the huge, club-wielding ogres.

"Yes, tell us you do." Dimitar added his voice to the conversation.

Momentarily distracted, Cal regarded him in surprise. "Where did he come from?"

"No time for that now." Jethro pointed in the direction of the ogres. "My God, they must be eight foot tall."

"At least. I've seen ogres who are almost ten foot in height, although that's rare. The biggest ogre is usually the leader. Their intelligence is limited, so the tribe will follow orders from their leader blindly. Moncoya must have struck a deal with the leader of this particular tribe."

"Can we stop them?" Stella asked. The ogres were getting close to the gardens now. Once the giant figures reached the open ground, it would be a massacre.

"We can try. If we can take out their leader, they'll begin vying with each other to take over. An ogre leadership contest is nasty and bloody, and it can last for weeks. The good thing for us, is they'll be too busy fighting each other to do anything else." He looked down at Stella. Her eyes glowed with love and trust and his heart swelled in response. "This changes our game plan. Can you get Grindan here at once?"

Stella nodded. Moving away from the three men, she held her arms out wide as if in supplication. "Grindan the Faithful. Come to me, my friend. *Hidercyme.*"

Immediately, the ground beneath their feet began to tremble then shake wildly. The lake waters roiled as though coming to a boil. Cracks appeared in the surface of the grass, swiftly marring the perfect lawns. These joined and became one huge fissure, out of which Grindan and his army arose. Within seconds, the ranks of thousands of mounted warriors were lined up in front of the palace.

The ogres, startled by this new turn of events, halted in their tracks. Clustering like gigantic confused children around the tallest of their number, they seemed to be seeking reassurance from him before continuing. Cal nodded with grim satisfaction. At least they now knew which of the ogres was in charge.

"What are you waiting for?" Moncoya's impatient tones broke the absolute silence. "Ignore this distraction. Your orders are to kill all of the other necromancers...but bring me the star!"

On hearing those words, Stella gripped Cal's arm. "Lorcan is still down there."

"Lorcan can look after himself," Cal assured her. He hoped to God he was right. He and Lorcan had fought their way out of many a sticky situation, but they had never encountered anything of this magnitude before.

Grindan rode forward, his hand on his heart. "We are yours to command, *breguróf steorra.*"

"Thank you, Grindan. Kill the ogre leader." Stella pointed to the towering figure who was reassuring and rallying his followers. Then she swung her arm in the direction of Moncoya. "Then defeat the faerie king."

The ghostly warrior bowed low. "It is done."

Grindan rode back to the head of his troops and issued his commands. As the first of the ogres set foot on the lawns, the mounted warriors charged, meeting the giants in a head-on attack. Cal hoped that Lorcan wasn't somewhere in the middle. The ogres set about clubbing everything around them. The only consolation was that they lacked any sense of judgment and did not have the intellect to distinguish their allies from their enemies. Cal noted, with a certain wry satisfaction, that Moncoya was jumping up and down and screaming with rage as some of his own sidhes and vampire servants were felled in the path of the ogres.

"Do I need to call upon the corpse army?" Stella interrupted his concentration.

"Not yet. Let's see how this unfolds." Although some of his men were falling beneath the onslaught, Grindan was systematically driving his warriors toward the towering figure of the ogre leader.

"Good. Many of them have been through enough in their living years. I don't want to expose them to this carnage unless I have to."

Just when he didn't think he could possibly love her any more, Cal felt his heart expand with the strength of his feelings. She really was the star the world had waited for. Even in the midst of this battle, her thoughts were for the souls in her care. He reached for her hand and she returned his clasp gratefully.

"Is this what you saw all those centuries ago when the prophecy was born?" Stella asked.

"What I see is always annoyingly vague." Cal turned away from the battle momentarily to look at her. "The detail eludes me. I can only hope that this is the great chaos from which peace will be born."

"Grindan is gaining on the ogre leader," Stella pointed out.

Because of their limited intelligence, the ogres had not realized Grindan's intentions and had not thought to protect their leader. The tallest ogre was surrounded by hundreds of mounted warriors before he knew what was happening. Although they looked like toy soldiers in comparison to his bulk, their combined firepower and relentless harrying soon had him howling like a wounded dog. Minutes later, the ground shook as the ogre leader was brought crashing down. Stella turned her face into Cal's shoulder as Grindan's men drove their swords into his body over and over until the grass around him was soaked with a pool of dark crimson.

The other ogres stopped in their tracks, turning to look at the still-twitching body of their leader. Instead of mourning his loss, their habitually blank expressions became a combination of pleasure and sly cunning. Their mission was forgotten. With one purpose only, they immediately turned their clubs on each other, raining blows onto those of their tribe who were nearest to them.

"You were right!" Stella exclaimed. "They are fighting among themselves."

Cal released the breath he had been holding. Taking the ogres out of the fight gave them a better chance but, even with Grindan and his men, it was by no means a foregone conclusion. Moncoya had spent centuries building up his army in readiness for this fight. His sidhe forces were legendary throughout Otherworld for their discipline and viciousness. Speaking of Moncoya... Cal risked a glance in his direction. He was just in time to see the faerie king conferring with Niniane. They were pointing at Stella and Cal.

As Cal watched them, Niniane nodded and then began to make her way across the battlefield. Despite the bloody fight raging around her, she remained unscathed. Nothing harmed her. How could it? She was the most powerful sorceress Otherworld had ever known. And she was heading their way.

"Take Stella somewhere safe. She won't get hurt if you get her away from here. It's me Niniane wants," Cal said to Jethro, as the two men watched the sorceress glide up the incline toward them.

"Merlin Caledonius speaks sense." Dimitar nodded his agreement.

"Merlin Caledonius speaks crap." Jethro's voice and expression were scathing. "You think I'm going to abandon you to face her alone?"

"Leave her to me." Stepping in front of the three men, Stella cut their conversation short. "I've been looking forward to this."

As Niniane mounted the incline toward them, Stella moved forward, blocking her path. The sorceress halted. "Out of my way, little necromancer. This does not concern you."

"Oh, but it does." In contrast to Niniane's harsh tones, Stella kept her own voice soft.

Niniane paused, looking from Stella to Cal. Her eyes narrowed into black, soulless slits. "You and he? No, that cannot be. I will not allow it."

"Too late. Time for you to finally move on." Stella stood her ground in the face of the icy fury that seized the ancient sorceress in an instant grip.

"Never." The word resonated with hatred and misery.

Stella braced herself for whatever demonstration of Niniane's supernatural powers was to come. Instead, she was propelled backward as the sorceress launched herself at her, trying to claw at her face. Remembering Lorcan's words about using her size to her advantage, Stella hooked her foot around Niniane's ankle, bringing them both crashing down onto the grass. She was able to use her speed, agility and the element of surprise to her advantage to pin the larger woman down so that she could straddle her, holding her arms at her sides.

Niniane's shrieks and curses filled the air around them for several minutes.

"You should think about how you look." Stella shook her head sadly. Lorcan had said Niniane was the vainest being to walk either world. She hoped he was right.

Niniane subsided, panting. "What?" The question was laden with suspicion.

"Well, you obviously want to impress Cal here—or do you call him Merlin? But, even if he wasn't around, there's Jethro, whom you must admit is serious eye candy. Even Dimitar is quite easy to look at when he's not doing the mean, moody scowling thing. Yet here you are, rolling around on the ground with your hair all mussed up, your face blotchy and your eyes all puffy. And that language. Tut, tut."

"What is your point?"

"I'm just saying you're going the wrong way about getting yourself a man. You could be quite pretty if you gave yourself half a chance…"

"Quite pretty?" Niniane was almost spitting with outrage. "I'll have you know I am considered the most beautiful woman in all Otherworld."

"Really? I can't see it myself." Stella shook her head. She was aware of Cal watching her closely and somewhat nervously. Probably wondering what the hell she was doing. She didn't blame him. *She* was wondering what the hell she was doing.

She risked releasing Niniane's hands. Stella allowed herself a small, inward sigh of relief when the sorceress did not instantly claw her face off.

"I *am* beautiful." Niniane's vanity was such that she refused to allow the matter to drop. Which was exactly what Stella had been counting on.

"If you say so." Stella shrugged, rising to her feet.

Niniane stood, facing her. "Look at me. You must see it."

Stella made a pretense of studying her thoughtfully. Her heart was hammering so loudly she thought it might give her away. She would get only one chance at this. Mess it up and they would all die. *Keep her distracted. Use her vanity against her.* She repeated the words to herself.

"Do a twirl." Stella made a circular movement with one finger and, to her never-ending surprise, Niniane obediently spun around in a circle.

It was now or never. The instant Niniane had her back to her, Stella raised her hand. *"Fýrwylm."* Fire shot from her fingertips and engulfed Niniane's clothing. "Feel free to join me, boys."

Cal and Jethro hurried to her side, adding their own flames to hers. The sorceress writhed and shrieked like a witch at the stake. The blaze consumed her, starting at her legs and working up her torso. Stella had the strangest feeling that the fire was building to an inferno inside Niniane. As though the sorceress's body had no substance and was nothing more than a shell that allowed the elements to enter and grow out of control within her. Like a hollowed-out tree stump or the skin a snake has shed.

"Are we strong enough to destroy her?" Stella had to shout above the roaring, hissing sounds of the flames.

Because if they couldn't crush Niniane completely, they were in deep trouble.

"We can bloody well try." Cal's face was grim. "Join hands. We'll be more powerful that way."

The three of them held hands while Stella kept her right hand extended toward Niniane. She felt a jolt as Cal's and Jethro's energy surged through her, redoubling her own powers. The strength of the streak of fire leaving her fingertips lifted Niniane off her feet and sent her hurtling partway down the slope.

"There's no smell," Jethro commented, looking down at Niniane. Her once-pale flesh was blackened now, the shriek fading to a thin whine. But she was still upright and trying to fight her way back to them against the wall of flames. "You'd expect there to be a terrible smell of barbecued flesh when someone gets burned alive."

"Niniane has never been alive." Cal's voice was grim.

Just as Stella was beginning to think she could no longer sustain the mental energy needed to continue, to keep being the conduit for these two powerful men, Niniane stopped moving. The flames faded to a dull orange glow and her charred flesh began to cool to a light gray.

Stella lowered her hand. Slowly, with a curious grace, Niniane's tall figure collapsed into the ground, leaving behind only a pile of ashes. A slight breeze stirred the grass, blowing the ashes across the green stalks.

"We did it." Dimitar held up a hand to high-five Cal and got a bleak look in response.

"I'm going back down there." Jethro scanned the battle below him. "Lorcan may need help."

"I'll come with you. You'll need someone to watch your back in that madness." Dimitar appeared not to notice the surprised glances Cal and Stella gave him. Jethro, on the other hand, grinned at them and shrugged his shoulders.

It seemed Prince Tibor's hold over his human servant was not quite as strong as the vampire ruler might believe.

"Is that it?" Stella looked at the gray patch of ash on the grass. The only sign that Niniane had been there at all. "Are you finally free?"

"Free of Niniane? Yes. Free of myself? Never."

Stella frowned, wanting to ask him to explain. Then a sidhe spear landed close to their feet and she decided that now might not be the best time for an in-depth discussion. She turned back to view the battlefield, her eyes seeking Moncoya, but she could see no sign of him.

Chapter 25

Throughout the long hours of fighting, Lorcan caught occasional glimpses of Tanzi and Vashti. From what he could see, the Valkyries had taught them well. While Vashti swung a mace above her head like a fury, Tanzi fought hand-to-hand with a broadsword that was almost the same height as she was. She thrust with this giant weapon while using her shield to parry her opponent's blows. Once or twice, Lorcan observed her bringing the shield crashing down on the head of an unsuspecting enemy and bit back a smile. It might not be sporting, but you had to admire her style.

Lorcan himself had been in real danger only once. Backed into a corner of the palace wall by a group of bloodthirsty sidhes, his strength had been waning when Jethro and Dimitar had come to his aid. Fighting alongside Prince Tibor's human slave and the mercenary who gave necromancing a bad name had been a surreal yet rewarding experience. He was still unsure how it had come about.

Although the outcome was already decided long before they arrived, the ranks of what Stella would call the "good guys" had been swelled by the arrival of the werefalcons and the elves. The fight was waning now and Lorcan took the opportunity to look around and check on Tanzi once more. He was unsure why it should matter to him if Moncoya's daughter had survived the fray, but it did. Funnily enough, he didn't feel the same interest in Vashti's fate. At first, he couldn't see Tanzi. Then he caught a flash of her gold hair as she ran past him. The next thing he knew, she had been felled by a sickening blow to her shoulder from a club-wielding elf. She dropped like a stone into the mud while the carnage continued around her. The elf dealt Tanzi another blow while she lay on the ground before charging onward into the fray.

Lorcan paused. He should just ignore what he'd just seen, right? She might be a woman, but she was still a sidhe. The enemy and Daddy's girl to the core. He began to move away, back to help the group of Iberian sidhe with whom he had been fighting. People who mattered. Muttering a curse, he stopped in his tracks, turned and bent over Tanzi as she lay deathly still. Scooping her up into his arms—mere seconds before she was crushed under the hooves of one of Grindan's mounted warriors—he cast a swift glance around him.

They could chalk this one up to Team Stella. Stella herself was standing near the pagoda above the battleground, directing operations. Cal was at her side. Their hands were clasped. Stella's powers were so strong now that she held the undead troops in her control like the consummate maestro conducting her orchestra. Under her orders, Grindan and his men were sweeping through the valley, driving the opposing sidhe forces relentlessly back. The ogres were too busy fighting among themselves to notice anything else.

The elves and werefalcons were dealing with the sidhe forces on the ground. There was no sign of Moncoya or Vashti, who had obviously seen how things were going and made a sharp getaway. Lorcan decided no one would miss him or Tanzi.

The palace grounds were a vast, rolling expanse of parkland that swept past the huge lake before dipping down into a valley. Here, the open grassland gave way to pine trees, and a river made a meandering path between steep rocky inclines. Tanzi might be a lightweight, but Lorcan was staggering slightly under his burden by the time he reached the river. A few hours of strenuous fighting followed by a spot of weight lifting would do that every time. He found a large, flat rock on the riverbank and placed Tanzi on it.

Lorcan studied her thoughtfully. Her breathing was worryingly shallow. Each time she inhaled, her small breasts barely moved beneath the silk blouse she wore. Always pale, her complexion had become ghostly. First things first. He needed to assess the damage to her shoulder. Luckily, her blouse fastened at the front with a row of tiny buttons. His fingers felt too big and clumsy for such dainty fastenings and he hesitated momentarily at the realization that she wasn't wearing anything under the shirt.

"Too late for modesty. Next time though, maybe consider putting on underwear before you go into battle." Lorcan spoke to the prone figure in the manner of a schoolmaster scolding a badly behaved child. Tugging the blouse down over her injured shoulder, he lifted and turned her so that he could view her shoulder blade. He gave a soft whistle. The smooth skin of her back was already marred by deep, angry bruises. To say Tanzi had been beaten black-and-blue would be to seriously limit the color spectrum of blemishes defacing her delicate flesh.

As he was pondering what to do next, her eyelids flickered and she groaned. Lorcan lowered her gently down onto the rock. "It's okay. You've taken a nasty hit to your shoulder, but I don't think there are any broken bones."

She sat up abruptly and he couldn't help but glance at her high, pointed breasts, revealed in all their beauty by the open blouse. *Give me a break, God. I'm a man, after all, and they are bloody gorgeous.* To his chagrin, Tanzi caught the direction of his gaze. She attempted to clutch her shirt closed, and the action caused her to cry out in pain. Lorcan made a move toward her, wanting to reassure her.

"Stay where you are, necromancer! My God, what have you been doing to me while I was unconscious?"

"Ah, no. Will you catch yourself on with that? Did you think…?" He ran his hand through his hair in a helpless gesture. "Seriously? You think I'm the sort of sick bastard who'd touch you up when you were out cold?" He sat down on the rock next to her, shaking his head. "I didn't expect you to have much of an opinion of me, but *that*?"

"You are the friend of the other one. The ancient sorcerer who wishes to destroy my father."

This wasn't going to be easy. "Look, right at this minute I'm not taking sides. I saw you get hurt. I got you away from the battle. I brought you down here because I thought your wounds might need bathing or you might need a drink of water." He grinned, but her face told him he might as well have snarled. "What can I say? I'm good at the rescuing, not so great at the old first aid."

"Why would you save me?" The ring of fire around her irises made the pupils appear endlessly blue. Their expression was suspicious.

"Because I'm an idiot who hasn't a single brain cell in his thick Irish head."

"Oh, I see what you are doing. You are attempting to disarm me by being charming."

"I might be trying but, by the look on your face, I'd say I'm failing miserably."

"I would like some water." Her voice was regal. The princess commanding a servant.

Lorcan glanced around. There was nothing for her to drink out of. Yet another black mark for him, another reason for those glorious eyes to register their contempt. Going to the river's edge, he knelt and filled his cupped hands with clear, cold liquid. Returning to Tanzi, he held his hands out to her. The outcome was in doubt for a few seconds, then she dipped her head and sipped the water from his hands.

"Thank you. You may leave me now."

"I could do that, I suppose. If I was the sort of unfeeling bastard who leaves an injured girl to fend for herself in the middle of a war zone. Lucky for you, I'm not."

"You call this luck?" He could almost feel the anger shimmering through her slender body.

"Ah, come on now." He flashed her his best Irish-rogue grin. The one that worked nine times out of ten. "Things could be a lot worse."

Her disdainful expression didn't falter. It looked as if this was going to be that one-in-ten time when the good old Irish allure failed him. Tanzi made an effort to get to her feet, gripping her bottom lip between her teeth. A slight groan escaped her and she sank back down onto the rock. Her face had a definite greenish tinge to it.

"I think you'd better let me take a closer look at that shoulder." Lorcan reached out a hand.

"Don't you dare touch me, necromancer!" Some of the color returned to her cheeks as she recoiled slightly, gripping her blouse tightly closed.

"Do you know what? I can't help thinking this would be a whole lot easier if you'd come down from your high ropes. I get it, you know. You are a noble princess and I'm a lowly Irish sorcerer not fit to kiss the hem of your gown. But if you don't let me help, you might end up with some permanent damage. And, believe it or not—" he grinned "—I have seen a girl's shoulder before and managed to control my lust."

He sensed the debate raging within her. Finally, she gave a brief nod. Turning her back to him, she slid the blouse from her right shoulder. Lorcan ran his hand lightly down from her shoulder to her waist. Her skin felt cool beneath his fingers and she shivered at his touch.

"It's as I said, I don't think there are any bones broken but you're going to be sore for a while. Some cold water on this might help." He tugged his shirt over his head and went back to the river's edge to wet the garment in the fast-flowing water. After wringing it out, he returned to Tanzi. He folded the shirt into a wad and held it against her back.

He watched her profile as her teeth caught and held her trembling bottom lip. Who'd have thought he'd ever find a grain of sympathy within him for Moncoya's daughter?

"I must go back." She glanced fretfully back toward the palace.

Lorcan shook his head. "Look, I don't know how much you were aware of before you got injured, but I have to tell you it wasn't going well for your side."

"I know." He had to bend his head closer to hear the words. "What else can I do?"

"Rest," he said firmly. "We are going to go over to that little copse over there—" he pointed "—and you are going to try to sleep. Then, and only then, I'll take you back to the palace."

"Sleep?" Her voice wobbled with incredulity and, for the first time, she smiled at him.

Tanzi's smile was something Lorcan had not prepared himself for. It knocked him sideways. Knowing what they were capable of, Lorcan had always considered himself immune to the legendary enchantment of the faerie. Faerie glamor, as it had been called in the days before Moncoya had swept aside the old ways. Gazing down at her for an instant, drinking in the sheer beauty of her face, he realized he might not be as resistant as he believed. He gave himself a mental shake. *Moncoya's daughter. Sidhe princess. Poison wrapped up in a perfect face and body.* That was better.

"Best treatment for shock, so my mother used to say. Can you stand?"

Tanzi staggered slightly as she got to her feet, but she managed to stay upright. Lorcan kept his arm around her, steadying her and holding the makeshift compress in place while she kept her blouse closed. In this manner they made their halting way toward the copse.

"You and Vashti... I always thought you were alike. But you're not," he commented.

"No, we might be twins, but we are opposites in personality. My father sees Vashti as the son he never had. Me? I'm useful as a weapon but beyond that I'm just a girl. Unless I have my sword in my hand, my only value to him is as a pawn in the marriage game." She stated it as a fact, without bitterness or complaint.

"Feudal." Lorcan kept his voice neutral, although his feelings were anything but. Why should it affect him so profoundly? *It shouldn't matter to me,* Lorcan thought, as he trudged into the shade of the trees, supporting her against his side. Moncoya's family didn't interest him. This bright, brave girl meant nothing to him. Yet the thought of her being used in such a way made a spark of anger ignite deep in his gut.

Tanzi attempted a shrug, wincing slightly as the movement caused new pain in her shoulder. "It is the way."

"What if they make you marry a warty old man?"

"Are you pitying me, necromancer?"

"No. I think my sympathies would lie entirely with him."

Her laughter was low-pitched and musical. "As they should."

It was a strange end to a stranger day. Lorcan sat with his back against a tree trunk and held Moncoya's daughter in his lap while she slept. The perfumed mass of her hair tickled his chin, and her soft warm weight against his chest reminded him that it had been a very long time since he had held a woman. He reminded himself several times—and his errant body several more times—that this was not just any woman. Darkness was falling when he woke her and they walked slowly back to the palace.

The scene within the grounds was one of carnage, but the battle was clearly over. Except no one seemed to have told the ogres, who were still fighting among themselves. Already there were signs that a cleanup operation was under way. When they reached the palace doors, two elf guards barred their way, clearly signaling that a new order was in place.

"I am Lorcan, friend of Cal." The elf bowed his head in deference, acknowledging that he knew exactly who Lorcan was. "Take this lady straight to Cal. She is to be treated with respect."

Tanzi regarded him with surprise. "Are you not returning with me to enjoy the victory celebrations with your friends? I thought you would relish our defeat and look forward to reaping the rewards of victory."

He looked down into the deep, blue midnight of her eyes. "Then it's clear that you don't know me. I would never celebrate death. And I'm a wanderer, Tanzi. The road is my home. I need no other reward."

There was a flash of something other than distaste in the dark depths. Was it disappointment? Or was that his own wishful thinking?

"Thank you for saving me." She held out her hand and he took it between both of his. She glanced up at the palace, and a shadow crossed the marble perfection of her features. "Although I no longer know what my future holds."

He gripped her hand. The old allegiances had changed and new bonds had been forged today. Were they enough to overcome the hatred of centuries? Only time would tell. "My friends will treat your fairly, that much I can guarantee. And I will make you a promise of my own. If you need me again, I will come to you."

She scanned his face, her eyes bewildered. "How will you know?"

He smiled. "Trust me, Tanzi. If you need me, I will know."

Chapter 26

Stella stood on the balcony of her room and gazed across the parkland. Darkness cloaked the scene and hid any sign of the earlier chaos from her view. Grindan was gone, having renewed his vows of eternal loyalty before he and his warriors returned once more to their underground graves. She hoped their rest would be peaceful and uninterrupted.

Was Moncoya out there in the shadows? What was he planning? One thing was for sure, he would be planning something. Her skin prickled at the thought, but she refused to turn away. They had faced and defeated him. He was the man who had stolen her childhood. Stolen countless lives. If he was out there, let him see her standing here in the palace he used to call his own. Let him know how it felt to be the tyrant overthrown.

A movement behind her made her turn her head quickly. This was Moncoya's legacy. Until they knew his whereabouts, they would be forever condemned to look over their shoulders.

Cal slipped his arms around her waist and drew her back so that she could lean against him. Stella sighed, enjoying the warmth of his body.

"I'm about to get into the hottest, most decadently scented bubble bath in the history of the world. Join me?"

His lips traced the outer shell of her ear. "Tempting as that offer is, I remember making a promise that I would tell you everything once this was over."

"Tell me in the tub." She turned in his arms, pressing her cheek against his chest.

"We have a great track record in water, Stella, but it's never involved talking." He tilted her chin up so that he could look at her face. "I keep my promises."

"So do I. I promise not to distract you."

"You are a distraction to me all the time." She made a protesting sound and he smiled down at her. "I didn't say I was complaining. On the contrary, you are my favorite diversion." His face became serious again. "I'll do you a deal. You bathe while I talk. If you still want me to, I'll join you later."

If you still want me to? Something in his manner troubled her. Surely she knew all, or nearly all, there was to know about him by now? *No more obstacles. Please. We've fought so hard for this moment.* What more could there be? Cal's grave expression told her there was definitely something. It also told her it wasn't going to be pleasant.

The bathroom was self-indulgent, as befitted the faerie queen. Occupying the center of the room, the sunken bath resembled a small swimming pool. When it was full, Stella shed her clothing and slid gratefully into the scented water, feeling some of the awfulness of the day just gone wash away as she did. Cal took up a seated position on the tiled floor with his back to the wall. His knees were drawn up and his hands clasped loosely between his legs. His eyes remained fixed on Stella's face and a faint smile played about his lips.

"Don't look at me like that," she murmured.

"Like what?"

"Like you are rehearsing how to say goodbye to me." A slight tremor in her voice gave away the fear that had suddenly gripped her.

"Stella…"

"Please, Cal…what else is there that I don't already know about you? You are Merlin. You are half sidhe. Niniane turned out to be the ex from hell and imprisoned you at Darnantes. In order to get free you had to strike a deal with the angels to act as sort of Otherworld law enforcer. I know all of that and I still—" She drew in a shuddering breath. She wanted to tell him she loved him, yet that distance was still there in his voice and in his eyes. "—want to be with you. If you are going to tell me you don't feel the same, then please get on with it because you can't shock me anymore with revelations about your past."

"Moncoya is my brother," he said quietly.

"Oh."

"Shocked yet?" He quirked an eyebrow at her.

"A little bit."

"We have the same father, but different mothers. My mother was mortal. His mother was a sidhe princess, our father's equal. While Moncoya was raised as his heir, I only met our father once. My mother and I spent my childhood running from him." Although the words were stilted, he seemed to be gaining in strength as he spoke. Stella waited, sensing his determination to continue. He wanted to tell it all this time. "My father was ambitious and evil, perhaps even more so than Moncoya. He devised a plan to take over the immortal world. He believed that if he sired a child with a mortal woman and gave that child up to the devil to be raised as Satan's own, his reward would be to become the ruler of all Otherworld."

Stella regarded him in growing horror, sensing where the story was going. "So there really is a devil? Satan does exist?"

"Perhaps not in the sense that mortals generally understand the concept. It has suited his purpose to encourage the view of him as one who wields power over sin and darkness. But, yes, there is one demon who is stronger and more evil than all others and his name—or one of his many names—is Satan. In his eagerness to please this demon master, my father decided that only the purest and most virtuous mortal woman was fit to be the mother of Satan's child. So he raped my mother, a young nun, in her convent bed while she slept. When the other nuns discovered her pregnancy, she was beaten and cast out from the convent. No one would believe that she did not know what had happened to her. My father found her and explained how I was conceived and the glory that awaited me. Through his pact with the devil, he had already given me the greatest gifts and powers he could bestow." His lips twisted into a bitter smile. "My father did not bargain on the strong woman he had chosen. My mother ran from him and took sanctuary with a holy man, a hermit who lived in a cave. It has a nice symmetry that my cave-dwelling days began even before my birth, don't you think?"

"I think your mother sounds like a remarkable woman."

"Oh, she was. As soon as I was born, she rose up from her bed and took me to the nearest church to be baptized so that the devil could not claim me. Then we traveled to another part of the country in order to hide from my father's anger. Little did my mother know how very difficult it would be to keep me hidden."

"Why was that?" Stella was fascinated by the faraway look in his eyes.

"I was rather precocious. I could converse like an adult by the age of eighteen months and was able to read and write by the time I was three. Then, of course, as a child it never occurred to me to hide my magical powers. I became something of a legend, word spread wherever we went and my father eventually heard about me. It meant we spent my entire childhood on the run. No sooner would we settle in one place than I'd do something that was likened to a miracle and we'd have to pack up and leave."

Stella, whose own childhood had been a series of moves and changes, felt a rush of sympathy for the boy he had once been. "That's why you cared for me when I was I child. You knew how it felt." Her voice was husky.

"That might have been true at first. Later I cared for you because of who you are."

"You said you met your father once. What happened then?"

"He caught up with us when I was thirteen. My mother had become ill. The nomadic life we'd led had taken its toll and we'd been forced to rest in one place to allow her to recover. My father found us. He was delighted with me. Oh, not because I was the son he had been waiting for. I was a hybrid, after all. He already had everything he wanted in his other son. Moncoya was his heir, a true-blood sidhe to carry on his name. No, he wanted me the same way Moncoya wanted you, Stella. He wanted to use me as a weapon of destruction against his enemies."

"What did you do?"

"I killed him." He watched her face to see how she would react to the words. When she didn't speak, he continued. "It actually wasn't intentional. He kept badgering me to demonstrate my powers to him. When I refused, he called me a mongrel, a cur, the excrement the devil had scraped off his boot." He smiled. "We had much better insults back then."

"But he was your father! How could he speak to you that way?"

"Exactly. I lost my temper. I told him I'd show him an example of my powers that would make his eyes water. It did more than that. As a young boy, I didn't know my own strength and I didn't hold back. He died in a ball of flames. Do I regret it?" Cal considered that matter, then shook his head. "At the time I was in shock at what I'd done. Now I know I rid Otherworld of an evil despot. Unfortunately, another evil despot—his other son, my brother, Moncoya—was waiting in the wings to take his place."

"At least I know now why you and Moncoya hate each other so much." Stella sat up a little straighter so that she did not have to tilt her head back to look at him. "What I don't understand is why you think telling me this would change things between us."

He bowed his head. His voice was low and, within it, she heard some of the anguish of his troubled dreams. "Because now you know what I am. What I was created for. I was put on earth to destroy it, to be the son of the devil. The powers I have were given to me for that purpose alone. You couldn't love me—no one could—not knowing the truth about me."

Stella emerged from the scented water and, shivering slightly at the coolness of the tiled floor, knelt before him, resting her arms on his knees. She ducked her head so that she could look at his face. "That might have been your father's intention, but he failed in his bid to make you evil. You are the opposite of what he wanted. You've devoted your whole life to fighting evil. It doesn't matter what you were meant to be, it's what you are that makes me love you, Cal."

He did look up at that. One side of his mouth lifted slightly. "Then you do love me?"

"How can you not know that?" Her voice was shaky. "How could you not feel my love for you whenever you are near me?"

"I did. Although I knew how you felt, I thought that once I told you everything you'd change your mind."

"Well, I haven't and I never will. But you know what? Every time I have imagined myself telling you I love you, I never pictured a scenario where I would be naked, wet and freezing my backside off while you were fully clothed and not even touching me."

Cal started to laugh, relief imprinting itself onto his features. Rising to his feet, he picked Stella up and carried her back to the bath, wading fully clothed into the hot water with her. Bubbles clung to his face and hair and he blew them away as he knelt and caught her up in an endless kiss.

It was some time before Stella could speak again. "Cal?"

"Yes?"

"Two things. First, does this mean you love me, too? Because you haven't actually said so."

He started to laugh. "Haven't I? Ever since I spoke to you for the first time on that beach in Barcelona, I've rehearsed so many speeches and here I am forgetting every word of them. Stella, I've lived through thousands of years and yet, until I got to know you, I'd never lived at all. You brought my heart to life. You gave me a taste of the magic humans experience every day. You showed me what it was to love. Yes, I love you with every ounce of my being and, no matter what the next thousand years hold, or the thou-

sand after that, I want to face them with you at my side."
He kissed her again. "What was the second thing?"

"Take those clothes off and show me how much you
love me."

Chapter 27

The elves had done a remarkable job of restoring the palace gardens to something resembling normality. There was just one problem, which Jethro pointed out to Cal and Stella when they emerged into the morning sunlight.

"It's been a full twenty-four hours and we can't find anything to stop them. We turned hoses on them and they paused briefly to drink the water before carrying on. We fired rocks at them and they picked them up and used them as weapons against each other. We tried lighting torches and threatening them with fire, but they just swatted them away." Jethro regarded the warring ogres with disbelief. "When one becomes too injured to continue it wanders off into the forest while the others keep going. Nothing seems to deter them."

"I told you they would fight until one of them is established as the new leader," Cal said.

"But what are we going to do with them in the meantime?"

Cal shrugged. "There's not much we can do. If we leave them to it, they'll move on eventually." He nodded at Dimitar, who was coming toward them. "Got yourself a sidekick?"

Jethro grinned. "I thought human servants were tied to their vampire lords for life, but he seems to think there's a get-out clause. For some reason, he's switched his allegiance to me. I'm not sure I can cope with being called 'master' for all eternity."

"What will you do now?" Stella asked.

"Oh, you know. Places to go, people to see." Jethro kept his voice light. The message was clear. It was his business and no one else's.

"Stay safe. And, Jethro?" Jethro had started to walk away, but he turned back, raising a questioning brow at Cal's words. "Thanks."

"Anytime." Jethro sketched a wave at them both and continued on his way, meeting Dimitar in the middle of the lawn. The two men walked away toward the lake together.

If you discounted the ogres, the gardens were peaceful. The morning sunlight threw diamond shapes across the lake waters and highlighted the colors of the garden. Cal breathed in the scent of the flowers mingling with the tangy pines and held Stella close. He was one of the lucky ones. He had both worlds. And now he had someone he could share them with.

"When you consider the solitary reputation of the necromancer, you appear to have a remarkable propensity for generating loyalty, my friend."

There was only one person who could take a simple statement and turn it into a pompous speech. Turning slowly, Cal came face-to-face with the Dominion.

"You're a long way from home."

"I thought, given the events of the past few days, I

should make the effort to come to you." The prim smile appeared. "After all, we owe you a great debt of thanks."

"You owe that to Stella," Cal stated firmly.

The Dominion bowed his head in acknowledgment. "Indeed. You have achieved all we asked of you and more, Miss Fallon. The gratitude of two worlds is with you this day."

Stella returned the angel's smile. "You say that as though I had a choice." She twined her fingers with Cal's. "And yet, it didn't turn out so very bad."

He smiled down at her before turning back to the Dominion. "You haven't come all this way to thank us."

"I do wish everyone I dealt with was as astute as you, Merlin Caledonius. It would make my job so much easier." The Dominion looked gravely from Cal's face to Stella's. "The prophecy has been fulfilled. The heart of the necromancer has been claimed."

Stella gave a little start of surprise. "He's right, Cal. I never thought of it like that. My heart belongs to you. You are the one who has fulfilled your own prophecy."

"I don't want to rule Otherworld. That has never been my ambition."

"Come now. This was your prophecy. You must remember your own words. *He who claims the heart of the necromancer star will* unite *the delightful plain*. Others, notably Moncoya, have interpreted it to mean he who claims the star's heart will be in control of Otherworld. Yet all those centuries ago, when you foresaw this day you used the word *unite*, not the word *rule*."

Cal frowned. "What are you suggesting?"

"A pivotal battle has been won. But Otherworld is a long way from the peace it needs. Moncoya is defeated, but not destroyed. Others will sense an opportunity in his absence. The wolves did not engage in this conflict. Do you think they will stay out of the next? Prince Tibor will not remain lightly in the background. There must be a peace-keeping force in place, with an interim council set up to maintain order, a powerful presence allowing all voices an equal hearing. This must be overseen by one who commands the respect of all."

"You mean me, don't you?" Cal groaned.

"You had that respect anyway. Now you have the heart of the necromancer star and you have defeated Moncoya." The Dominion was relentless. "Your credentials are second to none."

Cal turned back to Stella. "What do you say? I'll go wherever you want me to. Do we stay here or do we go back?"

Stella rose up onto the tips of her toes and whispered something in his ear. Cal grinned and slid an arm about her waist, holding her close against his side. "Yes, we can go back now and then to do some shoe shopping and get the latest computer games." Turning to face the Dominion, he nodded. "Looks like you have yourself a deal. I'll head up your interim council. On one condition."

"What is that?"

"Get those bloody ogres off my lawn."

Stella spread her wardrobe options over her bed. Downstairs the leaders of Otherworld, called together by the Dominion, were gathering for their first council meeting. Before that, there would be another, even more important ceremony. And she had nothing to wear. *Story of your life.*

She glanced at the dress and shoes Moncoya had chosen for her. Remarkably, the outfit had survived the battle unscathed. The dress *was* beautiful. *It couldn't be blamed for the fact that it had been chosen by an evil, butchering tyrant,* she reasoned. It was that or her shorts. There was no contest.

When she made her way down the grand staircase and into the banquet hall, she wore denim shorts and a plain black vest. Cal was waiting for her. Predictably, he wore jeans. His eyes crinkled into a smile as he took in her outfit.

"It was all I had," she whispered, aware of the dozens of interested eyes upon them.

"Do you think I care what you wear? You look beautiful." The smile in his eyes deepened. "You always do. It's our choice if we want it to be a dress-down occasion."

They turned to face the Dominion. It wasn't every girl who had her marriage ceremony performed by an angel in front of the leaders of the warring dynasties of Otherworld. It was a pity there were no photographs for her Facebook page. *In a relationship with Merlin.* It might get one or two comments.

When the ceremony and the endless, wonderful first kiss were over, Stella examined the ring Cal had placed upon her finger. It was a Celtic knot, engraved with ancient runes. "It belonged to my mother," he explained. "She told me that she wanted my true love to wear it. It has been waiting all these centuries for you."

Before Stella could reply, Tanzi approached them. In Moncoya's absence, she was to be the faerie representative on the council.

"Congratulations." Although the word was stiff and cost her a lot, Stella admired her bravery in being the first to come forward. Her father's desertion must have hit her hard.

"Thank you. I hope your sister is improving?" At first it was believed that Vashti had fled the scene with Moncoya, but the elves had found Tanzi's twin injured and unconscious on the battlefield. Stella might have a stormy relationship with Vashti, but she had somehow never envisioned the belligerent little sidhe as the sort of person who would run away when things got tough. She was glad she had been right.

"I hope that, with careful nursing, she will make a full recovery." Tanzi turned to Cal. "Your friend…the Irish necromancer. He could not be here for your marriage?"

"Lorcan has a tendency to turn up when he wants to rather than when he is required to. Not conforming is his specialty."

Tanzi wandered away after that and Stella spent the next hour at Cal's side being introduced to the dignitaries who were gathering for the inaugural meeting of the peacekeeping council. She quickly lost track of who was who until she saw a face she recognized.

Prince Tibor dismissed Stella's attempt to explain why she was forced to put him and his vampires out of action during the conflict. "You are the star. It is what you were brought here to do. I suppose you have seen nothing of Dimitar, my slave?"

Stella returned a noncommittal answer and the prince, clearly disgruntled, moved on. The Dominion took his place, coming to stand beside them.

"The elves have agreed to lead the peacekeeping force. One suggestion that has been made is that elections should be held. There should be a democratic vote for the leader of each dynasty."

Cal shook his head. "I am not convinced that the faeries would vote against Moncoya. He has ruled them for too long. They fear him and don't know any other way than his."

"Perhaps the time has come to show them there can be another way." The Dominion looked around the room. "Are the rumors true? Is there a descendant of King

Ivo, one who can legitimately challenge Moncoya for the crown?"

The Dominion regarded Cal thoughtfully as though considering how much information to impart. "There is," he said at last.

"Then what is the problem? Bring him out of hiding. Let him challenge Moncoya openly."

"Well, for one thing, the identity of the true heir has been so well hidden that he himself is unaware of it."

"But you know who he is." Stella sensed that Cal was finding the careful formality of the angel's conversation frustrating.

"I do. Unlike the goddesses of fate, however, I am unable to intervene. That is not my role. The matter must be left to run its course."

"Why do I suspect you already know what that course will be?"

The Dominion's prim smile appeared. "You flatter me, my friend. I have an idea, nothing more."

Cal turned to look at the banquet hall. A huge circular table had been set up in the center and the council members were beginning to take their seats. "This reminds me of another round table, another century—" He glanced down at Stella. She looked up and grinned mischievously at him. His own lips curved into an answering smile. "—another life."

"If you will permit my familiarity, I think this life suits you better, my friend."

"It does. And it would suit me even more if I knew I would not have to share this table with Moncoya at any point in the future."

"I can offer you no guarantees. All I know is that, if it comes to it, you will deal with him as you see fit in order to ensure the safety of Otherworld. In the meantime, who knows? The true heir may soon emerge and stake his claim."

"Is there a way we can help him do that?" Stella asked.

"If there is, I am sure that the two of you will find it." The enigmatic words were accompanied by a slight bow. "For now, my friends, I will bid you farewell."

"Cal?" Stella caught hold of his hand as he was about to walk toward the round table. "This may seem like a silly question…but what's my name now? Am I Mrs. Merlin? After everything that's happened, tell me I'm *not* Mrs. Moncoya."

He started to laugh. "Back when I was born, we tended to choose our own names. I've always liked Merlin Caledonius the best. How about we go for that?"

"Stella Caledonius. It has a ring to it. When this meeting is over, can we go away for a few days? The Dominion said the elves will act as a peacekeeping force. Can't we have ourselves a honeymoon before we try to find this missing heir?"

"Where do you want to go?"

"I don't mind. Except Barcelona. That's the only place I'm going to veto."

"And I'll veto Darnantes. I do know a nice little cave in Wales. I have some fond memories of the mountain pool there…"

* * * * *

Look for next title in Jane Godman's
Mills & Boon Nocturne trilogy.
OTHERWORLD RENEGADE
available May 2016.

"Trust me, Tanzi. If you need me, I will know."

They were the words Lorcan Malone had said to her. It had been a bit of Irish blarney, of course, spoken in the heat of battle. He probably didn't even remember who she was, let alone recall their strange encounter on that fateful day. So why, in this moment—when she was in more trouble than she could ever have imagined possible—should she suddenly experience a fierce longing for the bad-boy necromancer with the twinkling blue eyes?

It's called clutching at straws, she told herself. *It's what you're doing right now instead of facing reality and finding your own way out of this madness.*

"What are you thinking, my daughter?" Moncoya, exiled king of the faeries, watched her face.

"I'm thinking that defeat has unhinged you. That you have finally done what others have whispered of for years and taken leave of your senses." Tanzi had never before spoken so boldly to him. Defiance was the trait her twin sister, Vashti, proudly exhibited. Tanzi had always been the acquiescent one. Until now. There were some things you could not bow down and agree to. This was one of them. This was the ultimate personality changer.

Moncoya's perfect features hardened with fury. His blue eyes, so like her own with their sidhe ring of fire encircling the iris, lit with a brighter inner blaze. His fingers tightened on the arm of his chair so that his knuckles gleamed white in stark contrast to the black polish on his perfectly manicured nails. Tanzi braced herself. His retribution would be swift and merciless. She couldn't hope to match him for strength, but she might be able to outrun him.

The outcome hung in the balance for seconds that stretched into minutes. Then Moncoya laughed. It was a brittle, mirthless sound that set Tanzi's teeth buzzing. She knew that laugh well. It had never boded well in her childhood. She didn't imagine things had changed. Unexpectedly, he relaxed back into his seat.

"My child, you are overwhelmed by the honor I have arranged for you. I should have foreseen this." He rose, draping a deceptively casual arm about her shoulders. "Walk with me awhile."

They stepped through a set of double doors straight onto a sand-and-shingle beach. The entire island seemed to be made up of sand. Even the ocher-hued cliffs looked ready to crumble into grit at the touch of a fingertip. Ferns, wild fennel and coarse bamboo grasses clung determinedly to soil that was a combination of granule and dust. Tanzi thought of her father's palace, of the precisely laid-out gardens leading down to the elegant lake. She glanced back over her shoulder at the beach-side villa they had just left. Sea breezes and salt water had taken their toll on its elegance so that it had a faded charm she doubted her father would acknowledge. In comparison with the soaring, white marble palace she had called "home" for all her life, it was a shack. Moncoya was as out of place here as diamond in a dung heap.

"You made sure no one followed you?" Moncoya withdrew his arm from about her shoulders as they walked along the water's edge. Secrecy surrounded this hiding place. If he was discovered, he faced trial and inevitable execution.

"Of course." Tanzi was offended at the question. Would he have asked Vashti the same thing? She doubted it. *Yet we both trained with the Valkyrie. We are both equally astute when it comes to warfare and subterfuge.* It came back to the same weary argument. The same reason Tanzi had been summoned to be the recipient of his latest piece of "good news" instead of her twin. Moncoya viewed Vashti as the son he had never had. Tanzi's only value to her father was as a pawn in the marriage stakes. *Not this marriage, Father. The sacrifice you are asking of me is too great.*

"Tell me what has been happening at the palace in my absence." Three months had passed since the cataclysmic battle that had toppled Moncoya from his throne. It felt like three years.

"There is a peacekeeping council known as the Alliance in place. Each of the Otherworld dynasties has representation on it. The Alliance itself is led by Merlin Caledonius."

Moncoya's expression hardened further at the name. "That half-blood cur will pay dearly for his part in this."

Merlin, the greatest sorcerer the world had ever known, was Moncoya's half brother and the man who had brought about his downfall. Cal, as he preferred to be called these days, had widened the existing gulf of hatred between the two men further by falling in love with and marrying the woman Moncoya had hoped to make his queen.

Tanzi paused, looking out across the turquoise waters toward the horizon. She drew a deep breath. "My father, you wrong him. He is man of conscience who is doing a fine job of uniting the dynasties…" Moncoya's growl of rage told her she had gone too far.

"Am I, the greatest leader Otherworld has ever known, to be forced into hiding while he lives in luxury in my royal palace? Am I to endure the knowledge that he has stolen the necromancer star, the woman I chose as my own, from under my nose? Must I kick my heels in this backwater while you, my own daughter, take the seat that should be mine at this pathetic council table—" He broke off, his voice ragged. When he spoke again, his tone was softer, the words a caress. "But you know nothing of these things, my child. It is wrong of these men to ask you to involve yourself in their political machinations. They seek to trick you."

Tanzi bit her lip. How could she explain it to him when he insisted on viewing her as a helpless dupe? Being part of the Alliance had brought her new life. Oh, she had been regarded with suspicion initially by many of the council members. She was Moncoya's daughter, after all. They saw her as the spoiled brat sidhe princess who had been his consort—his puppet—in the past. Together with Vashti, she had blindly carried out his wishes. But things had changed three months ago on that battlefield. She had changed. A pair of laughing Irish eyes came into her mind once more and she determinedly dismissed them. Cal and his wife, Stella, treated her as their equal and, from them, she was learning how to be the voice and conscience of her people. She was developing an understanding of compassion and democracy. Tanzi cast a sidelong glance at her father. She was learning that there was a way to rule other than Moncoya's ironfisted style.

"Let us leave this talk of the mongrel sorcerer for another day. I look forward to dealing with him when the time comes. This marriage I have arranged for you is the highest distinction ever to be bestowed upon a woman. Through this union, I will not only regain my crown, I will be the undisputed ruler of all Otherworld." Moncoya's lips thinned into a smile. "There will be no need for their puny Alliance when that day dawns."

"And what of me, Father? While you become all-powerful, what would I become?"

He paused then, perhaps considering for the first time the true implications of what he was asking of her. Such was his arrogance, she might have known he would not allow her feelings to influence him for long. "You will be revered above all others."

She shook her head. "I will not do it."

His face was set. The silken caress in his voice made the threat even more menacing. "You have no choice."

"By all the angels, Father, you cannot intend to force me into this!"

Moncoya's lips smiled but Tanzi's heart quailed at the look in his eyes. "Given the bridegroom I have chosen for you, might I suggest you refrain from speaking of angels in the future?"

MILLS & BOON®

nocturne™

AN EXHILARATING UNDERWORLD OF DARK DESIRES

A sneak peek at next month's titles...

In stores from 18th December 2015:

- **Captivating the Witch** – Michele Hauf
- **House of Shadows** – Jen Christie

MILLS & BOON®

**If you enjoyed this story,
you'll love the the full *Revenge Collection*!**

1015_MB514

MILLS & BOON®

Why shop at millsandboon.co.uk?

Each year, thousands of romance readers find their perfect read at millsandboon.co.uk. That's because we're passionate about bringing you the very best romantic fiction. Here are some of the advantages of shopping at www.millsandboon.co.uk:

* **Get new books first**—you'll be able to buy your favourite books one month before they hit the shops

* **Get exclusive discounts**—you'll also be able to buy our specially created monthly collections, with up to 50% off the RRP

* **Find your favourite authors**—latest news, interviews and new releases for all your favourite authors and series on our website, plus ideas for what to try next

* **Join in**—once you've bought your favourite books, don't forget to register with us to rate, review and join in the discussions

Visit **www.millsandboon.co.uk** for all this and more today!